The Favorite Kind of Wild Magic

Book 1 of the Coven Thirteen duology

Sophia-Rose Johnson

I0629652

The Favorite Kind of Wild Magic

Published: S.R. Johnson L.L.C.

Cover Design: S.R. Johnson L.L.C.

Interior Design: S.R. Johnson L.L.C.

Notes on the writing style of the Coven Thirteen duology

Firstly, the Coven Thirteen duology is edited in Modern Language Association (MLA) of America standards as opposed to the traditionally used Chicago Style used in most novels. This was a choice as the author that I made.

Secondly, throughout the series, I have minimized the use of italics. In times where sentences, dialogue, and paragraphs would otherwise and traditionally use italics as formatting, I chose to use double colons because of the readability of italics. I am not the first author to choose to use double colons instead of italics, though it may be your first time as a reader seeing this.

Italics, because of their slanted angle, can be hard for people to read, especially those who have reading difficulties, eyesight challenges, and are prone to migraines.

Also by Sophia-Rose Johnson

The Castle of Skull Series

Castle of Skulls

Counts Her Souls

By She Who Is Death-Touched

The Mermaids of Lake Superior Series

Beneath the Surface

Thaw the Heart

The MacLeod Trilogy with Susan Stradiotto

Fight for Darkness

Hunger for Darkness

Conquer the Darkness

Poisoned Darkness with Susan Stradiotto

Short Stories in Anthologies

"Bloody Mary's Day Off" in the *Twice Upon a Name*

"The Haunting of Neve Ravensblood" in the *Third Name's a Charm*

To those lost in the world,
just trying to find their way out of the woods

Content Note:

Before you begin reading, please be aware that parts of this book may be triggering for some readers. *The Favorite Kind of Wild Magic* depicts and touches on several difficult topics through either mentions or depictions: murder, animal death and sacrifice, anxiety, depression, violence, gore, and more. While the whole book does not pertain to such topics, please remember to use self judgement before reading.

Take care of yourself.

Chapter 1

Witches are not created but born. Magic
thrums through their veins. Witches are
neither good nor bad. They are just powerful.
– Unknown

The scent of death lingers in the air. The trees bring me visions of burning and screaming. I tilt my head north and then west. I've followed the coastline from the house and haven't seen a body.

Like every morning, I've taken off down the frosty forest path and headed toward the beach. Wind whistles through the trees, bringing the crash of waves from the Pacific Ocean, yet it doesn't tell me any secrets from last night. Or why it smells like death in my woods.

Sirens cut the silence. I stumble, startled, and a tree catches me. The leaves brush my back. I place a hand on the bark and say, "Thank you."

The emergency vehicle sounds pitch through the trunks and bushes. Birds flutter up from the canopies. The sirens are on the road, fading quickly. I run through the woods again.

Dawn has broken, but the clouds stay steady. I push through the backyard hedge. The vines and branches reveal brown veins. The tall bushes close after I enter.

The house looms above me. From the back side up the stone steps, floor-to-ceiling windows look out at the woods and eventual sea. Over the bedroom floor— I stop to see her on the balcony—is Daphne.

Blond hair curtains her face, but her head is turned east, where the smell of burned flesh rises from the trees. What does she see from her perch? Is there black smoke? I curl my hands into fists, not wanting to see what the trees can show me.

I quickly duck down the steps and through the back door, hiding in the kitchen. I'm not safe to be alone here. For such a large house, it is hard to find places of solitude. There are thirteen witches in the house. We practically live on top of one another.

"Maisie!" Johanna waves me over to the table she sits at with Lizzy. "Have breakfast with us."

I give them a non-committal smile, hoping it isn't a grimace, but Johanna never blinks. Her smile never falters. I walk over to the kitchen table, brushing my fingertips along the wood. My magic creeps along it. While the wood is no longer breathing like a tree would, it was alive once, so I can connect, even if minimally.

"What are you up to?" I ask in forced nicety, eyeing the books on the table. I haven't known Johanna to ever step into the coven's library.

Johanna giggles. "Lizzy thinks she got the omen of death last night in her reading."

My breath catches. Having kept the smile on my face, my teeth begin to ache. I don't tell them what I smelled in the woods.

"Johie doesn't believe me," says Lizzy.

She has two teacups sitting at the table. Neither have the death omen, but the leaves are also not dry. She must be trying to replicate it. Nonetheless, she has several books open and holds a teacup to the page to match the book.

"Because she was alone and didn't take a picture of it." Johanna leans across the table and lowers her voice. "I heard you were looking for a new coven."

Perhaps I should've run back out the door once I saw Johanna. It's too late now, but I could hide in the basement or in the hidden passageways. Unfortunately, the girls' voices filter down.

"Why do you think that?" I ask.

These rumors always fly in the house, but the strength depends on who starts them. It's a good chance it was Johanna.

"You've been here for a few years, but you never seem happy," she says.

I don't let my face fall, but I may have forgotten how to breathe. The seared scent of flesh is caught in my nostrils. It clings to my hair.

"You're powerful, Maisie," says Johanna. "I'm sure other covens have been asking about you." But she long *asked* to be in this coven.

"I'm very happy where I am. Thank you." My face hurts. How long can I hold this fake smile?

Other covens have asked after me, sure, but I'm comfortable here. I like it here. I like most of my coven sisters too.

Johanna downturns her lips, but before she can continue, Lizzy says, "See! Death." She's too excited for the omen.

Johanna whips the teacup from her hands. "That's not death."

"Yes, it is," argues Lizzy.

From my angle, it's not the death omen. Not that I tell them that or give Johanna the satisfaction of being right.

A bleary-eyed Susana almost knocks me out of the way with her desperation to get to the coffee. I back toward the door. This might be my only chance to escape. Johanna hasn't turned her steely gaze back on me.

"Have any of you seen Beatrice?" Susana asks, pulling out the carafe and a mug.

Lizzy peeps, "She went out with a local last night."

Johanna flips through the book pages and checks the teacup. "Probably her new love at first sight."

"You're right. She always has a new beau, and they take her to all the nice restaurants in town. She probably stayed over at his place." Susana yawns. "What are you working on?"

I escape before anyone can loop me in further. No one follows, but their voices fall into the muffles in the house. The steps I take upstairs and to the landing offer more voices coming from the ballroom or dining room. Perhaps it's the three staff members instead of my coven sisters. I brush my hands along the wall paneling, knowing I could push it in and hide. But I won't escape the voices. The sound only ticks up as I walk past the bedroom floor. Doors slam, and someone plays music in the bathroom. A shower sounds good, but I climb up the last set of stairs.

The doors to Daphne's suite are propped open. Knocking, I enter a lush living room connected with a kitchenette and personal bathroom. Behind the doors, she has a large bedroom. Everything is furnished with antiques: old, dark wood with bursts of pink, like entering a rose gold-tinted sunset.

Having changed since the balcony, Daphne wears a white dress without sleeves. Black buttons buckle up the middle. A large floppy hat with a black ribbon and bow hides half her features. She looks more like she's going to a horse track than stepping outside into late fall.

"Daphne, the smell…" I want to tell myself that it wasn't death—I don't know what burned flesh smells like—but do know what it is.

Daphne holds a pair of black gloves and a black clutch. "Do you know where Beatrice went?"

My tongue turns to sand in my mouth. "I only know what I've heard from Susana," I rush to say, because I don't want to know what she's thinking. But I do know. I don't want to admit it. Don't want to think about it. "Beatrice went out with a local. She goes on dates, a lot. She sometimes stays overnight. I can get Susana."

"That won't be necessary." Walking over to a golden basin sitting on her dining table, she swirls the red-tinged water with her finger. "Have you felt anything?"

My magic brushes the hair on my arms, but Daphne's balcony doors are closed. She has no living plant in her suite, so my magic clings to the dried herbs in her cabinets.

"Last night, there was pain from the trees," I say quietly, wishing the words weren't true. But the pain from the woods kept me up late, and I woke up earlier than usual to run. "But the locals like to have bonfires. They cut down the trees without a care, and then they burn them," I add quickly.

The pain is fresh, and it haunts my dreams. Roxie closed the window in the middle of the night, cutting me off, but it only helped a little. I'm sure I was still whimpering. My dreams took root from reality.

Daphne steps back from the basin. "Will you come into town with me?"

It is not a question I can say no to.

***

Girls are waiting by the front door when Daphne and I come downstairs.

Susana wrings her hands as Johanna brushes Susana's dark hair over her shoulder and coos softly, but then Susana steps away and says, "Lizzy got the death omen." She says it loudly enough that the whole house could hear her.

Daphne says nothing. No mention of us going into town or what we're doing. I don't even know. I just follow her.

"Lizzy didn't get the death omen," says Johanna. "But if it'll put your mind at ease, let's go with Daphne." She steps between Daphne and me without being invited. Her height and heels leave me in shadows. "Daphne, you don't think something has happened to Beatrice, do you?"

Without saying a word, Daphne bypasses them, and Susana gasps. Johanna rushes after Daphne, her heels clicking against the marble floor. I jog around them just to open the oak doors and step outside, taking a deep whiff of the fresh air and listening to the quietness of the oncoming winter. Thankfully, the burned scent has drifted off.

Daphne, Johanna, and Susana walk out. "Come along, Maisie," calls our leader from the train of girls.

I close the doors and hop down the steps. The old uneven stone is slippery from melted snow and the mist blowing sideways.

Windchimes sing in the breeze, and green vines twist around the old Victorian columns. The small gate between the rusted black fence opens for us to leave, and tire tracks from last night are visible in the mud. That must've been Beatrice's local's truck. Not many locals visit our house that is offset from the rest of the town, but we also don't participate. Just going into town and potentially being around mortals makes my hands slick.

"Johanna," Daphne said, "will you open the portal?"

With a smug smile, she steps forward. Her magic swirls in the air. "Where to?"

"The trees behind the police station in town," says Daphne.

Susana stutters, "What?" and Johanna's eyes widen.

I turn back toward the house, but Susana blocks my way. Tears well in her eyes.

"Daphne, why are you going to the police station?" asks Susana. Her voice cracks. "Does this have something to do with Beatrice? I just want to go into town to look for her, and I needed a portal to get there so I wouldn't have to walk. Maisie, did you know about this?"

"No," I say, and Daphne burrows her gaze into me.

I didn't know where we were going but suspected it. Beatrice is missing, and I know what I smelled in the woods this morning.

"Johanna, open the portal, or I'll have Maisie do it," says Daphne, words clipped.

Johanna opens a portal immediately. Daphne walks through and then waves me in.

***

We are a herd in the police station, Daphne at the head. People in office chairs swivel toward us. We are the "weird girls" from down the road, but "weird" is the least of what they call us. The house—and its inhabitants—have been the talk of this town for a century.

"We're here to report a missing person. I need to speak with someone in charge," Daphne says to the police officer at the front desk.

Johanna lingers only a few inches behind her, matched in many ways including clothing. Johanna's strawberry blond hair is even styled like Daphne's.

Susana is close to the desk too, peeking around the corner like she will suddenly see Beatrice.

One officer with a sky-blue shirt and navy slacks hobbles forward. Every time she moves, keys jingle off her belt. Someone types, a police scanner rumbles, Susana taps her shoe, voices hiss—the sounds pulse in my head. I twitch.

"Maisie, why don't you wait outside?" Daphne suggests. I move toward the door when Daphne adds, "Johanna, go with her."

Please not her.

Not anyone.

I push open the door before the police feel the magic. I scramble to get away from all the noise and stumble down the concrete steps.

The nearby trees dance in the breeze, and I fall into sway with them. But the sounds of the small town—people talking on the street, a bell tolling from the church, tires squealing when braking—creep into my peace.

Johanna slams the door behind her. "People are staring at you."

I can almost imagine myself as a tree, rooted to the earth and moving in the breeze coming off the waves.

"I don't understand why we came to the police," whines Johanna. "Daphne is acting like we're mortals, and Susana is scared. Beatrice went out with a boy, like she always does. Give her a few hours, and she'll be home, walk of shame and all. Anyway, we can find her ourselves. We're witches."

I close my eyes and try to focus on the natural world, but it's hard with my pounding heart. It's a chisel into stone, driving fear deeper into me until my breath is all but knocked out of my lungs.

"I mean, we need to chill out," continues Johanna. "It's not like Beatrice is dead, and if she is, well…. It isn't like Beatrice is a powerful witch—it would be easy for her to be picked off by some guy."

Swallowing a deep breath, I lose any nerve I had to tell off Johanna. This is not the time or the place. Johanna shouldn't have come. None of this should be happening.

Little did I speak to Beatrice, but I hope she is wandering the streets, heartbroken after a bad date. However, Daphne would've found her. Daphne can find anyone. It was what she had to be doing with the basin of water when I saw her this morning.

I eye a nearby tree. We're in the middle of town, but maybe it could lead me to Beatrice. The trees are always watching.

"This has got to be a test, right?" asks Johanna, filling the few measly seconds of silence. "See who can find Beatrice. Daphne does this stuff, I know it. It's how you got to be her favorite, right, Maisie?"

I thin my lips together. No, that isn't how I got to be her favorite. And Daphne doesn't have favorites. She just trusts me because she's known me the longest.

"I've been wasting my time at the police station." Johanna groans. "I bet Lizzy is all over this, and the other girls already know where Beatrice is. Damn it." She crosses her arms over her chest. "How can you stand the cold? You're not even shivering. Why did Daphne make me come out here with you? You're obviously fine."

I'm better but not fine. No longer twitching, I run my fingernails over the creases in my palms. I'm as calm as I can be with Johanna standing beside me.

"What is taking them so long?" asks Johanna. "I could've found Beatrice by now."

"No, you couldn't," I say.

No one could beat Daphne. She's just that good.

Johanna glares at me. "You don't know that. You don't know anything about me."

As the police station door swings open, Daphne walks out, a tearful Susana on her heels. My stomach drops. I didn't want to be right—why do I have to be right? This doesn't happen to us.

Johanna demands, "Well?" Disdain riddles her voice.

"The police will keep an eye out for Beatrice," answers Susana, dabbing under her eyes with her coat sleeve. "But she hasn't been gone long enough to file a report."

"I can find her," Johanna claims, turning to Daphne. She wears a smug smile, like this will be the chance she has been waiting for to prove herself. She'll fail.

She can't find the dead. Even the most practiced witches, like Daphne, can't find the dead.

Daphne trails her gaze along the street and toward the beach. I don't like how she eyes my trees. A cliff lingers over the beach. Was that where the scent of burned flesh had been coming from?

"I've already tried to find Beatrice," snarls Susana. Anger flashes in her glassy eyes. "Daphne has tried."

"Let's talk about this at the house. It's not safe." Daphne's halfway down the steps before Johanna catches up with her.

Chapter 2

There is nothing stronger than a coven,
except those sisters who hold it together.
—Guinevere Warren

It is now a competition to find Beatrice.

Johanna has taken charge of the whole thing. Roxie, one of my roommates, couldn't say no to a friendly— or *not* so friendly—competition. More girls show up. The word has spread like wildfire. Rochelle, Paula, and Ubah take part in the competition too. Mikayla and Kami haven't returned to the house since leaving yesterday and don't know about Beatrice yet. Astrid doesn't leave her bedroom.

Our coven used to be thirteen and will be thirteen again when Beatrice returns home alive. But I can't lie to myself. Nor can I lie to the girls huddled in the kitchen.

Each of them have their own idea to find Beatrice, mostly with tracking spells or a concoction of potions. Then the girls proceed to tell each other how they are wrong.

It's too loud, so I sneak to the backyard. The closed door holds back their voices.

The grass browns, but the trees—at least—stay green, healthy, and vibrant. Singing birds hop from branch to branch. In the summertime, the girls come out to sunbathe. One time, Beatrice challenged Susana to a somersault contest, and we were happy. I *was* happy.

A loud burst of laughter echoes out. They aren't going to find Beatrice that way… if they find Beatrice at all.

Slipping through the parted hedges, I empty into the woods and place a hand on a nearby tree. The rough bark is cold. I close my eyes and force my magic forward.

When Carmella—a former witch in the coven—went missing, Daphne tracked her. Our leader is a legendary tracker, but a witch's tracking isn't always reliable. Audrey once tracked someone incorrectly to the middle of the Indian Ocean, and the other girls made fun of her for weeks. Carmella had run from the mansion, and by the time I opened the portal, Daphne already had a crying Carmella in her arms. Carmella left our coven the next day.

The trees connect branch to branch. The whispers follow, the leaves in the wind fluttering. Flashes of fire clog my eyes. I jerk back before I'm thrown into the same pain as the trees.

"What are they saying?" a woman asks.

With a gasp, I spin around. The branches whack against one another, aiming for the intruder. I pull back my magic.

Daphne places her hand on my shoulder. "The police said there was a body found in the woods last night, in the ash of the bonfire up on the cliff."

Air whooshes from my lungs. "Susana acted like Beatrice was still alive."

"I sent her from the room to give pictures of Beatrice and a description. To Susana and the others—" she grimaces as laughter shoots from the house—"Beatrice is alive. Susana won't know until the body is confirmed to be Beatrice's or until Beatrice walks into the house. I'll leave you to the peaceful woods."

Daphne walks away like she is taking a stroll through the park instead of one of our sisters being murdered. Why did she have to tell me? I want the same innocence as my sisters, but I'm not like them. I've never been like the others in the house, no matter how many girls have come and gone.

Every ounce of pain threatens to topple me. I would rather hold to hope, which is why I stay in the tree line. I take the calm as long as I can, but the days are growing shorter. Night stretches out and wraps its tentacle around my neck. I try to ignore the cold.

Bright light sparks from inside the ballroom. The flashes of light mean the girls are no longer tracking—or trying to track—Beatrice. A boom shakes the windows. Laughter follows. Joyful, unapologetic, worriless.

Taking the back stairs, I pause on the main level. In the ballroom, Paula and Rochelle are having a dance off to heart-pounding music. Ubah shows off the pretty colors of her magic by reflecting the light against the glass chandeliers. Her magic has always been mesmerizing.

I trudge to my bedroom, only slowing in the sliver of light coming from Astrid's open bedroom door. I can't remember the last time I saw it open.

"No one believes me. Everyone thinks Beatrice's run off with a local. But she's been gone too long. She doesn't stay out all night and day," Susana sobs.

I don't know why Susana has gone to Astrid, who is the least maternal out of us. Perhaps it's because the others are ignoring how wrong this has become.

"I can't find Beatrice," continues Susana. "Neither can the girls. Or Daphne."

I tiptoe past the open door and lock my bedroom door behind me. Unfortunately, silence is the worst friend.

Chapter 3

Historically speaking, any witch killed in the
Salem Witch Trials was not actually burned at
the stake. They were either drowned or stoned
to death.

–Iain Skinner, *A History of Witches and Mortals*

The overnight snow has left a fresh dusting. The trees
and the woods on my right blur as I run. To my left is
the vast sea. Only red buoys bob in the waves. Stomach
hurting, I slow to a jog, but the feeling doesn't
dissipate.

Like a block of concrete on my chest, vines around
my body, I can't breathe. Beatrice has been missing for
the second day—probably dead—and the coven is just
trying to wait it out. I know this won't end well. How
can no one else see it?

***

I walk into the empty kitchen through the back door,
slick with sweat. Where the girls would be milling
about, drinking coffee, and eating breakfast is empty.

Red and blue lights flash through the house. I raise my hand, partially blinded, and creep forward.

Large windows sit on either side of the front doors in the entryway. Daphne stands outside, wrapped in a brown fur jacket. A police officer in a blue uniform stands opposite her. My sisters are nowhere to be found, but someone had to notice the police outside. I've never heard the house this quiet.

I sprint up the stairs and slink into the library above the front entryway. Three police cars outside the gates have their lights on, red and blue flashing across the gray clouds. Only two officers stand within the gates at the front of the house. Daphne is at the base of the steps while the officers stand on the gravel.

"Ears above, ears below. Let me hear what others wouldn't like me to know," I chant in a hushed voice.

The mansion groans, but the spell works. The girls are huddled in the ballroom, Kami calling Beatrice's death a vicious lie, Susana crying, Ubah praying, Roxie snoring. I twitch from the power of the spell. All their talking and loud crying almost floors me. I focus on the conversation below.

"Tell me, what are you doing to find Beatrice's murderer?" orders Daphne.

"Ma'am, we are hoping to contact her family," an officer pleads.

"We are her family. This is her home," she responds.

"We have nothing to go on besides her name and the pictures we've received from you. We are looking for Beatrice's killer, but we need to understand her better," explains the officer.

Daphne scoffs. "You're wondering if she deserved to be burned at the stake?"

"Ma'am, we're wondering who would want to hurt her," says the officer below me.

"I told you about the local boy who picked her up. I gave you the description at the station—"

A sharp pain shoots through my head. I'm thrown out of the conversation and back against the library floor. Daphne probably felt the magic the second I used the spell.

Still recovering, I join my sisters in the ballroom, but the sound and emotions make the room tense. The windows are closed, heat trapped inside. Lizzy, Mikayla, Kami, and Ubah sit with each back facing a direction, candles lit and Beatrice's favorite things. A chill runs down my spine.

A seance will not end well. Communing with the dead is dangerous.

Susana is hunched over, and Paula hugs her. Rochelle holds Susana's other side. Her face is wet, reflective in the dim light. I want to give my condolences, but my tongue swells in my mouth.

Sitting next to Roxie, I force myself to stay with my sisters. The amount of pain in this room is overpowering. The girls' cries echo in my skull, like I have thousands of voices inside, but I cannot leave. We are stronger together.

Through her dark eyelashes, Roxie mumbles, "This is so boring—but sad. Astrid woke me up for this. Made me come here. Shit, here a bitch comes." She closes her eyelids and lets out a soft snore as Johanna hovers over me.

"Who do you think should take Beatrice's place?" asks Johanna.

Roxie stiffens beside me, and I blink. My mind takes a few seconds to process, like I'm a computer loading a large file.

"What?" I ask.

"You know, who is the next witch Daphne is going to bring in?" Johanna rolls her eyes at the girls in the corner. "They can cry all they want, but we both know we need thirteen witches. It's not good for anyone when we're down a witch. You get that, don't you, Maisie? You've been here a while. Didn't Astrid take your friend's place? What was her name? Audrey?"

She shrugs, like it's no matter, but my heart has jumped to the base of my throat. I couldn't speak even if I wanted to.

"Who do you have in mind to join the coven? Any powerful witches?" asks Johanna.

My older sister, Marney, comes to mind, but I haven't seen her since before the Second Witch War. I left our parents' house when I was young, and I thought she would visit me. At least in my dreams if not during the day. She's a dreamwalker.

"I know a lot of powerful witches. Daphne will want a stronger witch than Beatrice," says Johanna, and Roxie snores a little louder. "It's probably how Beatrice ended up dead."

My fingers wind tight into my palms, but my magic is slow to the uptick. There is no life to cling to in the house.

However, Johanna is already pushed back to the far wall, dispersing the four girls doing the seance. Confused shrieks fill the room.

Johanna groans, her head hit the white plastered wall. Thankfully, there isn't blood. Roxie has opened her eyes, her hand pistoled from the quilt. I scramble out of the way as Johanna sends a rush of energy forward, a spell on her lips. She's a conjurer, so her imagination will be our downfall.

The spell stops suddenly. Astrid stands, scarred arms outstretched. She has collapsed all magic into nothing. The weight presses on my chest. My magic has dried up in my bones. I try to reach for it but can never grasp.

Wearing a quartz pink dress and a bow on the small of her back, Daphne doesn't look as much in mourning as she does as a ballerina. "What is happening here?" she demands, standing beside Astrid. "The police have only just left the grounds. You could have exposed the coven."

"Johanna started it," Roxie whines, throwing off the quilt. Her thumbs are hooked between the knots.

"You threw me across the room!" Johanna spits, now standing, and Lizzy checks the back of her head. "I didn't do anything to you."

Roxie storms out of the ballroom, but I hesitate to go with her.

Daphne lets her pass before turning to the now silent room. Astrid has her raised hands balled into fists, holding our magic hostage.

"Beatrice has passed," says Daphne, voice definite. "I'm sorry for the loss of our sister. Friend. A wonderful person. We will hold our witchy duties tonight. Once the body is returned to us, then we will hold a funeral."

"Is that all the police said?" Susana uses the back of her hand to wipe her tears away.

Daphne says, "She was dead previously to the burning, if that adds any comfort."

No.

Yes.

Maybe.

"We need to find the killer," Paula urges.

The other girls nod. Under that sadness is anger.

Daphne holds up her hand. "The police have assured me they are looking for her murderer. The mortals are suspicious of us, so undoubtedly, they will be watching us. We must be careful."

My stomach twists. She talks like this is the beginning of a witch hunt.

"What about the open position?" Johanna interjects.

Hate-filled eyes stare at her. Roxie won't be the only witch attacking Johanna.

"Johie, maybe we shouldn't," whispers Lizzy. "Beatrice just died."

"We need thirteen witches." A smile creeps on Johanna's face. "I know a few powerful witches who are available."

Curling her upper lip, Daphne looks more like a rabid dog than a witch. Perhaps she's part werewolf. She stalks from the ballroom.

Chapter 4

A soul wove with mine, sisters across blood,
life and death shall not divide us.
—An old witch saying

When the clock strikes seven, we sit in the dining room in silence and wear our darkest but nicest clothes: Kami wearing something new, Ubah in a black hijab, Astrid a black veil. While Johanna wears black, a fake diamond necklace hangs from her skinny neck. Still wearing the quilt, Roxie stares blankly down.

The old grandfather clock tolls as Daphne stands at the head of the table, her hair pulled into a stiff bun. Her clear face makes her look younger, so she barely looks older than me. That's not possible when she's been in the coven for years. The soft candlelight rounds her features, but she misses the harsh etches of age.

With Beatrice gone, the even sides of the table are lost. We've had girls leave the coven before, and Daphne has usually found replacements in less than a week. It's different now.

"I know this has been hard," says Daphine to my sisters wiping at their swollen eyes and red-tinted noses. Her voice is missing its normal vibrato. "Our sister has been murdered. Beatrice deserved better. We must respect and mourn her. We must also know that tomorrow is a new day. Life goes on." She sits.

We wait for something more, but then the food is served. As if we didn't have enough food to eat all day. It's like we are eating Beatrice's sins. We do it silently, ripping into freshly baked bread and drinking red wine. The color is too close to blood, and I don't like the taste.

Roxie glares at Daphne, and I'm caught between them. Not that Daphne shows that she notices how Roxie sneers. I snatch a roll quickly and sink back into my chair as food is passed around. We take from plates filled with red meat and bowls of sweet potatoes and soup. I try to pass to Roxie quickly, but she is slow to take.

Johanna sits on Daphne's left, Astrid on Daphne's right. I, her supposed favorite, am at the far end of the table. However, a mile couldn't space Roxie from Daphne enough. Her anger for Johanna has only been replaced by Daphne.

I put something bacon-wrapped on Roxie's plate. "Have you tried this?"

Her plate is full. I don't want to eat either.

She mumbles, "I spoke to Daphne. She won't do anything about Beatrice."

I'm not sure what our leader can do at this point, but I say, "Daphne wants justice as much as the rest of us do. Daphne picked Beatrice—"

"Bullshit," she hisses. "I want revenge on Beatrice's killer, so does everyone else. But it goes beyond that. Daphne knows her shit. She knows how to bring Beatrice back to life."

"No." I choke on the bread.

Daphne eyes me down the table. I drink water, and it clears the bread from my throat. Horror strikes me. I struggle to find something else to say.

"Or reverse time," adds Roxie.

The water glass lands with a thud on the table, and water sloshes over the side. Girls stare down at the end of our table. Every other soft conversation has flickered out. Open curiosity stares at us. I wipe my hands on my napkin. Slowly, the girls focus back on their grief.

I whisper to Roxie, "No."

There are so many ways necromancy and time travel can go wrong. Not that I doubt Daphne knows those witches or spells. A group of witches tried it after the Second Witch War to bring back the Council, and the weather was thrown into whack, such as snow in the Pacific Northwest in June.

Rolling her eyes, Roxie jumps to her feet. The chair falls against the floor with a loud clatter. Every head whips toward her, except for Daphne. She and Astrid have their heads bent together, still deep in conversation. Roxie screeches, making herself impossible to ignore—though Daphne manages it—and then storms from the dining room.

I've let her go once today. I shouldn't do it again. I stand, but Daphne commands, "Don't." Her tone cuts me like a knife. I sink into my seat.

Daphne turns to Johanna, and Johanna starts a conversation. Names of witches pop from her mouth as she pushes her friends into the coven. The rest of us eat in silence, heaving forks and scraping knives against plates. Heaviness weighs on me until I'm slumped over the table.

***

A couple of minutes before the witching hour, we gather in the ballroom. I look for Roxie. Even angry with Daphne and Johanna, I don't think she'll miss the ceremony. It isn't about us but Beatrice. I've disliked sisters in the coven, but I wouldn't miss what could protect them in the afterlife or the next life.

A hand touches my shoulder, and I jump. My dinner lurches into my throat.

"Steady." Lizzy stands behind me. "Johanna isn't here either."

Daphne, Roxie, and Johanna are missing, Susana and Paula also gone. That should make me feel better. Powers are tied to emotions, and we are a powder keg about to explode.

Susana and Paula enter the ballroom next. Daphne steps in behind them and scans the room, landing her gaze on me briefly. If we don't have the numbers, then I don't know how we'll send Beatrice to the afterlife.

"Get into formation," orders Daphne with an exasperated sigh.

I step to one of the points. My sisters move too.

We will have a proper funeral when Beatrice's body is returned to us. Until then, we need to put Beatrice to rest. Thirteen points are scattered across the floor, creating a symbol of a burning sun. The rays jut out. With Roxie missing, two points remain empty.

"Marina, Nancy," Daphne says, snapping her fingers.

Two staff members move quickly from the wall to the open spots on the sun. The three staff members—Marina, Nancy, and Shelby—have dabbled in magic but aren't coven members. Their magic may be as strong as Paula's or Beatrice's, which means to say that they do not have a power. Or perhaps the staff members are "crystal-gazers." I feel dirty thinking it—they are my family as much as any girl conventionally in the coven—but the other girls say it.

With us facing the center of the sun, Daphne grabs sage, pine, vinegar, dried daisies, burnt cloves, and mint. Fresh garlic has been placed in the doorways and windowsills, mixed with salt. I don't know if we're trying to keep Beatrice out or anger her spirit. Daphne motions for the windows to be opened, and Shelby runs to the floor-to-ceiling windows.

The drapes have already been pulled back, and silver moonlight slithers into the house. The winter breeze blows through the now open windows. My hair curls around my throat, brought by my magic more than the wind.

Daphne brings the ingredients to her face, calling for Beatrice. When Astrid bends, the rest of us follow. The old woman gathers supplies, and we all stand straight, holding them to our mouths and noses.

When the breeze blows in from the open windows, the ingredients fall like snow. However, the wind brings something else with… a high-pitched scream filled with anguish. I hold my ingredients tighter. Whatever the voice tries to say is lost in a wind tunnel past my head. I twitch.

I need to do this. We are her sisters.

"Beatrice, we miss you, and we love you," says Daphne loudly. "If you can hear us, we want you to know that we are your family. We are your sisters."

The floor grows warm through the soles of my shoes, and I hold my filled bowl high. My arms tremble.

"We ask you, Beatrice," Daphne continues, "to move on. To find a new, fulfilling life. A life filled with love, respect, and kindness. Give to others what was not given to yourself."

The wind knocks over candles and blows the ingredients around our ankles. The flames flicker out. The floor has been burned numerous times. It'll take a lot to destroy this house. It has stood longer than any of us.

"Please, Beatrice," Daphne says. "It is time to move on. Think of the next life. Don't go down the path of revenge."

The chanting bellows over the wind. I'm barely able to see through my hair. I hold the few ingredients I still have in my hands, but the wind whips them away. The hardwood floor burns under my feet. I'm too attached to this house—well, the wood of the house, infused with my magic. The whole thing could go up in flames, but we can't break the circle.

"Beatrice! Be free from this life. Be better than the monster that destroyed you!" demands Daphne.

The screeching wind halts. My hair falls down my shoulders and back. I stifle a shudder.

The floor glows as bright as the sun. The heat claws up my legs. We jump back. Daphne is the only one who remains on her tip.

She doesn't grimace or move. With her eyes closed, she is as still as a statue. She could blend into the walls.

Finally, she says, "It is done."

The lights go out.

Chapter 5

The trees have eyes. The ground has ears. The
wind has a voice.
–Unknown

On just a few hours of fitful sleep, I rush through the
trees. The branches try to catch me. I pitch myself
toward the town and eye the cliff where Beatrice was
burned.

I shouldn't go. I should stay away. I should go back
to the house. My feet drag across the sand up the
cliffside, and I think about more than once running
away. But I have to see this through.

The cliff is deserted of mortals, but the remnants of
the bonfire remain: broken wood, torched ground, wet
ash. Bushes and branches are singed. Drawing closer, I
catch Beatrice's burned body outline. Bile bubbles in
my stomach, and I double over, dry heaving. I have not
seen Beatrice's body and mostly avoided her ghost, but
I have already seen too much on the cliff.

In the dusty gray and green woods, the yellow police
tape hangs from the trees, blue gloves discarded, heavy
boot prints dug into the ground, white cotton swabs

left in holes like a landfill. They—the police, Beatrice's killer, and everyone else—have left this place in tatters.

Stroking the soil, I murmur, "What did they do to you?"

The scene is secluded at night but popular during the day, especially for tourists in summer. Every local has been up to this point at one time or another to get a beautiful view of the town and the ocean. It's one of the places we take any new girl that comes to the coven. We won't take them here anymore.

Placing my hand on a charred tree, I ask, "What did you see?"

My magic takes hold, and a vision transports me back to a few nights ago.

A dark film overcast covers my eyes. I am rooted like a tree. The natural night sounds silence after a snap of a branch. The person is clouded in shadows but pulls a large, heavy-looking duffle bag. I feel pain as the person begins to chop the wood like my body being cut in half. The person sets to work, building the pyre and throwing tree branches and brush on top. Before lighting, the person pulls the duffle bag over, unzips, and pulls the dead Beatrice out.

I don't want to see more, but my magic grips my hand to the tree and forces me to watch.

Once the body is on the pyre in my vision, the person lights the wood. They don't stop to inspect their work, but I have to observe Beatrice burn. The flames gobble up her body and spit out ash.

I refocus on the present cliffside. When I take a breath, I only smell burning wood and flesh. It coats my tongue. Images of Beatrice's body dropped on the pyre and set alight haunt my mind. They are forever seared into my brain.

I jump up, ready to run, but trip over my feet. Mud splatters across my face. My wild heart pounds against my sternum. It's a drum that keeps me moving. I sprint.

The branches reach out at the wind's behest. I focus my magic forward, building a portal, and escape to the beach. I fall face first into the moist sand. The portal closes behind me. The vines slink away like snakes.

That was the first time I was ever terrified in the woods. I was more scared of what I saw—what I asked for the trees to show me—but the feeling doesn't leave me. The trees wanted to show me more. What else could it show me? I don't want their pain.

A hand touches my shoulder. "Hey, are you—"

The sand opens beneath her feet, a sink hole with a gaping mouth. She yelps as the sand starts to swallow her whole. My magic continues to open the ground while I stand taller than I ever have before. My magic moves itself, like it's living and breathing.

"Stop," I order, and the sand freezes.

My magic dissipates, falling back into me. Where it belongs. The sand relaxes, though a hole is dug. Thankfully, Lizzy has only been eaten to her knees.

I rush over. "Lizzy, I'm sorry."

"It's okay. I didn't mean to scare you," she says as I help her out of the hole.

"It wasn't you." How do I explain? Do I even want to explain?

No one should have to see what I have. It's too painful to talk about.

Lizzy shakes her sand-covered hair out. "Is that your power? It's cool, a bit scary but cool."

Why I'm Daphne's favorite is unknown to the coven—myself included—but my magic has always been a draw. Specifically, my powers. Covens aren't supposed to poach witches off other covens until someone's eighteenth birthday, but Daphne arrived at my parents' door when I was fifteen. I haven't returned since.

"What are you doing at the beach?" I ask without answering her question. The sand fills the hole.

Lizzy picks up her dropped black camera. "The rolling clouds are cool. They match the waves. Should I ask about your run?"

Lizzy is still newer to the coven. She's my sister, but I have many of them. I'll get a new sister soon. It seems I always do.

***

Back at the house, I take the stairs two at a time and bang on Daphne's door. The visions cleared my mind as soon as I entered the grounds, but when I blink, fire launches across my skin. I could be Beatrice burning, but I'm only the trees pulled from the dirt and set on fire.

"Come in," Daphne calls.

I push the suite door open. I need to get away from the thoughts.

"I'll be out in a minute," she says through a closed bathroom door.

"Take your time," I murmur, closing the suite door behind me. As if that wood will keep out what I saw.

Daphne has swing music playing. The saxophones whine from the vinyl track. The balcony doors are closed. The sound can't escape, but it drowns out my intrusive thoughts instead of being too loud.

A spell book and ingredients lay out on the table. I inch closer to see what she's working on. Daphne hasn't mentioned anything to me.

"Maisie," she says.

I spin around. Daphne pulls her pink robe around her. Her wet skin and hair are tinted red. I probably interrupted bathtime.

"What's going on?" she asks.

"I went to the cliff—" It dies on my lips as I recognize what she has laying out. I've seen her do it before. "You're going to get a new witch?"

She crosses her arms over her chest. "Maisie, you know we need to be a complete coven."

I know.

Other girls have left the coven on their own, and we found another witch to replace our sisters. If we don't replace Beatrice in this situation, there is a chance we end up like her. Perhaps her death was a random circumstance, but Beatrice was kind. Sweet. Caring. Why her and not any of us?

Why not me?

"I need to finish getting ready, and then I'll be going to see about a new witch. Will you join me?" asks Daphne.

I hesitate. She's right about Beatrice and the coven—Daphne is always right—but this is very soon after our sister's death.

"You don't have to come," continues Daphne. "If you don't want to meet a potential new witch to the coven, Johanna has been keen to go."

"I'll be ready," I say.

Waiting outside the house, I curl my hands into fists and pace across the gravel. It crunches, disturbing the natural peace, and I grimace. If I listen close enough, I can hear the waves on the beach as well as the hum of the cars of the nearby highway. It makes me want to hide deep in the woods forever. I could go up into the mountains and never be found.

Walking out the front doors, Daphne wears a large round hat and a navy dress with flowing sleeves. She's pristine, makeup touched up and dress ironed. She holds a clutch in one hand and a cream-colored index card in the other. She's professional, and I'm wearing a baggy sweatshirt, muddy running shoes, and a pair of black leggings. This is half of the outfit that I wore to dinner last night when the others were in their mourning outfits.

Outside the gates, Daphne extends the card to me. "If you would like to do the honors."

I study the address. I'm not familiar with southern California. I have traveled to the wooded and mountainous areas, places far away from people. This address seems embedded in mortals.

Focusing my magic, I open the portal. Green vines curl around in an arch. Daphne steps through the portal, and I follow. The door to the misty woods closes.

The scent of fresh flowers fills the air. Large mansions with clay roof shingles and manicured lawns are spread out before us, straight edges, large windows and balconies. The houses look too much the same but all so unique. And flamboyant.

"You're a block off," Daphne says.

"Sorry," I mumble, cheeks burning.

"Don't be." Daphne takes a right down the street. "I'm only helping you with geography if we return to this location."

As I stand between multi-million-dollar mansions, I'm very sure I'll never be coming back here. Why did Daphne choose a witch with this background? This is Council money and privilege.

Walls—concrete, glass, or plants—separate the properties. The houses stack on top of each other, layer by layer, on the hillside. A mixture of new money and old money matches each house like a personality. In the mix of creams, grays, and oranges, splashes of pink and purple show off high income.

"I used to live in a place like this," Daphne says absentmindedly, like she's reminding herself.

To me, Daphne has always lived at the house in the Pacific Northwest, in a little town and in a style that people want but can't achieve. I have never lived anywhere like this. At my parents' house in Minnesota, Marney and I shared a bedroom until we hit our teenage years and started more than a few fights. But then, she would appear in my dreams, or I would hang out in her room. Even when separated, we wouldn't actually leave each other. Or so I thought.

Daphne walks up a driveway to a mansion with a gate outside the four-door garage. Another driveway curls around a small patch of bougainvillea flowers. Up the stone steps with palm trees hanging over is a door made completely of pink mosaic. The whole house is an off-color white with an orangish mix of roof tiles.

Daphne rings the doorbell, and the musical note tolls inside. "Maisie, think of this more of an interview. We're not taking her home today," she says, even though she was the one pushing urgency before. Maybe she has more witches in mind to join our coven.

The witch has to choose to come with us. For most witches, depending on their strength, they have their choice of covens. Johanna came immediately. Ubah took a week. I snuck out in the middle of the night when my family wasn't looking.

A teenage girl opens the mosaic door hesitantly. We are an opposite sight. Maybe I should've changed after I saw what Daphne was wearing.

After removing an earbud, she says, "Hello?"

"Amira." Daphne smiles dazzlingly. "My name is Daphne Duvay, and this is Maisie. We've come to speak with you." She is already stepping into the house.

Amira stumbles out of the doorway. "Can I-I-I help you?"

"You like tarot cards," Daphne says, and Amira takes out her other earbud. "Sometimes, you have friends over and talk to spirits."

With Beatrice's recent death, it makes me uneasy. But I step into the house.

"Yeah, I try to read tarot cards. I like them," mumbles Amira.

"And you like lighting fires," says Daphne.

I didn't know we were coming for a fire user. Is this one of Johanna's friends?

Fire users are... rare. Powerful. Incredibly destructive. What else have I read about firestarters in the books in the library?

Amira gulps. "I don't know what you're talking about. What fires? I don't..."

Daphne walks further into the house, but I wait. My coven leader has her head tilted back, dragging her eyes across the high walls and artwork. The house feels unnaturally sterile. While the outside has a sweet tinge from the flowers, the house only smells like unscented laundry detergent.

Besides the few family photos, the house doesn't look lived in. The white tile matches the white furniture and white countertops. Not a speck of dust floats in the air. Pillows are plump, dining table set for ten guests.

Daphne turns back to Amira. "We have some things to discuss."

Amira rushes to say, "I can explain the fires. They're not—"

"Amira," Daphne interrupts, "Maisie and I are part of a very special group of people. You may not know it yet, but you have the ability to do things that seem impossible to others. Now, it is time for you to decide: what do you want your life to be?"

Her eyes widen. "I'm only eighteen. I don't know...."

I'm eighteen and not equipped to make big choices.

"I haven't graduated from high school. I'm supposed to be there, but I hate it. The kids hate me." Amira fiddles with the white earbud. "Do you want to see my room?"

Hopefully, it's better than the living room and kitchen.

Her bedroom has its own full-sized bathroom and a door to the patio. Unlike the rest of the house, Amira's room has more color: walls with music posters, some signed; schoolwork piled up on her desk, a textbook open; things stacked on top like she had run out of space. It feels homey, like Marney's bedroom was when she was a teen.

"Are you home alone?" I ask as Amira digs under her bed.

"Parents are at work. Siblings at school." Pulling a box from under her bed, Amira smiles proudly. It is her prized possession.

The edges are rubbing away, revealing its natural pale wood shade. Amira flicks up the cover: two sets of tarot cards, lots of incense candles, several spell books, charms, potions, and idols. One of the potions is chunky, unlike how it should be. I hope she isn't planning on drinking that. I don't know how much of what's in the box is witchcraft.

"Amira, what about the fires?" prompts Daphne, and her smile falters.

While the house is cool from air conditioning, heat increases in the bedroom. My magic rises to the challenge, so I interlock my fingers around my back. Daphne raises her eyes, waiting, and Amira's jaw dangles open. We're caught in a stare down, I in the center of them. Daphne wants something, but Amira doesn't own up to what she can do with her magic. It's the first step for any witch. Amira can't hide from who she is—she has to embrace it.

"We'll be going now," says Daphne, turning on her heel.

She didn't take off her shoes when we entered the house, like she somehow knew this wouldn't last long. Maybe it's because she has interviewed so many witches before.

Amira stands quickly. Her box falls to the side. The contents spill out. "But you just got here. Let me show you what I have done. Let me show you what I can do. Please!"

I follow Daphne, too slow for anyone's good. It feels wrong to run in this house, but I want to escape the whiteness.

Daphne is already out the front door, and I swoop down to grab my tennis shoes. Amira latches to me, and I still. Why do people have to touch me? Her clammy hand sticks to my sweaty skin like glue.

"Tell her to take me," pleads Amira. "I need to go. Wherever. I can't stay here. Please."

I tumble to the side and barely catch myself on the white wall. My wet handprint is now an artwork. I just decide to put on my shoes outside. "Sorry." I pull away from her and run out the door.

Daphne is halfway down the street, and I jog after her. The relentless sun scorches the earth. Everything is so bright and glinting. I stumble while trying to put on my shoes but manage to do it. The dry grass turns green where I was just standing. I catch up with Daphne.

"Amira's an option for the future but not now. She's not ready," Daphne explains without facing me. "She wouldn't be my first choice in an everyday case. We don't need more destruction, but we live in dangerous times. Any form of protection is good."

If we can call a firestarter *protection*.

We walk downhill. Birds chirp. Palm trees rustle. Somewhere in the hills, a dog yips. We'll be heading back to the house and may not be alone, so I have to speak now. Or regret will eat me alive.

"I went to the cliff where Beatrice was burned," I say.

After a few long seconds, Daphne asks, "What did the trees have to say?"

"It was more what they showed," I say. When I blink, another memory flashes before my eyes. "Beatrice's body was dumped, like an afterthought. The pyre wasn't built. It was all in haste."

Daphne purses her lips. "What would you do next for our coven?"

This is more of a quiz than anything else. She asks for our opinions, but I think she already knows everything. Daphne's plans are already in motion. I'm just on the ride but the designated driver.

"I would tell the others to be on high alert, but they already are. I would offer comfort because they just lost a sister. And," I say with a sigh, "I would fortify our defenses. With an open spot brings a new opportunity for a powerful witch to protect us." I don't like myself for saying it.

Under her long eyelashes and big hat, Daphne raises her eyes, impressed. A thrill of satisfaction runs through me for acing her test.

Chapter 6

The last known witch hunt in the United States was a singular witch in northern Minnesota. Penelope Ravensblood was burned at the stake while her young daughter watched on.
–Stewart Powell, *Notes on The Witch World from the Council*

A black hearse pulls into the gated courtyard, carrying Beatrice's body. The body in a black bag is wheeled into the house on a creaking gurney. The smell of sterilization follows, masking the scent of every potion we have made in the last month. The hearse's tires kick up gravel as they speed off. The black gates slam shut behind them.

Astrid stands in the doorway, watching Beatrice's body on a table in the dining room, and Daphne places a hand on the crinkled black body bag and says, "Maisie, why don't you go? Astrid and I have work to do."

I leave the dining room. The words don't sit well with me. A different girl may ask, but I don't want to know. We do everything as a coven, especially in death. But the rest of the coven is asleep, and I don't want to be close to Beatrice's body.

Settling back in a seat in the library, I read. My fingers fly over the pages, and I soar through the words. The heavy book lays on my lap, and I'm practically absorbed into the cushions. When my hair tumbles down from my bun, I realize my day has transformed into night. My body is still, and my eyes are sore. How long have I been reading by moonlight? I place the book back on the shelf and exit the library to a quiet house.

The house has been often this quiet since we learned of Beatrice's murder. Life has been leeched from the walls. Fresh air has been sucked from the hallways. The house is stifling. Normally, I like the peace, but it feels as sterile as Amira's house.

Something moves from the corner of my eye, and I jump. Beatrice, now wrapped in a white satin sheet, lays on the dining room table. Nearing the doorway, I root to the floor as someone bellows a sob. On the back end, where it pushed from her lungs, is anger. Something I fear and don't want to draw nearer to, but I have never heard one of my sisters cry like this. Not even Susana.

"I'm sorry," blubbers one of my sisters. "I shouldn't have let you go off with him. Knew he was going to break your heart. Didn't know he was going to kill you." Roxie's cries grow louder. "I picked you up the last time a guy broke your heart. Willing to do it again. Didn't know I was going to have to care for your body."

I peek around the corner. Roxie leans against the table, the rainbow knitted quilt wound around her shoulders. She wears the quilt like a shield, though it has no magical properties. Beatrice loved to knit and made each of us a quilt. Mine sits in a cabinet in my bedroom, collecting dust.

I study my memories of Roxie and Beatrice. I don't remember them speaking, but I didn't speak much to Beatrice. She was kind and often spent her time with others. After seeing so many sisters come and go, I didn't want to get attached to another sister who would leave me.

"Trixie, I'm sorry. I'm going to find your killer. I'm going to make him pay. Make him scream and cry." Roxie settles beside Beatrice's satin-wrapped body. "Do you remember when we first met? You were so pretty. I thought I'd drop dead. I was so nervous to speak to you that I ran off. Later, you found me, apologizing, thinking you had offended me. Like you could ever offend me. Remember when we went to Paris. You got one of those dumb hats, but damn, you looked hot. It blew off in the wind. I love you, Trixie." Roxie sniffles. "You didn't have to love me back. I only stayed because of you. Don't know what I'll do without you. You are my sunflower."

Silently, I slip away before I hear anything else, yet what Roxie has said follows me all the way to my dreams.

* * *

In the morning, we stand a wall of black in the backyard. Lizzy lowers Beatrice's white-satin body into the makeshift grave. Leaves dangle from trees, but no breeze blows them away after I spent an hour cleaning up before my sisters arrived outside. None of them are focused on the perfect flowers or how the grass and the leaves are still green when the nature outside the backyard is brown and gray.

Roxie wears the quilt and a stoney face. She reveals nothing of last night, and I'm too much of a coward to ask.

"Would anyone like to speak?" Daphne hides under her large black brimmed hat like a turtle.

Susana steps forward, toes dangling over the edge of the grave. Paula holds her back, like Susana will tip into the hole. Lizzy has raised her arm out too, like she expects it to happen. I keep my hands firmly hidden at my sides. My magic has been wild since my sisters stepped outside, jealous and territorial for what has long been only mine.

"We are all family here, but the truth is Beatrice was my sister. Not by blood but love. I felt closest to her here. We shared everything, which is why—" Susana's voice cracks— "this is so hard. I didn't know…." She turns into Paula's waiting arms and cries loudly.

A shiver runs down my spine. Should I be doing that for Roxie? But she reveals nothing.

Daphne nods solemnly. "Anyone else?"

We have nothing else to say. We have stood outside in the cold, the snow just barely holding off, for the last thirty minutes. The girls from the South are wrapped in heavy coats and hats, wearing mittens. Their cheeks have pinked. The funeral was quick, but we've had our time to say good-bye and mourn our friend. This is only a formality. One that I would like to be over.

Johanna is the first back to the mansion, Lizzy following on her heels. The rest of the girls trickle until Roxie and I stand alone. I need to put the dirt on Beatrice's body, or I would be inside. Or in the woods. The emotion that rolls from the girls leaves me hunched.

"Do you want a few minutes alone with Beatrice?" I ask.

"Why would I?" Roxie steps away from the hole. "Can you give her sunflowers?"

Nodding, I focus my magic on the natural surroundings. Lizzy could do this too, but I didn't have to touch the body. This is our silent tradeoff. The dirt covers Beatrice's body at the bottom of the hole. The ground becomes even, and my magic starts to grow sunflowers. The green stems and budding leaves sway in the breeze.

I kneel, wanting the best for Beatrice. Like I have done for others. The green stems ease themselves toward the sky. The yellow petals encompass the brown centers. Beautiful. But the petals aren't even. The color is too dull. I twist my wrist and push my magic a little more. The color still isn't right.

"Thank you." Roxie walks back into the mansion before I have finished the sunflowers. The kitchen door slams shut.

I look at the bare gravesite beside Beatrice. My hand springs up from my side, and red poppies rise from the

ground, full and luscious. Poppies were Audrey's
favorite.

Chapter 7

Never judge a book by its cover.

–Unknown

I sit in the library with a stack of books to my left and a notepad to my right. These are the good days. I need to focus on something when everything is spinning around me.

The book is filled with stories of how witches used power-inducing potions to amplify their magic, especially in battle. However, when the witches came down from the high, it was almost torture: convulsions and vomiting. Their powers started to eat them alive. I've seen this before. It's another thing to haunt me.

"What are you working on?" Lizzy strides toward me.

I hadn't heard her enter the library. I itch to cover the books, but she's already eyeing the open pages and my notes. "I'm just doing some research. It's always good to learn more," I mumble.

"Power expansion," she murmurs over my shoulder. "Why this?"

"I need something to do with my afternoon."

"Is there anything I can help with?"

I close the book. It'll be too suspicious to hide my notes. "Have you found any information about Beatrice's killing?"

She draws her eyebrows together. "I've been looking but haven't found much. I've called the police, but they won't tell me. There's nothing in the local newspaper. None of the girls have said anything. Why?"

"Beatrice's killing... I'm not a detective, but things aren't lining up," I say, recapping my pen and setting it on my notes. "She was dead prior to being burned. She was picked up by a guy she trusted—"

"But we don't know if he did it," Lizzy interjects.

Or who he is.

If the girls suspect this guy killed Beatrice—or even found out his name—there's a good chance he would end up dead. I don't know which of the girls would be the one to kill him, but the police would blame us. With everything going on, we don't need the police at the house. They are likely suspicious of us anyway. They haven't found any evidence of our wrongdoing or would be searching the house. It would be fruitless. Besides finding proof that we practice witchcraft, none of my sisters are murderers.

Nancy pokes her head into the library. "Maisie, Ms. Duvay wants to see you."

I get up, ready to put my books back, but Lizzy says, "I got it."

"Thank you," I say.

I jog up the staircase toward Daphne's suite but pause when a voice roars, "I'm leaving, Daphne! I hate it here. You've done nothing to help. Are you even looking for Beatrice's killer? Johanna said you are already looking for her replacement!"

The suite doors are open. Roxie—the yeller—stands near, fingers curled like claws. Twenty feet away, Daphne eyes me. I doubt she summoned me upstairs for Roxie. I'm usually the last one people want for a fight. I consider backing away. Daphne may have spotted me, but Roxie hasn't.

"You're free to leave if you like. It is your decision," says Daphne, voice calm. This probably isn't the first time she's had a girl screaming at her in her suite. "We need thirteen witches to be a complete coven. It offers protection. I want to give you all time to mourn, but I need to protect the coven."

"You're replacing her, so replace me too!" Roxie whirls around. Her eyes are wet.

If I was any other girl in the house, Roxie would be getting a hug. Instead, I hold my hands behind my back. I should be able to offer her more, like Paula or Rochelle would, but I'm just me.

"Maisie, we need to talk," Daphne calls.

A sneer pulls up the left side of Roxie's face. "Run to her, *favorite*."

Her shoulder knocks into me, and I stumble back. Pain shoots up my arm as Roxie stomps down the stairs. Her footfalls are like rumbles of thunder. The storm is passing now.

"Maisie." Daphne waves me in.

Closing the doors, I shuffle into her suite. I should've stayed in the library. It's safer.

A large bowl of shifting water sits on the bar, reflecting palm trees and something black. The images blur together, swirling in orange flames at the base of the basin. A face appears before disappearing into flashing red and blue light. The scent of magic waits in the room. It isn't Roxie's.

"Amira set another fire, which killed two people," says Daphne like this happens every day. So calm. Almost not human.

I freeze. It's too soon after Beatrice's death—and burning. Flashes of what the trees show me roar in my mind. I can smell burnt flesh and feel the damp ash on my skin. I scratch my exposed arms to get it off. It's not there. I'm not in the woods.

"We'll need to go back to California," orders Daphne, splashing the image away.

* * *

The plants hint a green tint but are mostly brown. Things are ready to burn, like they know there's a firestarter in their mix. Everything is slowly dying. One match could burn everything down.

Killing anyone is wrong—mortal, witch, or other. There has been enough death in the history of witches. Amira is a young and unexperienced witch, so she couldn't have known what she was doing, especially in a home that didn't appear to know about the existence of witches. Another reason why Amira should've found a home in our coven. She needs someone to teach her the ways of being a witch and how to coexist with those who are different but also like her. She has a strong and wild power. She needs an ally.

The fire—while extinguished—draws a crowd as Daphne and I round the street corner. Gray steam rises from the blackened brick and guts of a building. The scent churns my stomach. Too soon. Palm trees reach toward me, but I wave them off.

"Amira! It's good to see you." Daphne slithers an arm around Amira's shoulders.

Amira, for her part, looks confused. I am too. But Daphne had said…. Maybe Daphne knows that this was an accident.

The crowd glances toward Daphne with her loud outburst, but then they turn back to the fire department and the police. No one suspects Amira of being the firestarter or us as witches. Two local news stations roll their cameras. I duck my head away from the cameras, but one lens has followed Daphne. She does look more like a celebrity than a normal woman.

Daphne totes Amira toward an ice cream shop away from the crowds but still in public. Its *open* sign blinks in the window. She practically throws Amira into a booth. I slowly slip into the booth seat. Why have we come here? I don't openly judge her or Amira but don't know what we're doing. Daphne didn't say—I didn't ask. Based on how Daphne acts, everything must be okay.

The waiter takes our orders and returns promptly with our milkshakes in a diner that mirrors the 1950s. Red vinyl seats match an old jukebox in the corner. I pull my orange milkshake toward me, pushing aside the whip cream and cherry. Daphne and Amira haven't said a word to each other since entering the ice cream shop. I curl my lips around the paper straw, slurping to break the tense hold on the three of us.

"I wasn't expecting a milkshake from you." Amira presses her lips to the chocolate milkshake straw and sucks. "How's your shake?"

Daphne hasn't touched her strawberry milkshake that's still piled high with whip cream and a cherry, so I say quickly, "Great. They don't have this flavor where I come from. I was tempted by the pineapple flavor. We really stick to chocolate and vanilla. Maybe strawberry. Have you ever had a malt?" The words spill out of my mouth before I can stop them.

Leaning across the table, Daphne says, "You started that fire, Amira."

I hold still. The orange taste is now unnaturally sour.

Amira begins, "N—"

Daphne holds up a hand. "Don't lie to me."

Amira glances toward the door. Sliding to the edge of my seat, I hold my milkshake glass. The coolness rolls through me.

"I want to know if you meant to purposefully kill those people," says Daphne.

"I—" Amira pushes up from the booth and runs. Her sneakers squeak on the linoleum floor.

Daphne sighs. "Go after her, Maisie."

Pushing out of the booth, I run after Amira. My legs stretch out, and my heart pumps. I jog—don't sprint—but it's like I'm flying. I make sure my feet hit the ground again.

Amira barely makes it down the steps of the diner before I reach her. "Wait, Amira!"

She spins around. Fire springs from her fingers. I reel back. She knows how to use her magic more than I thought. The heat licks my skin. The palm trees start to bend toward Amira, almost snapping in half. The smallest flame will light everything on fire.

"What do you want?" Amira yells.

She'll expose magic. Only one mortal needs to see how she wields her power. The firefighters will drench us in a moment, and the police will have questions. Have the news cameras turned to us yet?

"To talk." My voice is surprisingly calm, but my knees quake. "Please. I don't want anyone hurt. That includes you."

She needs help, a sister and a coven. Daphne can say that I grew attached to her, but I saw Amira in pain. How she was missing a part of herself.

"Please," I add, hoping it will make the difference.

With her hands in her pockets, Amira trudges back inside and slides into the booth across from Daphne, who looks to have not moved an inch. Her milkshake, though a little melted, still looks pristine. The mortals ignore us, watching the firefighters across the street.

"Welcome back," Daphne says dryly. Almost like this whole thing has bored her. "Amira, did you light that fire on purpose, knowing there were people inside the building?"

I flinch at her pointed words and then grab my milkshake again. It doesn't taste as good now.

Tears swelling in her eyes, Amira leans back in her seat. "You don't understand."

"What don't *I* understand?" asks Daphne. Her tone has lost the sweetness.

"You probably knew your whole life that you are a witch. Something better than mortals. But I've always been the freak. At home and at school," says Amira. "My siblings are perfect. And the kids at school are always mean. They know I'm different. They won't leave me alone."

There are parts that I recognize from my own life: school, sibling, freak. I brush perspiration off the side of the clear milkshake glass.

"And the fires?" Daphne prompts.

Amira bobs the paper straw in her milkshake. "At first, I didn't realize it was me. I thought it was just crazy coincidences."

"Did you ask your family?" Daphne questions.

Amira snorts. "You've seen the house. Do you think they're witches?"

"No," I murmur.

Daphne stiffens beside me, and I clamp my teeth shut. I'm not helping. I don't know why I'm here anyway. Maybe Johanna would've been better?

"What about the fire today?" Daphne asks.

Amira eyes her melting milkshake.

"We know it's not the first fire you've lit on purpose, but it's your first with victims," says Daphne. "I've been watching you. I've been impressed with how powerful you are. Why the victims now?"

I still. How many fires has Amira lit? How long has Daphne known? Yet she still chose to seek out Amira for the coven.

Glancing toward the burned-out record store, Amira says, "It was a kid from school and his friend. He's always been a dick to me, and this morning, he just… made me so angry."

The griddle in the kitchen flashes orange flames, making the cook jump with a small yelp. The fire dissipates as quickly as it starts. I stuff my hands under my thighs.

"He and his friend went into the store. What are the odds we all cut school on the same day? I took the chance, and boom." A small smile lights up Amira's face.

The orange milkshake boils in my stomach. I think I'm going to be sick.

"I know it was wrong, but I don't care. I once lit Ms. Fernando's cat on fire, and I feel bad about that. But these assholes…." With a shrug, Amira slurps her milkshake until it's only the remnants of whip cream.

"You should go home." Daphne stands and places money on the table.

I jump to my feet. We haven't helped Amira, but I don't want her in the coven now. She'll put my sisters in danger. But we're telling her to go back to her old life? She killed two people.

Beatrice is dead too. Would Daphne say the same thing if Beatrice's killer is a witch? Would Daphne let the killer go? At the same time, if I call the cops, I don't have any evidence besides saying Amira is a witch and has started other fires. I would only expose witchcraft.

Amira widens her eyes at Daphne. "Don't I get to join your coven?"

Heading toward the door, Daphne shows her back.

"Hey! I'm talking to you." Amira reaches out, fingers twitching.

I'm caught in the middle of Amira's wrath toward Daphne.

My magic jumps to the brim, but I can't fight fire. I thrive on nature and peace. I make things bloom. I cannot fight—

No fire.

No destruction.

Amira stands there dumbfounded. Her hand is still outstretched.

My thundering heart stops.

Daphne arches an eyebrow. She knew how this was going to end the whole time. Like she orchestrated it, I was one of the violins to be played. I sang for her.

Daphne slips an empty vial into her pocket. The smells of rusty blood, clove, and foxglove burn my nostrils. It's part of a potion I now recognize.

Amira is no longer a witch, and Daphne has taken it from her. Her powers are gone.

Chapter 8

Daphne Duvay is a legendary witch. I knew I had to join her coven when I had the chance.
—Lada

When we get back to the house, my mind is still stuck on Amira. Daphne holds her head high as she walks inside. She changed Amira's life in a few moments. Who's to say if it was for the better?

Would Amira be fixed? Would she pay for her crimes? She's still a killer, and I feel complicit. First with Amira. Second with Daphne for committing a crime against a fellow witch. We've bound her powers.

I want to change and go for a run, needing a break from everyone. When I get to the bedroom, Roxie has a suitcase on her bed. Her stuff doesn't fit in, no matter how much she shoves down. The quilt she has been wearing lays next to her suitcase.

"Don't try to stop me," she warns. "I'm leaving. I'm done."

I sit on my bed. The mattress is too soft, and I feel myself sinking in. That is when my thoughts start to pound my skull. The orange milkshake slithers up my throat. I can't stay here.

"I mean it." Roxie packs slower. "I'm leaving."

I tie my running shoes. Through the loop and back out. Perfect bunny ears. I double knot them. Safe and secure.

Roxie stomps over to me. Her shadow crosses my shoes. "I'm talking!"

"You're lashing out because you're hurt. I don't think you'll leave." I stand, and Roxie stares at me like I'm speaking another language. Normally, I wouldn't say this, just let Roxie leave, but I have missed my chance to say other things. "I heard what you said to Beatrice last night."

"What?" Her cheeks redden. "You were eavesdropping! It's not what it sounded like. I was just saying bullshit. I was drunk."

"I know what I heard. I'm not going to tell anyone." I head toward the bedroom door. I'll send in one of our other sisters who mourns openly. Who can care for Roxie better.

After a second, Roxie orders, "Close that fucking door."

I turn, unsure if she meant with me in or outside the room.

"We need to talk," she says. "Fuck. Didn't you have friends growing up?"

Not really. Coming back inside the bedroom, I close the door behind me and sit on my bed. The last bed in our room belongs to Mikayla, but she rarely spends time with us or in the bedroom.

"Trixie." With a huff, Roxie picks at the quilt. "She was the first girl I've ever had a crush on. The day she showed up—did you see her? She was fucking gorgeous. I ran away like an idiot." She smiles. "When we spent some time alone, it was the best feeling in the world. She's perfect. And then she got killed. The end." She settles on her bed.

My heart sinks. "Did you tell her how you felt?"

"No," she says. "She liked boys."

I draw my eyebrows together. "But you liked her?"

"I *love* her." She pulls the quilt around her shoulders, like this is the closest she'll ever be to Beatrice holding her. "Have you ever told a crush you 'loved' them?"

"I've never loved someone. Like that."

I love my parents and Marney. I love my coven sisters. But I've never had interest in another human being like that. It seems weird.

"It didn't matter." Roxie runs a hand through her hair. "Did you see the guys she always went with? Emphasis on *guys*. I didn't want to be in love with her. Didn't want to be in love with anyone. And I didn't know it was going to be here and didn't know why it was her and it hurts so much—" her voice cracks— "to lose her. I wonder if she ever thought I was pretty or smart or funny."

I don't know what to say. Do I lie to her and say that Beatrice would've thought all those things? I didn't know Beatrice well enough. We missed our chance to ask before sending her to the next life.

We sit in silence for a few minutes. My legs still itch for a run, so I ask, "What now?"

Marney, if she was here, would know what to say. Any of the other girls in the house would know what to say.

"I don't know." She lightly hits her head against the wall. "I'm still leaving."

"Okay." I jump up from my bed.

"God, you're worse than Daphne." She flops on the bed, and the quilt falls over her head.

I run down the stairs and into the backyard. The sunflowers aim toward where the sun is supposed to be, but the clouds float thickly in the sky. The fall coldness is overtaking the backyard. It's only by my hand that the flowers continue to bloom. The plants leech my magic away, but I happily give it to them.

Chapter 9

Guinevere Warren had fourteen daughters,
spreading them across the most powerful
families in the New World. While she was
married to a singular man, it is rumored that
each of her daughters had a different father.
Guinevere hoped to mate with different
witches and learn which power was
reproduced in multiple generations. Thus,
which power became recessive.
–Iain Skinner, *A History of Witches and Mortals*

A week after Beatrice went missing, things are starting to return to normal, or at least, that is what we try to do. Johanna always wears a smile, and she organizes events for us. Most of the girls are hesitant to go out in public, but Johanna uses me as an example: I've yet to be abducted and killed when I go for runs. I'm not sure I'm the best example. I'm not around mortals in the woods.

Roxie is still around because every day I find our room disorganized, but I never see her. I haven't seen

Daphne lately either. Nor Astrid. They could be missing for all I know.

Back at the house after a run, I cut through the kitchen. Paula pours soup from a can into a bowl, and it plops with a splash. The odd orange color looks more like old squash than tomato.

"Hi, Maisie," she says, smiling.

Giving her a nod, I take off my muddy shoes.

"I wish I could be like you." She puts the bowl in the microwave. "But I hate running and working out. And being sweaty."

Paula is naturally lean with curly blond hair and piercing brown eyes. Freckles dot her face and exposed skin, like small constellations. She is usually with Ubah. I used to have a best friend like that.

"You should hang out with us," Paula offers, waiting for her soup to heat.

"I need to take a shower." My clothes stick to my skin, and my hair is a damp lump on my scalp and shoulders.

"After then, join us," she says. "We're in the ballroom."

Without an excuse, I go to the ballroom after showering, brushing out my hair, and changing clothes. I slowed myself down just to take a long time, but the girls are still there. Forts have been erected. Pillows and blankets are piled into a makeshift bed. A projector plays a love-like reality TV show on a wall, and girls play a board game on the floor. Out of the two choices, I sit between Lizzy and Ubah and scan the crowd of girls.

"Who are you looking for?" Lizzy asks.

"Roxie," I say.

Susana snorts.

I eye her, unsure if I've ever heard Susana do anything like that. "Wasn't she invited too?"

The doors are open in the ballroom, and most of the coven is here. Except for Daphne and Astrid who never come. Sometimes, it's easy to forget they live here too.

"Roxie—what a drama queen. She hated Beatrice, never said a word to her, and now she is all upset." Susana shakes her black hair off her shoulders. "I heard she's threatening to leave. She should just get on with it. Leave." She grabs the dice and rolls.

I'm taken aback by her words, so I look at the others. I should defend Roxie. She's my roommate. My sister. No one should be saying this about another sister. The rest of the girls around the circle nod. I'm the odd one out.

Suddenly, someone whistles, and Johanna stands in front of the projector, the images falling over her. "I have an idea," she squeals. "We need a party like the one we had a few months ago!"

The guest floor was buzzing that night. Locals were let inside, their curiosity palpable. Witches and other magical creatures traveled from far away to be at the party. The coven has had parties long before I arrived, and I stay away when I can. That night a few months ago, the mansion was so packed that it was hard to move, and the voices carried through the house. The music was loud, shaking the bones of the structure, and dust fluttered down. I tried to escape to the basement to get away from the noise.

"Beatrice just died," gasps Susana.

Johanna frowns. "I'm sad about that too, but think of this as an opportunity to find her killer. We can lure him out, bring him on to our turf. He won't even know what hit him."

Audrey dragged me out the few times there were parties when she was here. She had a blast, and I went to sleep quickly that night and stayed asleep long after.

"How do we know the killer would come?" asks Lizzy.

Johanna shoots her a stoney look, but it's a valid point. Would we want the killer to come here anyway? By the looks on my sisters' faces, the answer is yes. They'll tear him limb from limb.

"How are you going to get Daphne to okay this?" Ubah interjects. "You know how on edge she is. I doubt she'll want a party and to allow strangers into our house."

Johanna flips her hair back. "Let me handle that."

I stay with the girls, but when Kami and Mikayla leave, I follow. I walk up the curve of the spiral staircase to Daphne's floor. The doors are closed. I raise my hand before dropping it. This is ridiculous. Just something small in the grand scheme of things.

I turn away when Daphne calls, "Who is it?" The floor creaks under my weight.

I cringe. "Maisie."

"Come in. I'll just be a moment."

Inside her suite, the balcony doors are open. Sage, garlic, dried roses, pomegranate, and lemons scents fill the air. Something metallic too. Daphne has a bowl of water out and four calling cards face down. *Four potential witches*. I wonder if she plans to bind their powers too. Many potions have crossover ingredients, so it could be that Daphne tries to mask the smell of a binding potion with garlic and lemons. I don't let the thoughts go further. I trust Daphne, and I know she does what she needs to do for our safety.

I wander slowly around her suite. Hanging on her wall are framed photographs protected from the sun and wind, tucked away from prying eyes. The middle of the wall has pictures with water stains, yellowing edges, fingerprints, faces blurred out. Old newspaper clippings with black and white photos are lucky to be protected against time.

The lettering is small compared to the massive bold headline: A prohibition-era moonshine-ring club broken up in New York City. The photo below shows police officers leading two men in suits out of a club. A woman poked through the two men. The bright light of the camera seemed to have caught her by surprise. I don't know if it was the photographer's bright burst of light or the alcohol she probably drank, but she looked pale. Her features are like Daphne's.

"Find anything interesting?"

I jump back, cheeks burning. "Sorry." I shouldn't have been snooping.

"The pictures are on the wall for a reason." She wears a checkered black and white jacket. "What can I help with, Maisie?"

The party is on the tip of my tongue, but I swallow it. I'll leave that conversation for Johanna. "Have you found a replacement for Beatrice?"

"I've been looking." She walks to the basin of water reflecting the ceiling. She is not watching anyone for the moment.

"And Amira?" I curse myself for asking, but it has been days and Daphne and I still haven't spoken about it. I'm not sure I'm looking for an explanation. I'm not sure what I'm looking for at all.

"She's been arrested for murder," says Daphne.

My heart jumps to the base of my throat. "The police found evidence?"

"There is no evidence, just suspicion," she says simply. "Amira will get out of it. Her parents are wealthy."

"But she won't have her powers." My voice is harsher than I intended. My magic may be at bay, but my anger isn't. It boils inside me.

"I didn't steal her powers," she reminds me. "I only suppressed them. If she works hard and practices, she could be up to full strength again."

While we know that, Amira doesn't. She hasn't been trained by witches or been in a coven. She doesn't have any witchcraft knowledge. Nor would she know how to make a counteractive brew against a binding potion, including ingredients, dosage, and consistency. Potions go wrong often, which could make the drinker unintentionally ill. If Daphne hadn't brewed with perfection, then she wouldn't have gotten another chance to give Amira the binding potion.

"The rest of the candidates are in process, but I'm unsure of which one now." Daphne touches two of the four facedown cards. "I'm having a difficult time choosing who should join our coven."

"Are you hoping Roxie will leave?" I ask, and Daphne's mouth pops open. "I'm sorry," I rush to say. "I don't know where that came from. I'm just...." I need to stop talking.

"It's a stressful time," says Daphne with oozing sympathy. "And, no, I don't want Roxie to leave. I see how hard this is for her. Beatrice and her were... *close*." Somehow, Daphne knew about Roxie's feelings toward Beatrice when the rest of us were blind. "Roxie is allowed to leave if she wants. Like any of the girls are. You too."

I don't want to leave. This is my home.

My coven.

Daphne takes a handful of ingredients and lets them sink in the bowl. The colors morph together, and the flower petals rise to the surface. She places a finger into the water and twirls it until a tornado spirals to the bottom of the basin. The ingredients merge, but a potion doesn't brew. She has created a small transportation portal, unlike those powerful witches use, allowing her to look through reflective surfaces.

"Pick a card." Daphne pushes two of the cards toward me, and I flip them over.

Studying the pictures and limited information listed on the connected cards, I try to choose the best witch to join our coven. They are both powerful. One is a coven witch, like me, so she would've been taken away from a coven. The other seems to have no affiliation, but her parents were part of the Council—something that no longer exists after the Second Witch War. I need more information about the witches to know if either of them would fit into our coven. They would need us as much as we need her.

"That one?" I guess, pointing to the one on the left. It could go either way.

"Interesting," she says like she wasn't expecting me to choose that card. I knew I should've chosen the other witch.

Daphne picks up the card, pressing it to her nose and taking a breath. She puts another handful of ingredients in the basin. I lean over.

"Show us the witch we want to find, travel the world, space, and time. We call on our ancestors and the forces of all to find the witch to fix the pitfall," chants Daphne.

In the swirling basin, a fuzzy image starts to appear. The witch has a scarf draped around her neck, a heavy dark parka covering most of her and high boots to protect against icy rain coming in sideways. A wind blows her scarf off. She reaches out her hand, and the scarf flies back to her. The portal blurs until it returns to the shade of the basin and concoction.

"Telekinetic," I say.

Lizzy has telekinesis. It's a popular power, seemingly passing down through witchy generations.

Daphne steps back from the basin. "I thought you would look at the coven witch."

"She's the smarter choice, less likely to say no, and she's used to the coven life, but this witch—" I point to the basin— "had parents in the Council, so they must've been strong."

Just like Daphne wants. Maybe it's what we need too.

***

I don't know how Johanna convinced her, but Daphne agreed to the coven hosting a party. Maybe Johanna is more of Daphne's favorite than any of us think. So the next day, we go to the local mall. I was dragged here but didn't kick and scream. Maybe that was where I went wrong because I'm blinded by neon colors in store windows and the harsh fluorescent lights.

The mall is loud, even in the middle of the week. Children throw tantrums. Music plays overhead, only to be drowned out by music playing in stores or the high-pitched beeps from arcade games. A cell phone rings, and someone is yelling across the racks of clothing to another. My brain wants to burst from my skull, my ears leaking the fluid. I try to look for the nearest exit that won't set off a fire alarm.

"We should just go to Milan. Or Paris," says Kami to Mikayla as they shift through dresses. "Much better style."

"We already have dresses," says Rochelle on the other side of the rack.

"That's not the point," says Mikayla. "New dresses, new me. But, yeah, this mall sucks. We should go to Europe."

I peel back my glitter-covered hands and am unsure where to wipe them off. I slink out of the racks.

"But you have to get a mask, Lizzy! That's the whole point of a masquerade." Johanna throws open the dressing room door and struts out. She wears a skin-tight black dress.

"It looks great," Lizzy says.

Johanna scrunches her nose. "It needs more flare. Everyone can wear a black dress."

Lizzy holds a pink dress in her lap and a mask to go with it. "What do you think you'll wear, Maisie?"

Shrugging, I don't like any of the dresses the girls have suggested I wear. They say "this will bring out your eyes" or "this will show off your boobs." I don't want to wear a dress. I hate the idea of the party. I hate all of this.

"Are you going to match one of the themed rooms?" asks Johanna, returning to the dressing room. "We finally settled on the theme for the ballroom, which took forever. But then again, we stayed up all night on the invitations and sent those out before dawn. We have over three hundred reservations."

The number turns my hands slick. How will we be able to keep track of all the guests? Besides some locals invited, past coven witches and other witches are coming too. I only sent one invitation—to my blood sister—but it came back undeliverable. She's the only reason I would go.

I rub my hands on my pants. "I think I may just read in my room." Or hide in the basement.

"You're going to the party, Maisie! I'll drag you down myself." Johanna now stands in front of the mirrors, wearing a red sparkly dress with a train. "I've got dresses you can borrow. And we need all powerful witches on deck if we're going to get Beatrice's killer."

I nibble on the inside of my cheek. I don't think Beatrice's killer will come to our party, and we won't know who he is anyway. Since we're all wearing masks, it will be a good chance we won't recognize anyone either.

Lizzy leans over to me. "You don't have to dress up. Just come down for a little bit."

"I don't have a mask," I say, looking for an excuse. Even if it's lame.

Lizzy pulls a white mask from a bag. "If I didn't find the perfect mask to match my dress, I was going to make my own. You don't have to decorate it."

"Thanks." I hold the hard plastic.

The cut-out eyes stare at me. I run my thumb over the high ridge of the nose and under the eye holes, unable to fathom how to create something that showcases me.

Chapter 10

A witch in her element is the most dangerous
witch of all.
–Unknown

Cars line the street outside the house. Guests gather before the appointed hour, invitations in hand. Their voices vibrate the windows. I hide in the curtains, peeking out the front of the house.

While there are many people below—each wearing a mask—the witches are easy to pick out of the crowd. Magic rolls off them. They look off the tips of their noses at the mortals, who herd together and press closer to the gates. People will swarm the house and go where they shouldn't. The party will spiral out of control. Another reason I don't want to be here.

The coven giggles loudly. While it's nice to have some normality back in our house, what is the cost? Their excuse for the party about luring out Beatrice's killer is the last thing on their minds.

"Maisie, come on." Paula grabs my hand as the rest of the girls gather at the top of the stairs.

"Oh, so that's what you chose." Johanna eyes me through the slits in her mask.

Kami's dress hugs me tighter than I like, so I cross my arms over my chest. "You said everyone could wear a black dress," I mumble.

In the dim lighting, the dress looks black but is actually a dark green. I pull the long sleeves of the dress across my palms and hold my decorated mask. The green moss matches the color of the dress.

Out of the choices the girls already owned, I chose a dress that covered me as much as possible. However, Kami is skinnier than me in the chest and has less defined muscles. My breasts almost topple out.

"Masks on, girls," Johanna orders, twirling on her heel.

Her dress is floor-length with red sequins that dips low in the front and ever lower in the back. It looks like Susana's dress, much to Johanna's complaining. The rest of the dresses have taken on the personality of each of the girls, who have matched their masks to their ballgowns.

Johanna walks to the front of our line. "We need a grand entrance."

The girls giggle and gossip, excitement on the verge of climax in such tight quarters. Kami and Mikayla push their way to the front, Rochelle acting as their shadow. Susana, Paula, and Ubah laugh non-stop. At the back of the line, I could still make a run for it and lock myself in my bedroom. The girls might not notice me gone for a few hours, and if they do, I can slip down to the basement or hide in the woods.

"Hey." Roxie pops up beside me, putting on her shoes. Her silver dress sparkles like a disco ball.

My jaw drops open. I haven't seen her in days, but Daphne would've said if we need to find another sister for our coven.

"Roxie, where's your mask?" demands Johanna at the front of the line.

"Mind your own fucking business," Roxie spits.

Johanna's cheeks flush as red as her dress, but she faces forward.

Roxie whispers in my ear, "Nice mask by the way. Very you. Are those leaves from the backyard? Line's moving." She steps in front of me to keep it going as I stand there, stuck. "Come on."

Somehow my feet spur into action. The voices increase on our approach. We stand on the grand staircase, lined up. All the people stare up at us through their masks: awe and wonderment, lust and hunger, anger and fear. The eyes flicker to each of us. I'm being consumed by mortals and witches. Maybe a couple of other creatures linger in the mix. Too many people.

I turn to run back upstairs and hide, but Daphne stands at the top of the staircase, blocking me in. She wears a cream-colored flapper dress that swishes with her every move. Her mask is so small that it covers just her high cheekbones and her eyebrow bone. Everyone will know who she is.

Astrid sticks to the shadows at the top of the stairs, wearing a plum-colored dress. A net covers her face. She sends an icy glare my way. There is no escape.

"Welcome," Daphne thunders, cutting Johanna off before she starts her own practiced speech. "I'll keep it quick. Refreshments are in the dining room. Party in the ballroom. Couches in the library."

Chuckles echo through the crowd, and I shift uncomfortably. I don't want anyone in our house. Witchcraft is scattered around if someone knows what to look for.

"Now, let's boogey!" Daphne throws herself down the stairs, and electro-swing music roars to life in the ballroom.

The crowd surges forward like a tidal wave, and I hang onto the railing. The girls fly into the crowd with screeches, squeezing each other's hands to not be lost by the swell. Johanna remains by the handrail. By her grim face, this isn't what she planned.

People gather around Daphne like moths to the flame. Their words are lost in the boisterous noise. People touch Daphne as she passes, and she smiles at them, gliding through the crowd like a shining angel. She shimmers as if made of diamonds.

Colors brush together as bodies press into a herd. More people enter the house through the front doors. Beatrice's killer might be here. If the girls won't look for him, then I will. Setting my jaw, I plunge into the crowd.

In the dining room, mortals fill glasses in the champagne fountain. One mortal sticks his head under the flow. People drink until they are stumbling over the trembling floor and then cram together in the ballroom. Lights flash across the room, reflecting off the three disco balls hanging from the ceiling. I stagger out of the ballroom and into the library, hoping for refuge.

Kami and Mikayla are straddling men on the couches and consuming their faces in kisses. Their moans are as loud as the music. I'll never be able to unsee that. Why did they use the library? How did they get mortal boyfriends that quickly anyway?

I back into the hallway and almost knock a plate of food out of Rochelle's hands.

"They said they were going to get me laid tonight, but they're doing that," she says in a disappointed tone.

I stifle my gag. I don't want to hear this. I don't want to know. How can I get away from her? There's nothing wrong with Rochelle, but she smells like sweet champagne too. How much has she had to drink? Some of the girls were talking about pregaming beforehand.

"I really want a baby but not to tote it around and stuff," continues Rochelle. Her words slur together. "I know how much work babies can be, but I'm twenty-five. I'm getting old. I have eight siblings. My younger brother already has a baby. I'm doing it to further us witches, you know—to rebuild our numbers—after the Second Witch War. My grandma died—had her skin stripped off. Did you know anyone who died?"

I don't want to hear her words and don't want to think about the Second Witch War or who had their skin taken from their body. The war didn't affect our coven, but my old coven wasn't so lucky. Then again, there was no luck in the war.

I walk away from Rochelle, ignoring her calls to me. I can't care how rude I'm being. She may not remember in the morning depending how much she has had to drink. I've already seen a few of my sisters, and none of them are hunting for Beatrice's killer. So I have to.

Bodies crush each other in the packed ballroom. Making myself smaller, I propel through the humping crowd.

A foot almost kicks me in the face, and I jerk back. Daphne swing dances with a gentleman, and he lifts her. She laughs.

"Maisie!" Someone grabs my shoulder, and I jerk away. "What the hell are you doing?" asks Roxie. She takes my hand, sweat leaking between our palms.

The crowd parts for her, or maybe Roxie pushes them out of the way. Someone has opened the windows, letting the cold wind in. A wall separates the ballroom and dining room, but the music seeps through. The house rattles until it feels like it will implode. Voices encompass me. The bass drops, and the chandeliers tremble. I cover my ears.

A person presses his body against mine at the counter, and my magic builds. There are a lot of witches at the party. I don't want to start a fight. But if another person touches me, I may explode. I push away from the bar, taking the exit to the stone balcony.

The clouds have cleared off, revealing the moon. I blow out a deep breath, and white condensate flutters around my face. There is a perfected wildness about nature. My magic rises, and I shove it down and then sway with the breeze.

"You ditched me!" Roxie arrives beside me, drink in hand. "Motherfucker, it's cold out here."

"You can go back inside," I mutter.

She scoffs. "I know you'd just go to bed or some shit."

The basement. "I'll be out here a while." The cold air clears my mind, and the music isn't so loud.

"I'll stay." She stares off into the dark backyard.

A gasp breaks the silence, and memories flood my mind, digging their claws into my brain. It's like I'm touching the tree all over again—all I see is Beatrice's burning. I shake the thoughts from my head, but trees don't gasp.

"Did you hear that?" I ask.

Roxie hesitates. "It's not what you think."

A thud.

A squeak. A grunt.

My mind races my legs. I run down the steps into the grass as Roxie yells, "Maisie, don't!"

My pounding heart and raging thoughts have pulled my magic from the depths of my being. As a witch, my magic is never far away.

The grass shifts. The trees in the woods lean toward the backyard.

Another scream, high-pitched but not bloodcurdling.

Squinting in the darkness, I whip out my magic as a large man holds a young woman against a planter. Another one of my sisters is being attacked.

"Hey!" I stomp over.

The hedges and vines coil, growing closer to the man.

"Stop!" I rotate my wrist, and my magic twists.

The vines latch on to him and wrench him back from Rochelle. I loop my hand into the air. The vine throws him into the middle of the yard.

"What the hell?" Rochelle gathers her dress.

Roxie rushes to me, laughing.

Rochelle sets her deathly gaze on Roxie, but it flickers back to me the second I speak.

"What? He was attacking you," I say, losing my voice as the words spill out. I helped her, didn't I?

"Attacking me?" screeches Rochelle, storming past me.

She kneels at the man's side, but he jumps back. Terror glistens his eyes, and he runs. He won't be coming back to the house. I cringe. I didn't want to hurt a mortal. At least, he isn't too beat up.

Rochelle spins toward me, hands into fists. "What the hell was that for?"

"Calm down." Roxie steps in front of me. "She didn't mean to interrupt your love tryst. He wasn't even that good looking."

"I'm sorry," I mumble. My cheeks flame, and I glance toward the woods. Could I make it? The woods are always better than the house.

"Whatever." Rochelle stalks back to the ballroom.

I should go after her and apologize again, but Roxie continues to laugh, holding her stomach like it hurts so much. The woods are sounding like a better idea.

Chapter 11

What is considered safe? Day or night? In numbers or alone? People can only count on themselves.
—Guinevere Ravensblood

Around five in the morning, the house quiets. With a few people drunkenly dancing to music in the ballroom, I slip from the balcony and jog through the woods. I run for only half a mile when I hit a wall, about to fall over in exhaustion. The party lasted way too long, and I couldn't go to sleep even when I escaped Roxie.

I cut through the woods toward the house. This nature is left mostly undisturbed, except for the roar of the nearby highway. Shy animals hide in the green and brown environment. I intersect with the trail outside the mansion and follow it back.

Broken branches dangle from trees. Bushes have been trampled. Heavy footprints—a couple different shoes and sizes—are engraved the dirt. A wake of destruction. The footsteps lead to the fence. Crusted maroon stains the wooden door above the fence hatch, drops in a splatter pattern.

The hedge parts, and I sprint to the house. The music has stopped, and I check the ballroom for witches. No one. I fly up a spiral staircase and reach the top floor, the suite doors shut. I pound.

No answer.

The girls say I'm Daphne's favorite, but Astrid is her right-hand woman. I knock on her door, and the sound reverberates down the long hallway. The rest of the bedroom doors are closed. Who's missing?

Astrid demands from the other side, "What do you want?"

I whisper into the crack between the door and frame, "I can't find Daphne." Any louder may wake the girls. I'm scared of what I'll find and how they'll react. I'm not ready for this.

After a heavy pause, Astrid opens the door, robe wrapped around herself. Her scarred hands are exposed. "I haven't had my coffee yet."

"I think there might be another one of us missing. Or dead." The words physically hurt.

"Let me change." She closes the door in my face.

"Wai—" I stop myself from talking to the closed door.

My stomach clenches. I think I'm going to be sick. All I've had to drink or eat in the last twelve hours is water. I couldn't eat anything at the party, my anxiety controlling me. I step back from the door, and my tennis shoes squeak on the floor. Did the girls hear that?

Astrid walks out of her bedroom in a new outfit and veil. I lead her down the stairs and into the backyard, but she walks slowly. Already using a cane, she isn't a fast mover, but she doesn't look like she's trying to hurry along. She stifles a yawn.

I open the hedge for us, and she leans toward the struggle. Her gloved hand touches the dried blood, and she massages it between her forefinger and thumb.

"Who else have you told?" she asks.

"Only you. I couldn't find Daphne," I reiterate. "I think it was Daphne—"

Astrid scoffs.

Daphne is the head of the coven. She would be a prize to any killer.

"Believe this: *Daphne* is a hard lady to kill. People have tried. If there is a dead witch, it's not her." Astrid straightens. "In my younger days, Daphne went home with a guy after every party. We had parties all the time."

Confusion contorts my face. "You only joined the coven after the Council fell and after Audrey…" I choke on the words.

Astrid's smile reveals her gums. "Beatrice wasn't the first murder here, was she, Maisie?"

Vines twist like snakes near prey. I coil my fingers into my palm, feeling the bite of pain, but my magic nips at her heels as she leisurely strolls back to the house. It doesn't quicken her pace.

"If someone was kidnapped, then they're already dead. Look for the smoke." Astrid walks upstairs toward her bedroom.

I'm officially left to my thoughts. What will I do next? In a house as silent as this, my thoughts rage in my already pounding head. My magic curls around me like my hair curls around the base of my throat. I can't breathe.

I can't think.

The words seem to escape me, but I've said them once. I can do it again.

Knowing Roxie's in our bedroom, I start with her. "I think someone else is dead."

She pops her head out of the blankets. "Who?"

We go door to door, spurring the girls into action and fear. By the end of the hallway, we have six out of twelve, missing Kami, Mikayla, Rochelle, Johanna, Lizzy, and Daphne. I count the girls one more time. I look in their rooms in case they are hiding. The girls can be… idiotic when drunk, and they were very drunk last night. It's possible they are still drunk. But no one is hiding. No one is in the shared bathroom. Where is half of our coven?

"Did you check downstairs?" asks Susana.

"I checked the ballroom and the dining room," I say. And the library, kitchen, front entryway, and closets.

"A little higher than that," says Susana, and I cringe.

For the three years I've been in the coven, I've avoided the guest floor. It's not like we have that many guests anyway. We're grown women and should have our own rooms, but we bunk together like we're in dorms in college. Daphne says it builds our relationships. It has also destroyed more than a few friendships and left other girls packing.

All the guest room doors are shut. The five of us here—minus Astrid—stare down the hallway like it is a tunnel and we're unsure what's on the other side. Susana cries quietly, holding herself. Paula pulls her into a hug, Ubah hanging off her other side.

Roxie runs down the hallway, throwing her fists against the walls and doors. "Wake up!"

One door swings open, banging against the wall. "What?" Kami yells, a white sheet pulled around her.

"Damn," Roxie mutters. "She was my third choice to be dead."

"What did you just say?" Kami gapes.

Roxie runs back to our group, kicking down a door in the process. Unfortunately, I see more than I bargained for, just like last night. Rochelle is lying under a man. Both are naked. I avert my gaze quickly, but I'm the only one who looks away.

"What the hell?" Rochelle screams. "Again!"

Roxie laughs. "Rochelle, if that guy told you that it feels better without a condom or his dick can't fit in it, he's fucking wrong."

At the top of her lungs, Rochelle screams, "Get out!"

Ubah quickly closes the door, and we all stand in silence. We've found two witches, but there are more still missing, Daphne included. Where could she be? And why didn't she take me?

People scurry out of guest rooms, heads down, as we tear this floor apart. Then we clear the rest of the house of all mortals and guests. We reconvene in the entryway. I can't do this without Daphne and keep looking for her to come down the stairs. Maybe she has her own hiding places?

Roxie barks, "Think. Where did we last see them?"

"I last saw Daphne before midnight." I push through the fuzzy memories.

I lost most of my sisters in the crowd. I had been looking for a possible killer but hadn't thought he would get another one of us.

Ubah says, "I saw Johanna and Lizzy together, and I think it was after midnight—"

"I saw them around four, I think," interrupts Rochelle. "I was heading upstairs, and they were going into the kitchen, whispering about something."

"What about Mikayla?" I ask.

All heads turn to Kami. Her best friend. They have always been inseparable.

Sitting on the floor, Kami picks at the carpet. "I was pretty drunk. She was too. I don't remember much until you woke me up earlier. We pre-gamed before, did like five shots of something gross. We came to party last night."

Anger flashes in me, but I bite my tongue before it explodes.

Rochelle jumps in, "I saw Mikayla after midnight."

"Where?" Roxie demands, stopping mid-step in her pace.

"In the backyard," says Rochelle.

I hadn't seen Mikayla outside. "Was she by herself?" I ask.

Rochelle shrugs. "I was a little focused on other things—"

"Was she by herself?" I repeat.

Tears swelling in her eyes, Rochelle bows her head. "I think she was with some guy."

"They didn't stay in the backyard?" Kami asks.

"No. I was already there," says Rochelle. "They went through the gate."

My eyes widen. That was where the struggle was. The blood.

Rochelle scrambles for words. "Roxie and Maisie were there too. You had to see her."

"We were focused on you!" Roxie says.

"It was Beatrice's killer," Susana gasps. Her body trembles.

"Did anyone see what the guy looked like?" asks Paula.

"It was a masquerade, dumbass," Roxie snaps.

"Don't call her a 'dumbass,' bitch," says Ubah, standing in front of Paula. "You were out there. How come you didn't see anything?"

Roxie lurches forward, but I grab her hand. "Don't," I say, hoping she'll listen.

She wouldn't win in a fight against Ubah—none of us would.

I raise my voice: "We need to stick together." The words sound odd even as I say them.

I don't normally like to stick together. Being around all my sisters now is draining me dry. I can only blame myself because I didn't see Mikayla last night or who she was with.

Ubah groans. "Where's Daphne when we need her?"

Roxie paces the length of the front entryway. "We need to find this sick fuck."

"How?" Susana wipes her hand under her eyes. "He was in our house, and we didn't even know he was here. We had this party to lure him out, and he got one of us instead."

"Exactly," says Paula. "He was in our house, so he had to leave some clues behind. While we wait for Daphne to get back, we need to look for clues. I'll take the ballroom. Susana, take the dining room. Ubah, please stay with Kami and Rochelle. Maisie, take the backyard."

"What about me?" Roxie asks.

Ubah offers, "Stay in the kitchen with us."

From the back steps, I look from the garden to the changing trees to the hedge. Broken bottles and glass litter the path. Rochelle said Mikayla and her abductor were making out. The glass grounds under my feet, announcing me with every crack-filled step. The gate swings open with a high squeal, rattling the metal. The music had been loud last night, so maybe the squeal hadn't seemed out of place—or maybe the killer had come through the front door with the rest of the guests. We weren't checking invitations. So many things we did wrong.

Stepping between the nearest trees, I place my palms against the bark. "Please show me what happened last night."

The trees show me moonlight and Mikayla in her blue jumpsuit and blue mask, kissing a man. He's huddled in the shadows of the night. Mikayla too, though I recognize her outfit. His arms wound around her, pulling her through the gate. Then he grabbed something from the ground and hit her over the head. She fell.

Swallowing a scream, I stretch my magic and make the roots connect under the soil. "Show me more."

Last night, the man dragged Mikayla along the path and stopped at the tree line near the highway. His truck was parked on the tar, and he lifted her into the trunk. Leaving the lights off, he drove down the twisty road.

I return to the gray clouds and the morning chill. Where he was parked is nearby. Shivering, I jog the path the man took. A root sticks out of the ground, a piece of blue jumpsuit caught on the nub. Gold flecks from her heels sprinkle the soil. I hit the road.

The highway is further inland with multiple exits: one toward the interstate, one toward the beach, one toward the next town over, private roads to houses and cabins, and then the highway that connects like arteries to other highways. The man could've gone anywhere.

A semi-truck rumbles past me on the road, and the trees blow in the breeze, waving good-bye.

Chapter 12

What's the most coveted power? It depends
on the witch. Witches can dreamwalk and
timewalk. Fire is destructive. What about
flying or strength?
—Iain Skinner, *A New Order for Witches*

Smoke billows through the house, and I bound
upstairs. I reach the landing.

Lizzy hides behind a pillar, knuckles white. Girls run
out of the dining room, Susana stopping a fireball
before it hits Paula. Instead, it hits the wood and begins
to burn. Dark smoke wafts toward the ceiling.

"This is your fault!" calls out Roxie.

Another fireball shoots between the doors, probably
conjured from a burning candle. With a flick of my
wrist, the wooden door shuts. The fireball hits. *Boom!*
Pain sizzles my skin.

I whip open the doors and dash through. Roxie and
Johanna have torn most of the dining room apart: the
tables and chairs flipped, dangling glass like sharpened
teeth, curtains on fire.

Roxie yells, "The party was your idea!"

"To catch Beatrice's killer!" Johanna wears last night's red dress, but the matching red lipstick is gone. Dark mascara has smudged around her eyes.

"And now Mikayla is dead!" says Roxie.

We don't know that, but didn't I see it? The trees showed me images of last night.

"Not my fault!" snaps Johhanna.

The magic is building. They'll tear the whole house apart.

"He was in our grasp, and he took another witch. You left," says Roxie.

"You were drunk!" Johanna conjures another fireball from a flickering flame. She's backed up against the windows, half of them still open from last night.

"It was your fucking idea." Roxie deflects the fireball, sending it careening toward me.

I sprawl out on the floor. The fireball hits the wall behind me. Something crashes.

Johanna shoots off another fireball. Embers fall like discolored snowflakes.

Where is Astrid? She must hear the noise from her bedroom.

Balling into the fetus position, I cover my head with my hands and peek out. Johanna sends more fireballs toward Roxie. One nicks her in the arm. Roxie releases her fury with a screech. The windows burst, and Johanna is pushed out of the dining room windows that are twenty feet off the ground.

I release my fingers from my palms, and my magic responds.

A tree branch slams into Johanna. She screams. The wood and the leaves catch her and swoop her up before she splats on the ground. I scramble to my feet as Roxie charges forward and grabs a shard of glass.

"Roxie, no!" I chase her, but she launches out the window.

Roxie raises the pointed glass shard at Johanna, bringing it down inches away from stabbing her. A tree branch grabs Roxie's torso and whips her away.

At the window, I hold my hands the width of me. The two witches are separated for now.

"Fucking bitch!" Roxie thrashes in the air, digging her nails into the bark. It pinches my arm. "Maisie, when I get out of here, you're dead to me! I hope he gets you next."

Like a branch, I snap.

I'm the third witch out the high window. My magic beckons nature to me.

The world twirls. Dirt sprays us in the face. The green plants close in, red poppies and yellow sunflowers. The world rises around us, the dirt becoming a tornado.

I could tear this whole place apart. More than this yard but the town.

I am nature.

It flows through me. It listens to my magic. The wildness strums through my veins.

"Maisie."

I slam to Earth.

Air whooshes from my lungs. Something cracks in my body.

Then everything else drops too. Thuds and screams, all combining in my ears.

Raising my head, I blink dirt from my stinging eyes. What happened? Where did my magic go? I shove my fingers into the ground and try to create the world to my image.

"Maisie." Daphne looks between me and Roxie and Johanna. "What the hell happened here?" she demands.

Astrid stands over her shoulder. All the magic has been seeped away. Johanna wouldn't be able to conjure anything now.

Roxie sputters, "Mikayla's dead."

I don't want to hear those words, no matter how true they are. The truth is the worst. Such as the truth around me. The horror of destruction comes into focus: everything torn up, rocks and black dirt, fallen trees, dying poppies and sunflowers. The world has been remade by my magic.

I have destroyed what I love.

Closing my eyes, I try to ignore one of the worst things I have ever done. I want to say the worst, but I have done worse things.

Poppies litter the ground under me, their stems poking into my sides. Pain aches my chest and spreads across my body, as if I've torn my skin away from my bone and muscle. I press my hands into the ground, but it feels different.

Wrong.

The soil is exposed, cool to the touch, but it cannot fight the steam on my face. Heat coats me as anger burns me alive. Roxie is right: let me be the next witch killed. I deserve it for what I've done.

Daphne stands before me as the rest of the girls cower. "Inside now," she commands.

Astrid walks toward the back doors. Rochelle rushes inside, Susana and Paula follow. Lizzy walks down the steps, helping the limping Johanna. Roxie picks herself up, flipping me off. Daphne trails them all.

Curling into a ball, I try to make myself small. Hopefully, the grass will grow over me, and I will be buried. I'll be one of the bodies in the backyard.

Chapter 13

Daphne Duvay knows spells and potions,
sure, but she also helps the underdog. She has
taken in witches who have no active powers
or no specific power, like me, to create me
into a better witch. And isn't that what it
means to be in a coven?
–Paula

I want rain to wash it away. Wash me through the hedge and the trees, down the hill, and into the ocean. I lay on the ground, collecting dust. No matter how many times I have closed my eyes, I see more than I want to. Beatrice, Mikayla, Amira, Carmella, Audrey, the backyard, Marney—all my past mistakes creating a mountain that I cannot climb.

When the world starts to darken, her shoes appear in front of me. The heels slowly sink into the dirt. I haven't been so lucky.

"You've laid there all day," says Daphne. "You've freaked out the other girls. They were fools to test you at all."

"I did it again. Like what happened to...." The memories flood my mind.

"Audrey wasn't your fault," Daphne says.

"She was my friend." My best friend.

The only best friend I've ever had.

Daphne huffs. "Maisie, you must get up. Roxie and Johanna are still trying to kill each other, Astrid is in charge of them. We haven't been able to track Mikayla. Maisie, you can find her."

"She's dead. I can't find dead people."

"When the flames start tonight, you'll be able to find them quickly. The trees will start burning. You'll feel the pain."

I don't want to feel the pain. I want to continue to feel nothing. It's the best feeling: to stare blankly at whatever and think of nothing. Like everything has faded.

Daphne bends beside me. "What do you know that the other girls don't? What did the trees tell you?"

After swallowing the soil on my tongue, I tell her about the gate and everything else the trees showed me. It is everything I wanted to tell her today but couldn't find her. Where was she? Daphne was gone when we needed her the most. I relive what the trees showed me by every word that pours from my mouth. My throat is raw. Dirt is deep in my nostrils and down in my lungs. Where is the seed when I need one? I'll plant it in my body, and nature shall take my blood and my bones. It will become a strong tree.

"Maisie." Daphne holds out her hand. "Let's get you washed up."

We step on to the top floor of the house, and Daphne opens her suite doors. She has something brewing, but the smells don't mix. I don't know this potion.

"Take off your shoes," Daphne orders. "I hate when Shelby comes in. She moves everything."

I leave my shoes in the hallway and close the suite doors. Dirt flutters behind me like a train on a dress. It's on Daphne's marble floor. It engrains itself into her pink rugs. I leave a handprint on her golden doorknob.

"Take a bath or shower. I'll have Nancy bring up clean clothes and food." Daphne spreads out more ingredients in the boiling caldron.

Little black pebbles vibrate in the glass container with a lock on it, and I pause. What could she be using those for? She has a vault to keep our more dangerous and pricey ingredients in. Those pebbles should only be used in potions that create booms. Is the potion for the killer or for someone else? My stomach aches, and I can't tell if it's because I haven't eaten today or because of what I see.

Daphne shakes the glass jar of explosives. "Do you want to make a potion?"

I shake my head. I've done enough destruction for the day.

Taking one pebble from the jar, Daphne keeps a firm grip on it. If she drops it to the floor, it will explode, and we will die. I step back five feet. She throws the pebble into the cauldron.

With a slight tap, the pebble hits the bottom and bursts. The cauldron shakes, and smoke plumes. The bubbles roll over the sides. The floral scent of the suite can't hide the rancidity. I lift my dirty shirt to my nose. The water absorbed the explosion.

Stepping up to the table, Daphne peers into the bottom of the cauldron. "You can use whatever you like in the bathroom."

After shutting the door, I strip off my clothes and leave them in a heap on the floor. Lush soaps, shampoos, and perfumes fill the pink-tiled bathroom. I grab the least fragrant soap in the shower as the hot water scorches my skin. The grime washes around my feet. I scrub until I'm pink and shiny.

Finally turning off the water, I step out of the shower and then just stand there for a while, dripping. Water runs down my legs, but I can't force them to move. Steam fills the bathroom, clogging up the vent and my lungs. I tiptoe out.

Daphne stands next to the basin. "There are fresh clothes and food on the table."

I take the clothes to her bedroom and close the doors. Pulling on my pants, I catch my reflection in framed photographs. No newspaper clippings but actual photographs, except for a chosen two. They are film posters from the 1940s or 50s: colors bright but fading, kept away from the natural light. To the left, the pictures look older. All of it looks like her. Blinking rapidly, I gather the damp towel and leave her bedroom. I'm more tired than I realized.

In the sitting room, Daphne has a card flipped over on the table and a martini glass in front of her. "People clamor to be in this coven. It's got a good and long history. It was here long before I showed up, and it will be here long after I go."

I hang the damp towel on the side of the shower. "You chose all of us to join the coven."

"I don't always choose," says Daphne.

I walk out of the bathroom. "I thought you didn't take recommendations?"

"I try not to, but there are people who really want to be in the coven. They'll do anything."

"Like who?"

"Johanna." She cringes.

I think back to that time. Johanna replaced Tori, who had only been here two weeks and then left. Johanna moved in the next day. Around Tori's time, there had been a few people that had come and gone. Audrey was already gone. Carmella had gone. Lana and Christina had come and gone. Maybe Kelly was still around. Jane was gone, Lada too. Grace and Michelle—maybe—were still in the coven. Those names only offer a jumble of memories. They are witches who walked the hallways and have not returned. Not even for a party. Many of the coven witches never return.

Daphne slumps her shoulders. "Johanna wanted to be in this coven for a long time. We had an opening, and she was right there. Always."

"Why?" I ask.

She runs her pointer finger along the rim of her martini glass. "Sometimes, they're friends of witches in the coven. Maybe they had mothers or aunts or grandmothers or sisters pass through the halls. Maybe they've been to one of our parties." Her smile isn't genuine.

"But Johanna really wanted to be in the coven," I prompt.

"Johanna would've done anything to get into the coven, and she did." Daphne gulps from the martini glass. A tendril of liquid leaks from the corner of her mouth. "Don't you remember Johanna hanging around a couple years back?"

"No." During that time, so many girls came and went; I didn't get attached to them. But I don't want to talk about Johanna. "This morning, when I couldn't find you, I told Astrid. She did nothing to try to help me. Or Mikayla."

"Astrid was part of the Council. A dead witch is less competition." Daphne finishes her drink. The burn of alcohol lingers on her breath. She walks over to the counter in her kitchenette and starts mixing another martini.

"Astrid said she knew about Audrey's death," I say. "She knows I killed Audrey."

She takes a swig of her drink. "You didn't kill Audrey."

"I lost control today, like I lost control around Audrey."

I can't ignore what I've done. I'm no better than the person who has killed Beatrice and presumably Mikayla. The girls want to hunt him—they should hunt me too.

I continue, "I snapped, and I couldn't get the control back—"

"Maisie!"

Her voice slaps me in the face, and I flinch. She puts her martini down on the counter and crosses the suite to tower over me. With her long legs, it only takes her two strides.

"You were in such a horrible state that night, so let me remind you: you didn't kill Audrey. No matter what Astrid says," says Daphne in a faint voice. She clears her throat. "When you left Audrey, both of you had been fighting and were in terrible shape. She was alive. You were in control of your powers. That was how you knew to stop."

"I wasn't able to stop today." My eyes water.

I'm scared I can't hold back my crying. If I can't control my tears, how will I ever control my magic? It will control me.

"And I stopped you, Maisie. We all need help." Walking back to her kitchenette, Daphne drinks from the martini glass. "Astrid is cruel because she doesn't understand friendship. I hoped when I brought her back to the coven that time had changed her, but the Council made her worse. She's now bitter to have been defeated, bitter she wasn't strong enough—even bitter that her 'allies' left her to die." She rolls her eyes.

I sit for a few seconds in silence. "Do you think if she had friends—"

Daphne barks out a laugh, and I shut my mouth. My cheeks burn from being laughed at, but Astrid having friends could be considered ridiculous, especially with the Council. Those witches often backstabbed and killed each other over the smallest infractions. It was a game of power.

"Most times, friends are good and necessary," Daphne says factually, "but they're not always healthy. You understand that, Maisie? You don't want friends that call you names, are mean to you, willing to hurt you to get what they want."

"I know," I grumble. I'm not a child, as much as her or the others might believe. I'm the youngest in the coven. Also, the shortest.

"I tried to be Astrid's friend once, but you don't get anything positive in return." She swishes the remaining contents of the martini glass, but the liquid has run low again. If she continues to drink like this, she may fall over.

"Maybe you should slow down," I say.

"Alcohol doesn't affect me like it affects almost everyone else." Her words slur together. "You must've realized that by now. Like you must've realized a lot about me by now. You're just too polite to say anything." She puts a handful of ice cubes in a metal cylinder.

I don't know how many more drinks she'll make tonight, but I won't be part of it.

"I'm going to bed." I grab my shoes by the doors.

"Good night, Maisie," Daphne calls after me.

Chapter 14

Witches, like any other magical creature, are
not believed to be real by mortals. Though,
you'll find an uptick of blood-related deaths in
large cities from vampires, mutilated animals
by werewolves in forests, and an abundance
of glitter wherever fae live.
—Stewart Powell, *The Council Manifest*

My woods are on fire. Heat claws at my skin. I clench
my teeth before I scream.

My eyes flash open to my darkened bedroom. I tear
the blankets off me and run to the window, opening it.
An old oak tree lingers a few feet from the house, and I
reach out my hand. A branch spreads toward me. After
how my magic acted earlier, I hesitantly take a hold of
the branch, and it slowly lowers me to the ground.

Moonlight illuminates my destruction. My toes curl
into the upturned topsoil. The dirt can take whatever it
needs in me to survive after I have all but killed it.

Running outside the torn-up hedge, I build a portal
and land somewhere deep in the woods. Wind whips

through the trees, and the heat and flames reach toward me. I skid to a stop.

The pyre is built like a bonfire: one tree trunk stands in the middle, a limp Mikayla tied to it. Cackling flames eat her skin and clothes.

She doesn't scream.

She's already dead.

The hair on the back of my neck rises. I spin around a second too late. Something whacks me in the head, and I crumble to my hands and knees.

My vision blurs. My heartbeat pounds on my skull.

I try to rise on shaking legs.

In the moonlight, a guy swings a wooden baseball bat. My magic thinks before I can. The baseball bat is flung from his hands, clanking far away in the bush. The trees rustle. The man in a black hoodie runs away into the shadows of the night.

Groaning, I place my hand on the back of my head. My hot blood slips out, scorching the back of my neck. It clogs my hair.

I urge my magic to do something—anything to bring Mikayla down from the pyre! Anything to stop the flames. My magic slips into the shadows of darkness as my vision tunnels.

***

Cold drizzle blankets my body, sinking me into the dirt. I will be consumed.

I swim in murky waters, never-ending black behind my eyelids.

The ground rumbles, a stampede of feet.

"Maisie!"

Hands flip me over.

"Don't do that," a womanly voice snaps. "She's injured. You could make it worse."

"Maisie, open your eyes."

I peek through my eyelashes. Faces swarm, darkened by dancing dots.

"Why is she out here?"

"Um, I think she found Mikayla."

A shriek.

Gasps.

Sobs.

"Oh my God, Mikayla!"

Someone whispers, "You don't think Maisie did it, do you?"

"Shut the fuck up, you dumb bitch," Roxie says. I know that voice and language anywhere. "She was with me when Mikayla went missing. And do you see the goose egg on the back of her head?"

Someone prods my head. "We need to get her back to the house. She's still bleeding."

"What about Mikayla?"

"Should we call the police?"

"They'll probably think we did it."

"Leave the body," Daphne orders.

It's another voice that I know too well. My last three years have been spent listening to that voice, waiting for Daphne to speak to me.

"I'll give the police an anonymous tip," Daphne continues. "They can't know we've been here. Roxie, Johanna, get Maisie back to the house. The rest of you, look for clues and cover our tracks."

Hands grab me. They could be Roxie or Johanna or one of my other sisters. My head teeters back, brain moving in my skull. Pain shoots across my body. I groan.

Daphne snaps, "Be careful."

"I got her head." Chilled fingers hold my neck.

"Lizzy, go with them," Daphne commands.

They jerk my body with every step. I'm a doll in their hands.

Darkness swarms around me. Slivers of silver moonlight turn to electrical buzzing. The air warms.

"Where should we put her?" Johanna asks.

"Her bed?" Roxie offers.

"She needs to be closer to the potion-making. Let's go to the library," Lizzy says.

They move, and my head lolls. I'm falling left and right. Then they place me down. I try to peel back my eyelids, but they're crusted with blood. I only see red.

"What now? She looks strung out," says Roxie.

"We need to clean the wound," Lizzy says. "Johanna, get me betony, chamomile, coriander, feverfew, hemlock, lavender, and lesser periwinkle from the potion stores. Roxie, go get the medical kit. Make sure there is gauze and ibuprofen."

The doors bang shut. I shudder.

"Maisie, can you hear me?" whispers Lizzy.

Another groan escapes my lips. It's my proof I'm awake, but I've yet to decide if I'm alive. Death waits in the shadows.

"Okay, Maisie. I need you to stay awake. Can you open your eyes?" She wipes something wet across my eyelashes. "There you go."

Several Lizzy heads float in my vision.

"Don't worry. We'll clean you up and you'll be back in action," says Lizzy.

The memories blur in flashes of orange. Pain sears my body, numbed by my throbbing head.

"Fire. Mikayla." The words rub the back of my throat.

Lizzy hushes me. "You're okay. We were so worried about you. Thankfully, Daphne is good at tracking. Sorry it took so long."

Roxie clunks back into the room and hands the box to Lizzy, who says, "There's no thread and needle. She's probably going to need stitches."

"Then we should *probably* take her to the hospital," Roxie says. "She doesn't look good. I thought she was fucking dead in the forest."

Lizzy picks through the box and then orders Roxie to get clean towels and hot water. Roxie leaves again, and it's quieter. Lizzy pinches the back of my head, acting like she is cleaning my wound. I hiss. Coolness seeps across my skin.

"Keep your eyes open, Maisie," orders Lizzy, and I force my eyelids apart. "Good job."

Tears burn my eyes, but I make out Johanna reentering the library. She holds several jars and vials.

"Thanks, Johie." Lizzy spreads the items out on the floor. The jars are filled with things we've used before in potions. "Can you swallow, Maisie?"

"Yeah." I swallow my own saliva for good measure, but it lodges in my throat.

Lizzy places the two ibuprofens in my mouth separately, and I swallow each with a splash of water.

"Maisie, we'll clean the wound," says Lizzy. "I'll use lavender and periwinkle to make the swelling go down. Johie, do you know if Paula still has thread and a needle?"

"We can ask her when she gets back." Johanna hovers a few feet away.

"Johie, can you check, please? We may not have the time." Lizzy picks through what she has on the floor. "Where is Roxie?"

In the silence, my eyelids shut again. The blackness spreads out around me. It's so nice. And warm.

"Nope. Stay awake." Lizzy pokes my ribs until I open my eyes. "You have a concussion. Maybe Roxie is right, we should take you to the hospital? But they'll ask questions." She picks up vials and smells the contents. "I heard a rumor that sirens visit the beach outside the house in the summer."

"Mermaids too," I mumble. Moving my jaw sends another jolt of pain up the back of my head. "They migrate north when the water turns warm."

"Is there a difference between mermaids and sirens?"

Not many witches have run-ins with the sea. There have been enough drownings in our past. If witches exist, then mermaids, vampires, werewolves, and so on exist too. We're all connected.

"I try to stay away from sirens, but they come to the beaches by the house," I say. "Sometimes mermaids show up to parties."

Lizzy arches an eyebrow at me. "Mermaids coming to parties?"

"They can turn their tails into legs." I don't think there were any mermaids at our last party, but we were wearing masks. And I was distracted. "Daphne knows a few. You should ask her."

"But it's mostly sirens that come to shore?" questions Lizzy.

"They sunbathe. Or when it is mating season. They don't kill all the men they pull into the ocean," I say, reciting it like I am reading a book. That isn't where I learned the information, though there are a lot of books in our library about mermaids and sirens. Some of the information is wrong.

Lizzy runs her fingers through her light blond hair. "I didn't know you know so much about mermaids and sirens."

"Got it!" says Roxie.

I flinch at the sound. Even Lizzy jumps. Roxie and Johanna walk back into the library.

"I didn't need a babysitter," Roxie complains.

Lizzy takes the cloth and dips it into the steaming water. "Maisie, this is going to hurt. Sorry."

What hasn't hurt? She starts cleaning my wound, and I try not to lean away or scream. She brushes my hair aside. The pain throbs like its own heartbeat, pounding in my ears. I'm swimming in the ebb of my mind. I thin my lips together, but a groan reverberates through me.

"We should take her to the hospital," Roxie repeats. "She could have a brain bleed or a level five concussion."

"She would be in a coma if it was level five," Johanna interjects.

"What then, Doctor Barbie?" snaps Roxie. "You know everything because of *Grey's Anatomy*?"

"I need to clean and dress the wound," interrupts Lizzy. A final tone lingers in her voice. "After that, we will take turns watching Maisie. She can fall asleep but needs to be woken up every hour and checked on. Someone needs to stay with her the whole time. I'll take the first watch. When the others get home, everyone gets a shift. Roxie, get more blankets. Johie, get her some chicken soup. We need to see if she vomits."

"What happens if she vomits?" Roxie asks, voice rising an octave.

"Then she goes to the hospital. Go," orders Lizzy.

A few seconds later, the library doors slam. The tension presses on my head, the same that curls around my neck.

Through clenched teeth, I say, "I didn't know you had medical knowledge."

"I'm guessing I know as much about medicine as you do about mermaids and sirens. We are experts to the people who know nothing." Lizzy dips the washcloth in hot water again.

* * *

The murky waters shift to a summer day. My dreams bloom from memories. I recognize the day I saw my first siren. On the beach in the Pacific Ocean, Daphne asked, "Have you ever been to Lake Superior?"

I nodded. My parents used to take Marney and me often, and we had field trips there as children in school.

119

What our parents told us and what mortal teachers told us were very different.

"Do you know of the shipwrecks?" Daphne asked, quickening her pace as we trekked across the sand.

"They're famous," I answered. Many freighters pass through the Great Lakes, Lake Superior the largest of all.

"Do you know there are mermaids—or *sirens* as *some* people call them but they're different—living in the Great Lakes?" she asked.

I drew my eyebrows together, confused. My parents had told me many things, but mermaids in Lake Superior were never one.

"Did you hear about the death a few towns down on the beach?" she asked. "A man was killed, part of his neck missing, torso gouged out, heart missing, left leg missing. The newspapers say a shark did it."

"You think it is a… mermaid?"

"Siren." She pointed across the waves. "This is the migration course. They come around this time each year. They're adventurous creatures, but all of us have patterns. Down here."

We ducked behind a tree on the edge of the woods. The beach sprawled out before us, cut off violently by the gray-tipped waves. I raised to the balls of my feet to peek out.

Two women sat on the shore, facing the sea. They let out a shriek of high-pitched laughter that mimicked an off-tune song.

I moved from behind the tree and brushed away a branch from the view. "Are those…?"

Both sirens craned their heads toward me. Then one jumped in front of the other. Her mouth opened, a song blossoming out. I was enchanted, stepping forward as the harmony filled my ears. Daphne stepped in front of me, snaking a hand around my torso.

In a language that I'd never heard, Daphne spoke. More interestingly, the sirens listened. With a smile, Daphne stepped into the trees, dragging me along.

"What was that?" I asked as the sirens jumped back into the ocean.

"Their song," answered Daphne dismissively, trudging back toward the house.

"No. The language?"

"It's not used anymore. We're old friends," Daphne explained, and I blanched. "You should be happy about that. One of the sirens was pregnant. Her friend was going to protect her no matter what. That's probably why the man died. Sirens kill to eat, mermaids do not. Mermaids and sirens are very close, but there are subtle differences. Some might say a siren or mermaid can choose who they want to be, or maybe it is biology. They're alike like we are alike with humans. So close yet so far away."

Choosing my words wisely, I said, "We don't hear about mermaids and sirens often."

"As witches and mortals, we bleed into one another, but it's impossible to become a siren or mermaid. Back in the day, sirens and mermaids were hunted. Like us. Now, it seems they've been forgotten about, like the rest of magical creatures have." Her arm brushed my shoulder. "Maisie, I'll take you to other creatures sometime."

"Maisie!" yells a new voice, and my eyes flash open to the library. Roxie looms over me.

"What?" I squirm to find my feet under the blankets.

"I have to wake you up every hour. Lizzy's orders. You dying?" asks Roxie.

Did she have to wake me up like that? "No."

"Okay. Go back to bed, favorite." Roxie sits in a chair on the opposite side of the couch, pulling her laptop onto her thighs and presses play on a show she's streaming.

I roll my head to the other side, staring at the couch's back. I dive back into the darkness.

Chapter 15

If one does not value power in magic, then is
one even really a witch.
—Stewart Powell, *The Council Manifest*

Memories seep into my dreams, transporting me to
three years ago.

In the dead of night, Daphne instructed me to the
coven via a portal. I had left my family, letting a rash
decision overtake me. She said, "You can meet the girls
in the morning."

When morning struck, Daphne led me through the
sprawling house. The waiting girls eyed me in the
dining room, and I shrunk. They were older, taller,
prettier. This wasn't the coven I was used to. Twelve
young women glared at me like I was their competition.

"Come, Maisie." Daphne sat at the head of the
table, I on her right. "This is a lot to digest with a new
coven, so let's forgo the formalities for now. You'll
meet all the girls later. Let's eat."

The table was long and set. Food piled on top of
each other, much like the girls. Their bubbly voices

layered one another, held in by the high ceiling and closed windows.

"Hi," said a girl from across the table. "I'm Jane, and that's Lada and Michelle." She pointed down the table, and two girls waved at me. "We've heard great things about you. We're excited that you're here."

"Speak for yourself," someone mumbled, and my cheeks burned.

"Eva," Daphne snapped.

"I'm done." Eva's chair squealed across the floor, and she stormed out of the dining room.

"Anyone else?" asked Daphne, swirling a spoon in her tea.

No one else moved, but the glares dug into my skin. I wished I had the ability to be invisible or chameleon into my surroundings, or I could've had super speed and ran away. If I wasn't such a coward, I would've made a portal and gone home. We ate in silence, but I only picked at the food on my plate. My old coven never would've done something like this. Why was my new coven doing this to me? I didn't know them or the history, but when Daphne Duvay asked you to join her coven, you did. You weren't going to get the chance again.

Once breakfast was done, Daphne showed me the house. "I'm sorry about Eva. She thinks she deserves this and that, but the truth is no one deserves anything. You have to work for it."

"What did I take from her that she thinks she deserves?" I asked.

Daphne showed me the ground floor first. "I don't play favorites, Maisie, but the girls think I do. Eva is

124

powerful, and she thinks she deserves to be at the front of the line, to be the favorite, to stand above everyone else. That's not how it works here. It's not based on power level. We learn to better ourselves in the craft."

That was what I wanted.

"Maisie, I can teach you what your old coven could not," continued Daphne. "In many covens, there are witches with different levels of power. The covens expect to have one very powerful witch, and the lower powered witches do their bidding. You weren't going to learn anything unless you were to take the place of leader. Even then, it would be based solely on magic. I want to teach people witchcraft, not magic. Potions, spells, charms, hexes—our old ways."

"I know some spells and potions." But I heavily relied on my magical abilities. My sister, Marney, was the best in our whole coven at potions.

"Everything can be learned," said Daphne.

Eva stood at the house entrance, red in the face. Marina and Shelby stacked her plentiful suitcases beside the front doors. A vein throbbed in Eva's neck. Fury was written on her features.

"I'm sad to see you go, Eva, but I know you will land on your feet," said Daphne almost too politely. "This way, Maisie." The leader of the coven turned up the grand staircase.

I chased her. Eva burrowed her glare into my back, and my skin heated. I touched my shirt just to make sure she hadn't started me on fire. She hadn't. Daphne and I walked into the library, doors closing behind us. Immediately, I felt at peace.

"Maisie, whenever you like, you are free to come and go. Life is… short." Then she motioned around the library, but I was already marveling at the size. "I noticed you like to read."

"Yes." I stepped beside her.

"I don't ask much from the girls in the coven, but I ask them to keep areas clean. Our staff does much for the house, but it is old and needs upkeep. Magic can only do so much. I ask that you keep this area clean, but I will warn you: I haven't had someone in this area for a long time. Not many girls use the library."

Walking over to a far wall, I studied the bookshelves and found the books to be randomly placed. Panic spread through me. How was it possible that anyone found any books? Maybe that was why the girls needed more help with potions and spells. I would have to take every book from the shelves and organize the whole room. Perhaps even create a cataloging and checkout system.

"I'll do it," I said automatically. The library combined some of my favorite things, including being alone.

Daphne smiled at me. It was a soft but proud smile, like I had been graced by sunlight after days of heavy clouds. I basked in the smile for as long as it lasted.

"Thank you," she said. "Now off to the rest of the house."

The dining room, ballroom, the guest rooms, and where the girls slept. My stuff had been moved up to my new bedroom, and Daphne said, "You'll be with Lada. Eva *was* your roommate."

Thankfully, Lada was not in the room when I came in. My stuff was placed on the freshly made bed.

"Maisie," Daphne said, "if you need anything, let me know. I live upstairs. Supper is on your own tonight, but I think Lada may have some ideas. Do you want anything before I go?"

I looked back into the empty bedroom. There was so much that I couldn't put into words. "No."

She walked away, stilettos echoing with every step. Closing the door quickly, I got into bed and pulled the covers up to my chin. Tears streamed down my face. What had I done by leaving my family and my coven and all I had ever known?

***

My eyes flash open to the present. I'm alive. In pain. Not alone. I turn in the library.

Repairing a shirt, Paula moves gracefully to pull the needle and thread through the fabric. How can she work so nimbly?

"Oh, you're awake. How are you feeling?" She sets the shirt aside.

"Fine." I try to brush my fingers through my knotted hair. "Do you know if... um, Lizzy stitched my head?"

"She didn't but did ask me. My thread could probably do it, and you've got a lot of hair so no one would notice a scar—I just didn't think it was the best idea." Paula gags. "And Daphne agreed. Conversation over."

"I'm sorry about Mikayla." *And Beatrice and all my failures.*

"Me too." Her bottom lip quivers. "You should get more rest. I can report to Lizzy that you woke up and used full sentences."

I prop myself up on my elbows. "What about Mikayla?"

"Daphne made us leave her body in the woods. She said she left an anonymous message for the police. They'll find her body, *says* Daphne, but we just left Mikayla out there. We shouldn't have—" She gasps.

"Paula, I mean it, I'm sorry." Every time I move my jaw to speak, my head hurts.

She kneels next to me. "I've never lost someone before. All my family is alive. So when Beatrice died, I was confused. Even now, I think she is going to come through the front door. Mikayla has even... I can't... not another one of us." Tears run down her cheeks. "My grandmother is a... well, she's stronger than me. She's a necromancer. When Beatrice died, I asked her to bring Beatrice back. My grandma considered it, giving me all the options because the thing is they—the person, I mean, never comes back right. She saw the body: Beatrice charred, beyond recognition. My grandma couldn't do it. Saying it wasn't a life worth coming back to." She wipes her cheeks with the back of her hand. "Growing up, all I wanted was a power like my grandma's, but I never got it. I work my ass off, but I can't do it. I have no power. I try every day, running through the stretches and steps, hoping it might appear. Then Mikayla has an active power and

128

doesn't use it. Beatrice never stood a chance. I don't stand a chance."

"He's...." I don't know what to say.

I have an active power. I almost died.

"Sorry. He attacked you and I'm...." Paula stands up. "You should go back to sleep. I need to fix this shirt."

Chapter 16

Magic allows for impossibilities, but power
comes with consequences and responsibilities.
The stronger the power, the more control it
needs.

–Unknown

After a week of joining the coven when I was fifteen, Daphne waited in the backyard after my morning run, sitting on one of the benches. "Trying out the trails around the house?" she asked.

"Yes," I said.

The overgrown trails hadn't been used in ages. I hated to make my own. I was already destroying what the earth was trying to recover.

"Maisie, I was thinking we would work together today." She wore slacks and a puffy jacket.

"I'm a bit... rusty. I don't always practice," I admitted. Though I was sweaty after my run, my hands were especially clammy.

"You wouldn't be the first witch. We rely heavily on our powers, but we forget that they are much like muscles, needing to be stretched."

The backyard housed three old oak trees, green grass, a hedge with a wooden door, and a small garden. The grass and hedge were trimmed more like a manicure than actual care, turning brown.

I placed my hand down on the dry grass. The dirt wasn't gaining enough nutrients, one of the oak trees blocked the light. The magic flowed through me. Green grass tickled my palm.

"While that is impressive, that's not all you can do," said Daphne. "The grass was greening before you placed a hand on it. Why don't you challenge yourself? Your powers will only grow if you let them."

I balled my hands into fists. "What if I... lose control or—"

"You can control your magic, so it doesn't control you. What about the garden or the hedge?"

"They're in fine condition."

"I'll pass that along to Marina."

Turning her back to me, Daphne took something from her pocket. *Click.* The small hairs on my arms stood. Daphne stepped back. Orange flames crawled up the leaves and branches. *How could she do that?* I rushed forward, but Daphne took my arm.

"I don't think you have fire abilities." She grabbed the hose and doused the flames.

The scarred hedge slacked. Pain sizzled on my skin, but I grew closer to assess the damage.

Placing my hand on the hedge, I strained to breathe. "I'll fix you."

I pressed a finger to each of the burned branches, each like an artery. My skin tingled as my magic moved.

The charred branches shed the blackened bark. It dropped dead leaves.

"Maisie, don't push yourself too hard," warned Daphne. "Know your limitations."

I imagined green hedge leaves and then forced them to grow. They started to bloom. The leaves were crumpled and mismatched. I tried to make new leaves. Unfortunately, they came out the same way. I pushed my magic harder—

Rough hands pulled me away from the hedge.

I stumbled to my knees. The world blurred.

"You're trembling. That was too much," Daphne said.

Now that I had pulled back from the magic, I saw what happened to me. Weakness seeped across my bones. I needed a nap.

"Maisie, you want to prove yourself, but I trust you." Daphne brushed her clothes off. "If you don't mind, Maisie, I'll be off. I am picking up Eva's replacement today. Her name is Audrey."

***

Someone else is in the library with me. The smell is different. Not Paula's thick floral perfume.

Laying on the couch, I stare into the darkened shadows. "Hello?"

Ubah pops into the dim light. "Sorry for waking you, but you're basically the librarian. Where do you keep the werewolf books?"

I draw my eyebrows together. The skin pulls taut, and the back of my head throbs. "Are you looking for folklore or scientific?"

"Young adult."

I point in the general direction of fictional literature. My hand is as heavy as a boulder. "You may need a ladder. The young adult section is by author's last name, but there are several werewolf books."

"Thanks." Ubah walks over to the shelves, swinging her cell phone flashlight.

"Why are you looking for a werewolf book?" I ask.

"It's my job to look after you, and I'm in a werewolf mood. Roxie was watching this teen show earlier, and oh the boys.... I need a man with abs." She picks through the titles.

"There should be some books, a trilogy, with white covers. Look under 'S,'" I say. "Do you know anything about werewolves?"

"Full moons," she says, balancing on her tiptoes. "Don't like vampires. Usually hot."

"Smell like dogs."

Ubah laughs and sits where Paula sat, opposite me, like I am a plague. "You should go back to sleep. You're close enough to when Lizzy told me to wake you up that it should be good anyway."

"How about you?" I ask.

"I'm going to see how far I can get through the werewolf book before I end up taking my own nap." She cracks the book spine.

***

When Audrey showed up at the coven, we were roommates with Lada, and she was already friends with Jane and Grace. For the first few days, Audrey and I hung out with the three, but Grace didn't like Audrey. That made the other two girls not like her. The rest of the coven was slowly turning against Audrey. However, I had never known a girl like her.

"We should do something today," Audrey announced in our bedroom one day. "What's around here?"

"The woods, the ocean?" I offered.

"Ugh. I'm so bored." She flopped onto the bed beside me. "We could go to Berlin, Tokyo, Rio, Accra—anywhere. We have the power. The world is our oyster. Or some shit like that. What are we going to do? And don't say something boring, Maisie. I'll leave you."

"No, you won't."

"I'm very powerful. You wouldn't even know what hit you."

"I can take it," I said, placing the book I was reading on the nightstand.

She propped herself up on her hands. "Not my power. I am the most powerful witch here. Daphne's got nothing on me. I don't know what anyone sees in her. Maybe it's the boobs?" I blanched, and Audrey laughed. "What do you think is her biggest secret?" she asked.

I shrugged.

"Come on, Maisie. You've spent time with her. Does she secretly kill people? A whore?"

"Audrey, that's not nice."

"Don't be a prude, Maisie. I'm not judging." She huffed. "Maybe she isn't actually a witch?"

"I've seen her do witchy things," I said.

"Maybe, she's like a hundred years old?"

"A hundred?"

"Okay, so more like five hundred. Or a thousand."

I scoffed. "She looks barely older than either of us."

Audrey studied our bedroom ceiling. "We should go to Sydney. We can have lunch."

"It's midnight there," I told her.

"We're going clubbing."

"Audr—"

"Nope. We're going clubbing. Wear something slutty." After hopping off the bed, Audrey began stripping in front of me, and I looked away.

She wasn't the first woman to change in front of me, but I didn't like it either. I had asked Daphne to get a separator for changing, but I was the only roommate who used it. Then again, my coven sisters had walked down the hallway naked. In a house of all girls, I was the odd one out who didn't want to show off their body.

"Rude. I'm fucking hot. Now move," she ordered, kicking the side of my bed.

I walked to the wardrobe and looked through my clothes. I had nothing that Audrey considered *slutty*, but I had things that I considered loose. My parents never bought me anything revealing, but I hadn't wanted to wear anything like that. I shifted through the clothes.

"Let me guess, you don't have anything?" With one shoe on, Audry hopped to Lada's closet.

I pleaded, "Audrey, don't. She doesn't share." She could've been back any second.

"She's an only child. Of course, she doesn't share." Audrey threw Lada's dresses on the bed. "How about this? Oh, this one. This one is ugly, so is this one."

One dress crumbled to the floor in a heap, and I went over to pick it up.

"Don't!" said Audrey.

I jumped back, startled.

She turned back to the closet. "Ugly. Ugly. Ugly. Oh, that's cute. I'll keep that. Maisie, you should try this one on. You've got the boobs for it."

I wrapped my arms around my chest, yet my breasts bubbled over my arms through my high collar t-shirt. Why did they have to make their presence known?

"Don't be embarrassed." Audrey went over to Lada's vanity. "They're great!"

Looking down at Lada's dress, I said, "Audrey, we shouldn't do this. This is her home too."

"She doesn't like me. I showed up to the coven and tried to be nice but wasn't good enough for her and the others." She picked a lipstick tube from Lada's enormous collection. "Do you like this one?"

Having put on the dress behind the separator, I looked over at the shade of red. Too bright. "It's nice."

"And expensive." Audrey pressed the tip of the lipstick to the mirror and wrote something I couldn't read. Her handwriting was atrocious. She ground the tip down into the mirror until it broke and fell to the floor. With her shoe, she smashed it into the carpet. "Whoops." Audrey plucked another lipstick out of Lada's box. "You ready?"

As we went down the stairs, I saw Lada, Grace, and Jane hanging out in the kitchen. Lada's eyes came to me and then gave me a double take. I wanted to apologize, but Audrey towed me out the back door.

"Maisie, wake up," someone orders, and I'm thankfully thrown back to the present.

I prefer not to remember those moments with Audrey, but the coven didn't feel like a home until Audrey arrived and swung her arm around my shoulder.

"You're crying," Kami whispers, lingering at my side. "Are you in pain?"

My head aches, but it's been worse. "I'm sorry about Mikayla."

"Thanks." Kami sits next to me on the couch. "It hurts so much. I was sad when Beatrice died but didn't think Mikayla was going to be next. She was my twin, you know. Not by blood but...." She scrubs her face with her palms, her eyes glistening with tears. "We did everything together. I know it sounds morbid, but I thought we would die together. Like we were separated at birth but the whole cradle-to-grave thing. I should've been with her. I should've.... I just thought, if anyone, it was going to be Paula—because she's not very powerful. Or Rochelle—because she is sometimes just stupid. I never thought it would be Mikayla. She's strong, and she has power. She was hunted and killed."

"Hunted?" I repeat.

The word sputters in me. It might be because the word is so pointed. It strikes my chest.

"Like a wolf hunts a deer or something. I'm not very good with nature. I leave that to you." She shakes out her hair.

"Hunt?" I try the word out on my tongue like I've never heard it before.

"Okay. Maybe it was the wrong word. No need to be mean about it." Jumping to her feet, she storms from the library.

"That's not what I…." I trail off as the library door slams. A book falls off the shelf, and I flinch. However, my mind is working.

Things that hunt: sirens, wolves… mortals.

***

During a potion lesson, Daphne stood at the head of the dining room. Each of us had a cauldron of our own. Daphne was taking it step by step, making sure we followed along, especially the replacements for Lada, Jane, and Grace.

"Maisie, lead the seminar." Daphne stepped off to the side, and like before, I took her place at the front of the dining room. Daphne wove through the tables, and the girls attentively looked at their brews. Halting next to Carmella's table, she whispered, "This isn't the potion I'm making."

Shrinking, Carmella squeaked, "I'm sorry. I only wanted to try something harder."

I struggled with the technique, necessary attention, and speed of the process. There were too many ways this potion could go wrong. So what did Carmella want that was harder? What did I need to make?

"Watch the edges. They'll burn." Daphne walked on, checking Audrey's abysmal work. "Maisie, what's the next step?"

Looking at the potion at the front of the dining room, I tried to remember. Daphne had been reciting from memory, but we had a handout at our workstations. Having read the instructions three times before starting, I stirred the potion. There was a time limit, but if I could just—

A potion exploded with a rasping boom. We ducked for cover. Glass trembled. Slowly, I peeked around the corner of the table. A blob rose from Carmella's cauldron.

The plume, controlled by Daphne and a spell, inked black smoke and electrical lighting. Carmella had created a weather potion, but a spell would've been better. The actual power would've been the best. The plume—not storm-like now—stretched up and out. Daphne was merely holding it in place.

She roared, "Out of the room!"

We scrambled but weren't quick enough.

The plume poked the chandelier, shattering Daphne's spell. Purple and green slime that smelled like week-old feces left out in the summer heat soaked us. I gagged.

One of the girls screamed, "It's burning my eyes!"

"Good job, Carmella. Well fucking done," spat another.

Carmella hunched over. "I don't know what happened."

Their voices layered on each other: "You messed up." "You're not as smart as you think you are." "Screwed up an easy potion!"

"Girls, get cleaned up." Daphne pinched her nose.

We rushed from the dining room to get away from the stench and the goop falling from the ceiling. Everything was ruined, including the books. By the time I got upstairs—hauling Audrey—we were the last ones in line for the showers. Down the hallway, one of the girls was saying, "When I'm done with my shower, Carmella is not going to know what hit her."

One of her friends said, "She's so stupid anyway. Her potion was so off from ours."

"Did you see her crying? Like grow up." She pretended to cry, and I looked down at my slime-covered shoes.

The slime stained the floor, seeping into the cracks. The staff were going to have a hard time cleaning.

"Carmella acts so smart, only because she's powerless. Mostly mortal. I don't get why Daphne let her in anyway," said another girl.

"Shut the hell up! No, really," yelled Audrey. "You just blabber. Carmella is a shit-ton smarter than you. I would like to see you create that potion. Bet you can't." Her magic rolled through the hallway.

We were saved from any further awkward interaction when the bathroom door opened, three girls coming out. The three girls went in. Audrey and I stepped up to be next, the last two in the hallway for the showers.

We stood in silence for a full minute before Audrey broke it. "I know I can be a bitch, Maisie. I'm not the best person, but I've got rules of conduct, like don't fight a weaker person. Lada could handle her own. So can Angel, Maxie, and Laverna." She looked to where the three girls had been. "Carmella cannot."

I crossed my arms over my chest. "Why do you say that?"

"She's like you. You're book smart, will ace any test, but you can't win in a fight. Plus, you're small and a pushover."

What? "I'm not a pushover."

She scoffed.

"I could definitely win in a fight," I said.

"Against Carmella," she retorted.

"Against anyone."

"You couldn't win a fight against me."

"I could—" Hot breath rushes my skin like lava. My eyes flash open to the library, back in the present.

Johanna looms above me, and I jump. My magic jerks with me.

She smirks. "Did I scare you, Maisie?"

Ignoring her question, I rub my neck. "Is there any water?"

Johanna picks up the full glass. She looks like she is going to hand it to me until she stops and says, "Tell me what your dream was about."

I don't like the look in her eye, like she's on the hunt and I'm an easy target. "Did you ever meet Audrey? She was one of my friends. I had a dream that you and Audrey and me were hanging out—and Lizzy," I lie through my teeth.

She tilts her head to the side. "We were just hanging out?"

"Yeah. I think you and Audrey would've been great friends."

Johanna hands the glass to me like it's a reward, and I chug the water. Even after drinking it all, my throat is raw. Every part of me is warm, and I kick off the blankets someone has put on me.

"Lizzy said we need to keep your strength up," she says, "so you should sleep. I'll keep an eye on you. You won't die on my watch."

An icy feeling runs through my veins, but it awakens me. Unease clots my body, wound up by the memories of Audrey and what happened to Carmella. She left that night.

Chapter 17

They say don't mess with a scorned woman,
but they obviously never met a scorned witch.
–Unknown

The open shades reveal a sunny morning. The night
has finally passed, me being woken every hour. Head
hurting, I push myself into a sitting position. Pain
rushes through me, and I sway on the couch and groan.
That was too fast.

"Shut up. I'm trying to read their lips." Astrid eyes
the ground out the front window.

"But," I say, and she whips around.

Her crystal blue eyes are as hard as diamonds. Scars
extend the length of her face, disappearing under her
high collar dress.

"Shut. Up." She turns back to the window. Her
white hair bounces in its soft curls.

Drawing my fingers over the blanket draped across
me again, I whisper, "What's down there?"

"The police and Daphne. I'm stuck babysitting you
while the rest of the girls have their ears pressed against
the doors. I hope you're happy," Astrid grumbles.

"Did Daphne call the police here?"

"No, they arrived at dawn. They wanted to come into the house, but Daphne refused. She put on her charms. They make any man do her bidding." She scratches at her arms through her gloves and long sleeves. "They know the body is Mikayla's, and they are reporting it to Daphne. She plays the grieving and shocked woman well. Too bad her back is to me, or I'd know what lie she is spewing."

I lean back on the couch. The sunlight and her speaking add to my throbbing headache.

"The police will sniff around more now that two witches are dead," continues Astrid. "It was easier back when the police were dumb and easily paid off. They probably already think we're the ones who killed Beatrice and Mikayla. But you already know about that, don't you, Maisie?"

"I told you I didn't—"

"You're alive, so you can take care of yourself." Using her cane, she hobbles from the library.

"Wait, close the shades please," I beg, but the door shuts behind her. I flinch at the sound, and the sudden movement vibrates down my bones. My body jerks like I'm caught mid-seizure. White light bursts before my eyes from the pain. All I want to do is sleep.

The bright sunlight slants through the east-facing windows, and I crane my neck to look away. Even when I pinch my eyes shut, the light seeps through. It claws into me and holds my brain hostage. I need to close the shades.

I stumble over to the windows. My feet drag over the rugs, and my toes catch in the fabric. Each move of my leg blurs my vision and I use my muscle memory of the library layout to find my way to the windows.

Sunlight sears my body. I'm too warm. Is this a fever? I thought people got cold before death.

The sun is too bright. I grab ahold of the curtain, digging my fingernails in. Too late.

I land with a thud on the rug. The bright sun dances in my vision for a second before the curtain falls on me.

***

The day and night were calm with a thin layer of clouds covering the sky. Flowers bloomed wildly. I was ready for spring, but my magic was ready for it more. It wanted to stretch as much as I did.

Audrey roared, "You don't understand, Maisie! You live in this perfect little world. You are Daphne's favorite! You grew up so easily! It was just given to you on a platter."

"I had to work for where I am," I argued. Even after being friends with Audrey for a year, it seemed she didn't know me.

"No, you didn't!"

We stood in the backyard. I had been gardening. More herbs were needed for our next potion seminar. Audrey had sprinted out of the kitchen, her magic on high, and had started screaming, jabbing her finger at my chest.

"*Maisie, this. Maisie, that,*" Audrey went on, flinging her hands out. "What makes you so special? I've met enough girls in my life that are exactly like you: quiet,

145

average—and people just fall over you, don't they? You don't even have to try!"

"Audrey," I said.

The garden started to grow, the vines snaking up. I shook off my magic.

"Don't give me that tone! People look straight through me when I am a powerful witch. You are... forgettable? Useless," she spat.

My powers spiraled at those words, even though I brought my nails into my palms. A strong wind, aided by the open hedge, knocked Audrey off her feet. She landed on her side.

"Walk away before you regret it," I ordered.

I had never seen her like this before. She was relentless, like she smelled blood in the water.

On the ground, she was laughing and rolling around. She ripped out the grass, and it was like someone was plucking out my hair. Before I could order her to stop, the grass moved like a tidal wave. It pushed Audrey to her feet, and then she hit the ground and became two. Their movements mimicked one another.

A shudder ran down my back. I hated when she did this, multiplying into copies of herself. It was creepy. She used it on the coven all the time to freak out the girls.

"You've done it now." Both of her stood.

"Audrey." I put my hands up. "Let's talk about this."

This had gotten far out of hand. Neither of us were thinking straight.

They stepped toward me. "Are you scared, Maisie? The powerful and favorite Maisie is scared."

"I'm not scared." My wavering voice gave away my lie. However, my fear wasn't directed at her. The vines and roots were like snakes, and I tried to corral my magic. "I don't want to hurt you."

The Audries expanded again, creating four. I stared dumbfounded. She had only ever done three of herself, and she had sweated and breathed heavily through it. Her magic had been weak for the following week. They flipped their red hair over their shoulders.

"Hurt us?" they echoed. "Like you ever could. Your magic is cute, but do you want to see what an actual witch can do?"

The ground rippled up, putting distance between us. The wind was strong, wanting to throw me into the glass windows. The roots of the trees started to curl around my feet and legs, holding them in place, spreading up my torso and arms. She was using her magic to somehow control mine, probably conjuring this magic. But how? I had never seen Audrey conjure.

Their giggles slapped me in my face. "Not going to fight back, Maisie? I thought you were powerful."

"Audrey, this isn't you," I pleaded. "I'm sorry that I used magic on you first. That was wrong, and I was out of line. It goes against everything this coven believes in—what I believe in. I didn't want to hurt you. I'm sorry. Let's talk about this."

In the whirling wind, their next words were lost on me.

Eight stood before me. I gaped. How was this possible? It shouldn't have been.

"You said you were powerful," they mocked.

The eight turned into ten but looked less like Audrey. Their whole bodies were like melted ice cream on a summer day. Her faces drooped. Their hair had lost its shine. The ten turned into twelve. Only one more needed for a coven. She would be unstoppable.

"What did I do to you to hate me? What did I do?" I asked.

We had had fights in the year we had known each other, but we hadn't had any recently. Where was this coming from? Why today? And why couldn't I stop it? Normally, I would say sorry, and she would forgive me. We would move on.

"Audrey, I'm sorry for using my magic against you. I was wrong. But this isn't you," I said, flicking my eyes to each of the Audries.

Audrey was many things, but she wasn't cruel. She didn't pick fights with me. She took apologies. She was my friend, and we had been best friends since the day she showed up to the coven.

"It isn't me." Of the twelve hers, eleven turned to the original Audrey in the center. "What's happening? I'm scared." Her voice was soft and sad.

"It's okay," I said. She was my best friend, and I wanted to help her. "It'll be okay."

A devilish grin reappeared on her face. "You're so naive, Maisie."

Groaning, the bodies morphed. Parts of each of the Audries were ripped away and sucked into a new version.

The thirteenth Audrey.

"No!" I thrashed my hands into the dirt, collecting my magic.

The thirteenth Audrey started to merge into a singular being. Her limbs were backwards, her jaw slack. Her eyes were just holes in her moldy skin. The other copies had been at least a little better.

With my hands plunged in the dirt, I released my magic back into the wild.

Tree branches snapped. Roots, like a squid's tentacles, grabbed each of the morphing thirteen. Wind created a vortex, and the bodies were sucked up into it. Her screams followed. The magic twisted, but the roots held me down. The earth and I combined.

Audrey thought I created vegetables. That I was a flower child, one with only nature and peace. But I wasn't a pushover. I chose my battles. Specifically, those I could win.

Her screams morphed as the tornado grew faster.

My fingernails pressed into my palms. Blood oozed into the green grass. My magic and the hungry ground took it.

Her screams stopped.

My magic let go.

The roots receded. The trees stood back up in their place.

"Audrey?" Pushing off the torn-up ground, I stumbled to her.

She lay in flimsy sod. Her back was arched as if she was being pulled toward the sky by her hips. White foam oozed out the side of her gurgling mouth. Her bones broke and reformed together. What was happening to her? She had overused her magic, but I had never seen overuse come with these side effects.

Bleeding from the nose and exhaustion, yes. This was… monstrous.

"I'm going to get help. I'll be back." I ran into the mansion, yelling for help.

No stampede of steps. No one answered me. How was no one home now?

Audrey might've tried to kill me, but I couldn't let her die.

After rummaging through the kitchen cabinets for anything to help, I turned as Daphne stared at me. "You're here! I need help, Audrey needs help. She attacked—" I didn't know what happened.

Daphne went out the back door, keeping a relaxed pace. I nearly kicked at her heels to move her faster.

She halted abruptly, and I slammed into her back. Why had she stopped? I peeked around her.

Audrey stared up at the sky. Her mouth hung open in a final gasping breath.

I tried to go around the coven leader, but Daphne gripped my hand and warned, "Maisie."

"Audrey? Can you hear me? Audrey!" I yelled, but my best friend didn't move. What had I done? Oh my…. "I killed her. I didn't mean to. She came after me, and I was just, I had to, I didn't mean to—"

Daphne slapped me across my face, and I stilled. Her eyes hovered on the gate. The unlocked hatch tapped against the metal frame. It must've come undone when I opened the hedge, like all I had done to stop Audrey—but I hadn't wanted to kill her. The backyard was shredded.

I scrambled for an excuse, but the truth stared at me. I was a killer. "Daphne, I—"

"Shut up, Maisie." She gripped me. "Maisie… wake up."

Chapter 18

I give my blood to thee, keeping our secrets
between we. If one shall speak, then pain will
peak. Your secret is mine for all of time.
—A blood oath spell

I blink my eyes open to the sunlight that fills the library, and I'm blinded. Heat tears at my skin. I can barely breathe. Someone has their body locked on me, and I try to kick them off. Pain shoots up my spine.

"Is she seizing?" someone asks.

"Is she hallucinating?" another questions.

"She's hot." Daphne pulls back the blanket, and the weight is released off my body. "Open a window."

A rustling. A thud. The chilly air graces my skin, and I heave a sigh.

"Maisie, where does it hurt?" ask Daphne.

"Everywhere." I focus on the source. "My head."

Lizzy stands behind Daphne. "Overexertion. She was found by the window. She probably got up, and her body couldn't take the activity. Maisie, you scared us."

I swallow the dry acidic taste on my tongue. The police were here with Daphne, asking about Mikayla. Where is Astrid to take the blame for what she did?

"I need to speak to Daphne." My voice comes out as a whine, but I cannot escape the memories flashing behind my eyes. I have long pushed out these memories—not wanting them—but they have crept back in. I can't ignore them anymore. When no one moves, I bite out, "Alone."

The girls shuffle from the library, and Daphne stands two feet away. The doors shut, but the girls' soft and hushed breaths echo under the door. They're obviously listening, but they would try to listen anywhere in the house.

"Yes, Maisie?" Daphne asks. Her tone is outwardly polite, but I know the warning note.

I keep my voice low. "The night Audrey died—"

"Maisie." She shakes her head. "Don't do this to yourself."

"The police never came for Audrey. I can't remember anyone asking for her—no family, no friends. No one has come asking after Beatrice too. You really know how to pick us," I say.

No one would ask about me either. I don't know where Marney is, and my old coven is dead.

"It's not like that," says Daphne.

"The night Audrey died—" The words choke me. "You *never* talk about it. You pretend like it didn't happen. Like I didn't kill—"

"You didn't kill her." Red spreads up her neck.

"The night Audrey died, I remember it," I continue. "I have gone through it so many times, but I think I almost figured it out. I knew I was forgetting something. Audrey was looking for a fight, but it wasn't really her, was it? She was more powerful than I had ever seen her. After the fight, she convulsed, vomited—just started dying. I couldn't have saved her, right?"

"Yes," she says almost too quickly.

"Why did you never tell me she had taken a power inducer?"

She peeks from under her dark eyelashes. "Would that have made it better?"

"Yes, of course!" My voice slaps my ears, and I cringe.

"Fine. I'm sorry I didn't tell you," says Daphne without an ounce of remorse.

"You're not actually sorry." I huff. "Audrey wouldn't take that by herself. She… was more powerful than other witches in the house. But the power inducer doesn't kill people. It makes them weak afterward So, Audrey did die at my hands."

Power inducers can kill witches. They can go wrong in so many ways. But it was me.

Tears burn my eyes—but not for Audrey. I killed someone, I'm the monster. For two years, I had been volleying back and forth about whether I killed Audrey, but I know the truth now. And Astrid is right.

"No," growls Daphne. "You tried to help her, Maisie. She didn't die by your hands."

"My magic," I correct.

"No." She looks elsewhere, her pupils small. "Maisie, you must understand there are things no one should know. Just know you didn't kill Audrey. It wasn't your magic or hands." She turns her back to me.

"What does that mean?" I hurl a pillow at her, which misses wide. My hand slumps to my side, pain shooting up my bones. I regret the action, but she turns back to me, raising an eyebrow, unimpressed. "No more lies, Daphne. I'm begging you."

Her shoulders slump. "Girls don't stay with me long. They come and go. You've stayed with me the longest, Maisie, so it's only fair that I let you know some secrets. But you will not be able to unknow them."

Dread squeezes my body, and fear ebbs in the back of my mind. However, curiosity makes me ask, "How long have you been here? At this coven, in this house? How long?"

She sighs.

Leaning back on the couch, I brace myself. I think I already know. Astrid has made comments, and Johanna acts like she knows.

"I've been here since the middle of the last century," she says, and my breath catches in my throat. "I tried my hand at the movies, but I was told I wasn't very pretty and my acting was crap. I heard of covens in the Pacific Northwest, so I traveled north, stopping by and trying them. I can't remember the year I showed up."

I want to ask how old she is—so many questions about her life and why she looks a few years older than me and what else has she seen—but my next question bursts from my lips before I think: "Why me? Why am I your favorite?"

I cringe at how childish and shallow I sound, but it's the question I've been asking myself since she showed up at my parents' house three years prior. I wasn't eighteen years old or allowed to choose my own coven. I ran away with her.

Daphne smiles broadly. "You're trustworthy, not easily angered. I know you can get the job done. You're smart, Maisie. A hard worker. And if the time comes for me to go, I know you can be a leader here."

"When are you leaving?" I don't want to be the leader.

"No time soon. I've lived a long time. Survived many things. I don't think I'm going to be dying any time soon." She laughs.

"When were you born?" I ask.

She frowns. "I was in an orphanage in the South for a long time. I wouldn't give myself this accent. It may have been around the time of the Redcoats, but it is more like flashes of red. Everything is a blur."

I lean forward. "What do you remember?"

"The 20s—the *1920s* that is," she says, squinting into the shadows of the library. "I remember portions, but that may be because of all the moonshine. I remember some other things too. Like the 1880s was an amazing decade. I was up and down the East Coast. There were quite a few vampires."

"You've met vampires?"

Throwing back her head, she giggles. "When you're better, we can meet them. There are some in Seattle and Minneapolis—certainly in New York City. Depending on what pack you find, they are cordial. The older they are, the finer the taste they have." She sounds like she has done more than just *meet* vampires. "In my younger days, I was wild because I knew nothing could hurt me. That's probably why I don't remember what I did. Eventually, it catches up with you."

"Is that why you came to this coven?" I ask.

Coming to the edge of the couch, she kneels. "I had been searching for a long time for people like me. Not just witches. I had been in covens before, but none of the covens ever felt right until I came here. I can name every girl who has walked through that door. They leave me."

"I don't want to leave." This is my home. I can't imagine being anywhere else.

I don't have anywhere else to go.

She gives me a sad smile, like she has heard this all before. How many girls have there been before me? How much of a favorite am I?

"Is it only Astrid who knows about you?" I ask.

"She first stayed here in the late 1970s," Daphne explains. "Her parents were flower children, and she hated them for it. They only taught 'good' and 'light' magic, so she came searching for bigger and better things."

"Were you the leader?" I lean into whatever she says, piecing together the life she has told me about.

"No." She scoffs. "Astrid hated knowing less than me, and she left after two years. In the 80s, she came back, absolutely astounded by me not having aged. A witch's power is her weapon, and it keeps us alive. I swore her to blood secrecy."

I gulp. "That must've been difficult."

Blood secrecy isn't a joke. It can kill the most powerful witches. Daphne could die depending on the wording of the spell. My blood burns hot in my veins, but thankfully, the window is still open. Another cool breeze billows in.

"A blood oath is easier than you think," says Daphne. "Astrid wanted my knowledge, so I taught her the best I could. She cannot tell another soul without dying a painful and bloody death."

I sink back into the couch, but I can't go any further without falling between the cushions. "Are you going to make me do the same?"

"You are far more trustworthy than Astrid could ever dream to be." She pats my hand. "I know you have questions, but you need to sleep. And heal. I can't begin to explain the shrieks that followed when Kami found you on the floor."

Chapter 19

You'll never know a witch's power until she
uses it.
–Unknown

When deemed strong enough by Lizzy and Daphne, I move to my bedroom. I am only allowed to leave my bed when I need to use the restroom, and I spend most of my time sleeping or reading. My legs itch to go for a run, but when I stand, I sway. The back of my head throbs like I'm being hit by the wood bat all over again.

I am stuck like this for a week. While it's sometimes terrible, it's not horrible. This is the first time in this house that I've ever been alone. Mostly.

Roxie comes into the bedroom as the sun sets. She pounces on my bed, and I wince. My brain moves like jelly in my skull.

"You should've seen Johanna today. She was pissed," says Roxie a little too loudly. "Daphne has something planned for tomorrow, and I can't wait. Johanna being pissed off only helps. We need to dress nice."

I groan.

"What, you don't want to go?" she asks.

"I don't want to dress nicely," I say. It isn't a lie, but Roxie's talking also makes my head pound. It's easier when the door is shut and the voices muffled.

"Oh, yeah." Roxie laughs. "You can probably dress in whatever you want seeing that you're injured. Do you think you could get away with pajamas? Maybe a Halloween costume? You should see how far you can take it. I would love to see you dressed up in one of those inflatable t-rex costumes. It would make you a whole foot taller."

A yawn escapes my lips, somewhat forced. Whatever Daphne has planned, she hasn't told me. She hasn't visited me in my bedroom anyway.

"I get it." Roxie hops off my bed. "You're tired."

She leaves, and when the door shuts, the lights flicker out. Except for the silver moonlight that slips through the parted curtains.

The light illuminates the dishevelment of the backyard.

I rip the blankets off and grab my sweatshirt from the hook. Placing my feet on the carpet, my knees quake. When I try to stand, I use the wall and whatever else in the bedroom to keep myself upright. What has happened to me? I've been off my feet for about a week after my head injury. I teetered so close to death that I should've been in a hospital, tied to tubes and watched over by trained medical staff.

Through the open window, I call to a nearby tree. It reaches its branch over to me. My magic is strong even if my body is weak. I'm only a conduit for the magic anyway. The tree releases me on the torn-up dirt, and I fall to my knees. This isn't the first time I have destroyed something I love, and worst of all, this probably won't be the last time either.

"I'm sorry. I should've done better. You deserve more than me." A tear rolls down my face and plops on to the dirt. "I'll fix you. I'll give you whatever you want. Take me as your own."

Where my tear dropped, a small bud blooms.

I summon my magic, controlling it into the tiny blade of grass. "Grow."

The blade is only a few inches when I stop it. This is only one small step in remaking, yet sweat has gathered under my armpits. My hair lays damp against my scalp.

I place my hand on the topsoil. "A little at a time, please. I'm still healing."

The blades start to poke up like little razors. The ground and my magic move without me. I nearly fall.

"Control," I whisper to myself.

My magic is slower this time. It wants to show what it can do again. I don't have anyone to prove it to except myself.

The grass spreads in a wave of green. My magic travels through the soil, awakening the stagnant life. The sharp blades climb upward. I pull water from the dirt to make the grass soft.

Sweating through my sweatshirt, I strip it off and then set my hands back on the dirt, but then Daphne calls, "Maisie," from her balcony. She says no more, and she doesn't need to because I'm already pushing to my feet and heading inside.

How much has she watched? How long would she let me go?

My body trembles. Sweat dribbles down my back. After walking up the spiral staircase, I wheeze, each breath rattling my lungs. I brace a hand on the center column before climbing the stairs again. Stumbling through the open suite doors, I basically fall on the couch. My skin is hot wax slipping off my body.

Daphne mixes herself a drink in the kitchenette. "I know I have been absent of late. I want to answer your questions, but we've had higher priorities. I know you understand."

I nod. Two sisters are dead, two spots in the coven open. My sisters buried Mikayla without me. More girls talk about leaving, their murmurs slipping under the door at night. They are scared, like I am. Roxie has told me the police have visited the house more, and locals are driving by. Any time the girls are in town, they are stared at. The police think we killed our sisters, and the locals are close to starting a witch hunt of their own.

Pointing to a newspaper clipping on the wall of two men getting arrested with Daphne, I ask, "What happened that night?"

Tilting her head, she purses her lips. "I was very drunk. It was only the next day I saw the newspaper and me on the front page. Those two—I don't remember their names—they threw a lot of parties. Arrested every other month. Always got out of it."

I indicate to another picture. "What about that one?"

Daphne walks over to the picture-filled wall. While I want to ask about each picture, I don't know how much time I have. She has lived a hundred different lives before she came to the coven. Some of which she has pictures of, but that leaves much of her life undocumented.

Taking off the back of the frame, she pulls the picture out carefully and walks back over to me. "Boston, 1887," she reads from the back. "I think there was this Irishman and his wife... she was a witch. Her coven called themselves druids or herb witches. She spoke to the dead, *or* that's what she claimed. Pay her a penny and she'll tell you of your fortune for the day or the week or the month. Never longer than a year. If you give someone their life's fortune, they won't come back for more." She drinks from her martini glass. "Besides performing maybe a hex, I don't remember much. I didn't stay long. I was up and down the East Coast."

"Why?" I ask.

"I had the time." She shrugs. "Girls my age were getting married and having children."

"You've never wanted that?" Me neither.

She laughs. "I've been alive a very long time, so I bet I have wanted those things at one point or another. I used to be lonely a lot. I think that's why I went to so many parties and outings. I had a few boyfriends. During those days, it was a lot easier. You found a girl or a boy, called it good enough, settled down, and started a life. I don't think I was ever married." She draws her eyebrows together like she has to think about it. "That time isn't memorable."

"What changed it all?" I ask.

Finishing her current martini, Daphne walks back into the kitchenette. "I tried my hand at Hollywood, but World War II happened. It's cliché nowadays. It's hard to think what history will be and won't be history when you're living it. What will people remember?" She measures out the liquor and dumps each shot in. She puts in ice cubes and then shakes the metal container. I flinch—too loud—and she stops. "I think everyone knew, after the Great War, that a second one would be remembered. Here and now, it is memorialized where I think the Great War is forgotten or seen as lesser." She puts the brown liquid into the glass. "I worked in a factory during the day. Went to a coven afterward, where we did potions and spells to save the day. None of it helped. On the weekends, I danced with boys who would go off to die in war. A lot of virgins. They had good blood." A small smile plays on her lips.

A shiver runs down my spine. My mind tries to connect the dots about where she has been and what she has seen. She has lived through these moments, talked to now-dead people. History is written in her mind.

When she speaks again, her voice is sorrowful. "No one really came back. If they did, they weren't the same." She sips her martini and then adds more liquor, like she didn't make the correct concoction. "The following years, I stayed in Hollywood to chase those dreams of a cinema star. I wanted my name in lights, but my name wasn't good enough. I wasn't a good enough actress or singer or... maybe I just didn't sleep with the right people. I tried to date men, but they were so struck by the war. I couldn't fix them. They married, though. When my dreams officially collapsed of being a star, I went looking for a new dream."

I lean forward, resting my chin on my knees. "What other dreams did you have?"

"I think I used to want to be a doctor," she says. "Blood doesn't bother me, but I can't spend that long in school. I used to want to write novels, but I don't have the patience. I loved animals growing up. That reminds me." Walking over to the wall, she stands before the 1920s but after the 1880s. She takes a picture from a wall. "I used to be in the circus."

I couldn't take the picture out of her hand fast enough, wanting to see what I've missed before. The image is bleary. It could've been the circus or another random day that she wore a shiny leotard.

"What did you do in the circus?" I ask.

She licks the liqueur off her lips. "One of the biggest attractions was when the ringleader stabbed me."

I fling the picture on the table, disgusted. A dirty film covers my fingers, and I wipe them on my pants. It's no wonder she doesn't talk about her past.

"It hurt the first few times, but the pain numbs. To this day, I don't feel anything there." She prods her stomach. "I can heal quickly and naturally. By the next night, I was fine."

I still. "You let him do it?"

"The girls who got all the love letters rode the elephants. I, on the other hand, picked up trash and sold tickets. I wanted to be in the show, so I showed him what I could do." She laughs. "He didn't think witchcraft. Science was the craze, so he called me a freak. I became centerstage of the show." It's so nonchalant, yet her voice is filled with pride.

Chapter 20

In the new order of witches in the Council,
witches should be tested as children for their
magical strength. Those witches who have
enough power will be welcomed to the
Council.
—Stewart Powell, *The Council Manifest*

In the morning, I blink away the twinkling dust in my
bedroom. A flurry of hushed voices echo in the hallway
before someone knocks on my door and asks, "Maisie,
are you up? Daphne wants us downstairs in an hour."

In the ballroom, the girls grab food and sit at the
tables. Through the windows that surround the front
door, I see people lined up outside the gates. A shudder
runs down my spine at the thought of auditioning
witches to be in the coven, but we're desperate. It's no
wonder Roxie said Johanna wasn't happy: Her
friends—those she has been pushing to be the coven—
will have to audition like all other witches.

After scanning the coven, I take my plate of mixed
fruit and sit between Roxie and Lizzy. Other girls have

plates filled with food and mugs of coffee and notebooks with pens.

Potion stations and spell books line the tables opposite us. The middle of the room is cleared for a witch to show off her magical abilities. We are her willing participants and judges.

I've been to an audition at the coven before. It's always the same girls trying to get in. The current coven buzzes in excitement, but my stomach twists for how we got to this point. Two of us dead, a few of us missing.

"Where's Rochelle?" I ask.

Lizzy leans over. "Her parents called her home. They said it wasn't safe."

I gulp. Why hadn't anyone mentioned it? I thought the girls only talked about leaving.

Roxie rolls her eyes. "Isn't Rochelle an adult?"

"Rochelle must've felt she wasn't safe. I think she blames herself for Mikayla's death," says Lizzy. "Kami mentioned it."

Roxie and I were there that night too. We are to blame as much as she is.

Daphne walks into the room, her heels announcing her entrance. She wears deep purple, matching from her eye makeup to her heels. She sits between Johanna and Astrid in the middle of the table. Now that I know her secret, I know why every coven witch knows her name. Yes, it is her skills with spells and potions. What they don't know is how long she's had to master them.

We silence as Daphne writes the first name in thick letters at the top of the first notebook page. "Leticia," Daphne calls.

The auditions to join the coven begin.

Leticia wears shoes that click with her steps while she blurs from one side of the room to the other. I glance at Daphne keeping her eyes trained on Leticia's feet. With three openings, Daphne has the ability to choose a wide range of magic: Rochelle low-to-medium power, Mikayla medium power, and Beatrice no power.

Johanna leans forward on the table, tapping her pen on her notebook. "Cool trick. For a superhero."

Faster than a lightning strike, Leticia stands before Johanna. Our coven sister jumps back in her chair, her eyes wide. A few girls snicker. I try not to.

"Thank you, Leticia," Daphne says. "What is your knowledge of potions and spells?"

"I grew up in a coven in New Mexico," she explains. "I trained with them. We don't have a particular spell or potion level, but I did excel in training with the group."

"Are you in a coven now?" asks Daphne, scribbling down what Leticia says.

Others copy the movement. My blank notebook stares back at me. I curl my hands over my chest.

"Not right now," answers Leticia. "When I went to college, I left my coven and haven't found one that I have been interested in."

"Is there anything else we should be aware of?" asks Daphne.

The witch goes through some spells and potions, which are fine but not amazing. Johanna yawns. I've done the potion before, and it takes a medium amount of witchcraft ability.

Daphne sets down her pen. "Thank you, Leticia. We will have a decision tomorrow. Shelby, send in the next witch." The words are cold, but her voice is polite. If she knows she's going to let Leticia into the coven, she doesn't hint at it.

The next girl has her sleeves pulled down to her hands. She hides behind her dark, stringy hair. Her pale skin makes her look more ghost than witch. She mumbles something, and I lean in, as do half of the girls.

"Can you speak up?" asks Daphne.

"Can we close the shades? It's too bright," the girl says, shrinking away.

Daphne looks at Lizzy. With a snap of Lizzy's fingers, the curtains close, leaving us in the dim light from the open ballroom doors.

"Is that better, Kaitlynn?" asks Daphne.

"Kat." She picks at her sleeve. "Yeah. Thanks."

"Okay, Kat." Daphne puts her pen to her paper. "Show us what you can do."

Her eyes spark once she finds something across the room. The water in a cauldron starts to boil, heated by a small fire in the coals. A tiny amount of black smoke arises, and I avert my gaze, memories flooding my mind of both Beatrice and Mikayla's deaths. And Amira's crimes.

"Firestarter," Roxie mumbles in awe. "They're supposed to be rare."

I grimace. "They're not as rare as you think."

"Fire!" someone screams.

"That's kinda the point." But then Roxie jumps up from her chair, knocking it over.

Flames climb up the curtains that Kat asked us to close. The windows are shut. Most of us get to our feet, except Daphne. It's like she suspected this might happen. She writes in her notebook.

Kat is untrained and inexperienced. A firestarter, especially with two of us having burned on a pyre, seems like bad luck.

Smoke billows in the ballroom, and I cough. My lungs shake my chest. The fires under the cauldrons have gone out, and hot water is better than no water. Before I can run for them, Lizzy takes the water from the cauldrons and splashes it over the curtains. White steam rolls up. Someone opens a window.

"I'm sorry," Kat says, laying on the floor in a ball. I don't know when she fell. Fear is written across Kat's face.

"What is your experience level in potion making?" asks Daphne in a neutral tone.

"None," squeaks Kat.

"What is your experience with spells?"

"None." She pushes into a seated position. Her body trembles.

"How did you learn about our coven?" asks Daphne without looking up.

"A psychic."

The girls exchange glances. *A psychic?* Most psychics are frauds, especially when compared to witches. But what if it is true? Maybe another witch told Kat to come to this coven.

"She said you could help me. I really need help. Please." Tears roll down Kat's face. She wipes them away with the back of her sleeve.

"What's the psychic's name?" asks Daphne evenly.

Kat gulps. "Lily Melrose. From Grafton, Vermont."

Daphne writes it down in her notebook. "We'll have our determination by tomorrow. You can go now. Shelby."

Our staff usher the hopeless-looking Kat out, and I raise my hand to reach for her. She needs help. But then I drop my hand, just as I had done to Amira. We have to be fair to all the people who showed up today to join the coven. But what are the chances two firestarters don't know any potions and spells because they weren't raised in witchcraft? Witches take care of their own. Why are Amira and Kat different?

Nancy drags the last of the burned curtains away as girls write in their notebooks. Roxie mumbles, "I hope there's not a quiz later."

My pages are blank. My pen is unmoved.

When Daphne finishes writing her notes, she turns to a fresh page in her notebook. I trust Daphne to make the decision for our coven, like she always has, but I don't want to be at the auditions. Other girls are enjoying this too much, smiling and gossiping amongst themselves. I could never stand in front of a coven and share the secret of my power. I would be too nervous to perform any potion correctly.

Daphne declares, "Next."

This girl is smartly dressed: black block heels, slacks, and a suit jacket with red lipstick. Maybe not physical power radiates off her, but there is something powerful about her. It's natural.

Daphne begins, "Savannah—"

"Savvy," she corrects with a strong southern drawl.

"Savvy," Daphne amends, "what do you have to show us today?"

Savvy walks toward the potion and spells, and Johanna sits back, annoyed. Obviously, Savvy will not be demonstrating an active power. The smell of smoke lingers in the ballroom, so I'm okay with that.

Daphne has picked many girls at eighteen, but Savvy looks to be in her mid-twenties. It could be the confidence or the makeup. Besides Astrid—*and* Daphne—most of us are in our late teens or early twenties.

Without breaking a sweat, Savvy mixes, measures, and maneuvers with the ingredients and reset cauldrons. While one potion boils, Savvy starts a second. She lets the potions simmer for half a minute and then dishes them into small vials. The ingredients mask the burnt scent. I breathe through my nose.

Savvy places two vials in front of each of us. The girls pick them up. The liquid splashes in the glass, small bubbles rising to the rim. There are four of us who don't move: Johanna, Astrid, Daphne, and me. Personally, I don't know what the potion is, so I'm not playing with it. We don't need another fire in the ballroom.

"What are these?" asks Roxie, shaking a bottle.

"One of them is a powerful lust potion. Put in the intended drink, and it lasts in their system up to twenty-four hours," explains Savvy. "The other, you take off the topper, light it, throw it, and run."

"What does it do, though?" Paula swishes the liquid back and forth. It fizzes.

Daphne answers simply, "It's a bomb."

Girls slam the vials down on the table. That's a good way for the potions to accidentally explode. I squint at the vial to remember the ingredients Savvy used. We should technically try the potions to ensure they are what Savvy says they are, but I'm not willing to destroy anything else. Most of the girls aren't either. Except Roxie.

She has a devilish look in her eyes. Thankfully, she leaves the vial on the table.

"I've heard you've had trouble. That potion will get him." Savvy steps back into the middle of the room. "Any questions?"

"What is your experience with spells?" Daphne asks.

"I would say high, much like potions," answers Savvy.

Johanna jumps in, "Any powers?"

Daphne doesn't write that down. "We'll make our decision by tomorrow. Shelby will show you out."

"Thank you for your time." Savvy walks out with Shelby.

The girls are writing again, the vials untouched on the table. I look between the two vials and count back the steps, but Savvy had moved so quickly and efficiently. She moved between the two potions with ease without written instructions. I can't remember which ingredient she used for which potion. I raise my hand to take my pen to the blank paper and then place my hands back in my lap.

Nancy resets the stations for the next girl, but Shelby brings in an elderly woman. It's not that our coven is against the elderly, but Daphne usually brings younger women to join.

Daphne smiles. "Catrina, it's nice to see you again."

Catrina chuckles. "You haven't aged a day."

Both laugh, and my skin itches. It's weird being in on the inside joke. Astrid glowers.

"Everyone, Catrina used to be in the coven... sixty years ago, wasn't it?"

"Fifty-seven, but who's counting?" Catrina's laugh is more of a wheeze. She leans on her walker. Two bright yellow tennis balls are attached at the bottom. Her purse sits on the seat.

"I thought you were down in Florida," says Daphne.

"I was, but they're all retired witches." Catrina waves her hand. "They play and drink more gin than any actual witchcraft. Anyway, this is my home. I want to die here."

I still. More death? No. We can't take any more of it.

"How much time do you have left?" asks Daphne like that is a normal question and somehow a person would know.

"Sixteen days," answers Catrina in a dry tone.

The girls glance at one another. The movement isn't lost by Catrina, who gives a toothy smile. But *how* does Catrina know? Did a psychic tell her how many days she had left like one told Kat to come to our coven? We wait for Daphne.

She writes details in her notebook. "We'll get back to you tomorrow with a decision."

"Thank you." Catrina drags her walker against the floor.

Shelby tries to move forward to offer help, but Catrina shakes her off. They move slowly out the ballroom doors. The girls shift awkwardly in their chairs. No questions about potions, spells, or powers.

Daphne flips the notebook page. "Next."

Shelby shows the next girl into the ballroom. The auditioning girl sidesteps Shelby, standing in front of us. She wears a dazzling smile and a bright yellow summer dress in late fall. The window is still open from Kat, and the cool autumn air rushes in, fluttering the shredded curtains.

"Hello, my name is Julia. Thank you for having me today," says the girl. "I will be demonstrating my magical ability. Please leave any questions for the end of my presentation." She sets an apple, plastic bowl, and a red brick in front of her on a white-clothed table.

Our magic pools around us as much as hers does. The metallic scent fills the ballroom. The one open window can't clear it fast enough. My magic rears its head outside, and the trees sway without a breeze.

Picking up the apple, Julia holds the red skin. The apple shrivels like the moisture disappeared, and I squirm in my seat. Thankfully, I don't feel any pain from the apple, the same if someone ate it, but horror catches in the back of my throat to watch the destruction of nature. What could she do to the backyard or to my woods?

My magic rises, but I push it down. Lizzy peeks at me from the corner of her eye, and I shake my head. I'm all right, even if the back of my head throbs. Lizzy sets her jaw. She doesn't like something about this either.

Julia lays her hands on the cheap blue plastic bowl, and it starts to shrivel and... melt. A horrible scent comes from the dissolving plastic that never catches fire. I press my nose into my shirt. Nancy opens more windows. A few girls shiver, but I sit higher. The blue bowl becomes a blob on the table.

Then Julia picks up the red brick. We inch closer. The red brick starts to erode, turning to dust in her hands. The red sand lays on the table as Julia crushes the rest with her fingers. Wind from the open windows blows the dust away. Nancy and Shelby will have to clean it up later.

One of my sisters whistles, but I only shudder. It's the same destruction Kat can accomplish but in a different way.

"How are you with potions?" asks Daphne.

"Fair," answers Julia.

"Spells?"

"About the same."

Daphne records this all down on the page she's titled "JULIA" and then sets her pen down. "We'll have our determination by tomorrow."

"Thank you for your consideration," says Julia.

Shelby rushes forward to escort her out. Nancy already has a dustpan and broom. The bowl blob and apple will need attention, so Nancy retrieves thick rubber gloves.

When everything is clean and reset, Daphne calls, "Next!" A stream of girls follows.

Kathleen is from Virginia. She closes her eyes and stands very still in the middle of the room, and another one of her appears by the far wall. Unlike self-duplication, astral projection is a hologram image. If Audrey was here, she would've said something bad about astral projection. The whole thing makes me slink back in my chair. Astrid and Johanna look over at me, wearing near identical smirks. Kathleen's original form walks in from the hallway, and she receives applause from some girls. She has created three of herself.

Holly has bright orange hair, and freckles sprinkle her pale skin. She shows off her spell and potion skills. She makes two potions for us. The filled vials are a soft green and a murky yellow: to give someone good health and good dreams. When Holly casts a spell, it is directed. She is polite, answering every question with "ma'am."

Esme does lunges in front of us. Then she stands eight feet tall and still growing. Her arms stretch out like noodles, circling us. Johanna mutters, "Circus freak." Esme's elastic body twists, and then she settles back into her normal—but tall—height. I can't tell if it's her magic or genetics.

Identical twins—wearing matching outfits—Chelsea and Chloe come to our coven because we have multiple openings. The way they finish each other's sentences and seemingly know each other's thoughts unnerves me. I think back to Audrey's self-duplication.

"What do you have to show us today?" asks Daphne.

One of the twins—I can't remember which one— pulls out a kitten from their bag and sets it on the ground. The little orange furball crawls around, and Paula coos and Susana calls it over. The other twin places a hand on its back, and the kitten starts to shake, a whimpering scream echoing from its lips. It falls over, dead.

Screams erupt from my sisters. Paula starts, "What the actual fu—" Susana sobs loudly. Lizzy jumps from her chair, and I am biting down on my tongue as my stomach twists.

Too much death. Beatrice. Mikayla. Amira. Catrina. The Second Witch War—

The first twin places her hands on the dead animal, and a small meow fills the chaotic ballroom. The kitten is back on its feet, dazed but playful. The twin who killed it bounces a ball of yarn in front of the kitten, and the animal swipes at it.

I can't tell if this is necromancy or something else, but it's wrong. Magic isn't good or bad, light or dark, but I'm going to be sick. I don't often think about this kind of magic—necromancy or healing and the touch of death—but my magic is on high. I want to hide.

Daphne takes notes feverishly, her pen nearly slicing through the paper, and then asks very polite questions. None of us have the same calmness. My sisters cling to one another; Roxie has her hands balled into fists. With the kitten playing at their feet, Chelsea and Chloe give generic responses, and Daphne says we'll have a decision tomorrow. The twins take the kitten with them, though I want to snatch it away.

Agatha is a plain witch. After seeing what the identical twins can do, my sisters and I are okay with a witch spending her time brewing potions and working on spells. She fumbles, spilling some of her potion on the floor. It sizzles. Finally, she manages to put the potion in the vials. It is not enough for each of us to have a vial, and the liquid solidifies. We move to the next audition.

Taylor. Amanda. Kristina. Tricia. Marie. Mara. Isabel. Sydney. Out of the seven girls, only one is a strong witch. I want them to have a chance to join the coven, and they want a home. We have more than enough rooms to fill. The other witches have passive powers or no powers. Johanna yawns loudly at Sydney, who then turns red and shuts down halfway through her audition.

The next girl walks into the ballroom, chomping on pink bubblegum and cracking her fingers.

Johanna brushes her strawberry-blond hair from her face and smiles. "Ashley, I'm so happy you could come today."

The realization settles like ice over the table. Daphne said she took Johanna's friends into consideration, but obviously, the consideration didn't get very far.

Daphne writes a header on a new page. "Ashley, what do you have to show us today?"

Her feet lift from the ground, and she hovers in mid-air. She reaches the ceiling in a couple of seconds and then flies around the ballroom. She reminds me of a sports car with her sharp turns and abrupt stops. The witch lands on her feet silently.

Beside Daphne, Astrid frowns. "Can you make portals?"

"Yes," Ashley responds.

"Then why do you feel the need to fly? It's inefficient," says Astrid.

Cutting off that line of questioning, Daphne asks, "How are you with potions and spells?"

Ashley turns to Daphne. "Great."

Astrid scoffs, and Johanna narrows her eyes on the old woman. I doubt Astrid is intimidated. Their blooming friendship is quickly extinguished.

"We'll have our decision by tomorrow," says Daphne. "Thank you, Ashley."

Before Shelby can show Ashley out, another girl walks in. Much like Ashley, she acts as if she's already in the coven. She wears dark clothes, and her deep brown hair is pulled back. She doesn't introduce herself, but Johanna announces, "Robyn!"

Without an introduction or even a polite hello, Johanna's other friend morphs in ten seconds, turning into a tree. Robyn, a shapeshifter, stays that way for a minute before moving to her next shift: a dog. She walks up to Paula, who scratches her back. A couple of my sisters giggle. For her third and final trick, Robyn turns into Ubah.

Roxie jumps up and yells, "Fuck no," but Ubah remains seated, unimpressed. Robyn's Ubah reminds me of a wax figure in a museum. Just something isn't right.

Robyn turns back into herself, and Daphne writes in her notebook. "How are your potion and spell skills?" asks Daphne.

"Amazing," Robyn responds with a smug smile.

Our leader writes that down too. "We'll make our decision by tomorrow."

A third witch of Johanna's struts into the ballroom like this is a fashion show. Her hair is bobbed and sleek, and her skirt is short and stiff. She glows like there is constant glitter on her. Shelby stands in the center of the ballroom with Johanna's other friends, looking at Daphne, dumbfounded. This has gotten out of hand.

"I'm Zelda," announces Johanna's third friend to the ballroom. "Would you like to go on a journey?" She holds out a small white chess piece between her forefinger and thumb.

A crack starts to form in mid-air and then grows to look like a doorway, much like the portals powerful witches can make. It expands, showing what appears to be a window to another time. People wear long petticoats and bowler hats.

Zelda, the time traveler.

A rare witch stands in front of us, and she knows it. "Who wants to go?"

It's not like I want to go through the portal, but I want to be closer to it. Just to see. Respect is demanded with such rare magic. A few girls inch toward it, but I glue myself to the chair. I don't want to be sucked into another time and stuck. Zelda is a stranger, and I don't trust her to bring me back. Excited murmurs pass between my sisters, but Daphne frowns at Zelda and the portal.

Daphne has lived through a lot of history, even if she cannot remember it all. Here, Zelda is peddling adventures without really knowing real life at the time. Their powers and rivalries are like those of witches of self-duplication and astral projection.

Writing in her notebook, Daphne asks, "How would you rate your skills in potions and spells?"

"I have two other places we could go in the past or the future," says Zelda, ignoring Daphne's question.

"That won't be necessary. We'll have our determination tomorrow," says Daphne, waving her hand dismissively.

Shelby tries to usher the three witches out of the ballroom—hopefully the house—but they linger, looking toward a stoney Johanna. After half a minute, Johanna nods. Her three friends leave without further fanfare.

Auditions only happen in one day, so we audition other witches through sunset: Amy, Laurel, Karen, and Silvia. My stomach, back, and head hurt. The outside beckons me, but I'm stuck inside, feeling magic without being able to use my own.

The excitement we once had is gone, even as Mercedes—another auditioning witch—crushes a rod of metal bar stock. Daphne says, "We'll have our decision by tomorrow." Her tone is dull too.

Shelby ushers Mercedes out of the ballroom. We wait for the next witch to enter because there has always been another in a long line of witches today, but Marina walks in. I crane my neck around her. Maybe Mercedes was the last witch to audition? It's finally over. I don't know if I want to sleep or go outside first. Maybe I'll sleep outside.

"I'm here to audition for the coven," Marina announces, and I freeze, halfway to standing.

Marina is one of the staff who steps in from time to time with witchy duties, but she has never been part of the coven. She's been here longer than me but has never been chosen to join.

Daphne doesn't write Marina's name down, staring ahead at the woman who cooks most of our meals. Susana starts with a new page before Paula touches her hand. Everyone else doesn't move.

Johanna snickers, and Astrid smirks. They are powerful witches looking down on someone who doesn't have a power. Marina, from what I've seen while I've been here, isn't a witch. Any spell she says falls flat. Any potion turns to mush.

"I've been practicing, Daphne," continues Marina. "I've been waiting for many years. I've seen your seminars. I've taken notes. I'm not the same woman who walked in not knowing anything about witchcraft. I'm not a crystal gazer."

"No." Daphne collects her notes.

Marina whines, "But it's my turn. Let me show you what I can do."

"No." Daphne walks around Marina.

Tears swell in Marina's eyes. She should get the chance to audition like every other witch, but I clamp my lips shut. No one else says anything anyway.

"Daphne, if I don't get a place in the coven, I'm going to leave," threatens Marina.

"Then leave," says Daphne from the doorway. "Girls, eat supper now. We're not done yet."

Marina lets out a frustrated scream and then stomps out of the ballroom. How long has she been preparing dinner for us? How many meals have I eaten that she has made for us? A moment later, a door slams somewhere in the house. I flinch.

Roxie breaks the silence in the ballroom: "I think we just lost her cook. Our last meal better be good." She goes to get dinner. Others follow.

Chapter 21

The history of a coven does not only come
from the witches or the magic but the
knowledge passed down.
—Unknown

As Marina leaves the house, Johanna says, "She'll be back," but I don't know.

With our plates full of food, we sit at the dining room table and speak over each other: "What about Kathleen?" "Or Kristina?" "Mercedes." Names pop around me. Each one is louder than the other. The chorus of names screech, no matter how much I duck my head.

My untouched food waits in front of me, but I can't bring myself to eat it after Marina left. The girls eat and get second and third portions. It will be our last feast. We'll either have to make our own dinners or starve. The arts of cooking and potion-making are different.

"Catrina," one of the girls begs. "She only has sixteen days left. She wants to die here. It's her home."

"Does no one else think it's weird that she knows when she's going to die?" asks Roxie.

"Not Esme," Johanna says, ignoring Roxie. "Not Leticia or Mercedes. Those aren't real powers. Let them be superheroes in capes and masks."

Looking at her watch, Daphne stands from the head of the dining room table. "Write your top five choices. Slip them under my door by ten. Maisie." She leaves, and I push up from my chair, beckoned.

The murmurs of "favorite" trail me, but I wasn't sitting at Daphne's right or left hand today. I don't know her internal thoughts.

The back of my head throbs. Tiredness wracks my bones. I should be in bed. But I jog after the fast-moving Daphne.

Once we're outside the front gates, Daphne orders, "We're off to Vermont."

I nibble on the inside of my cheek. "Is this about the psychic Kat mentioned?"

Kat will be at the top of my list, but I don't know if Daphne will take our choices into consideration. Much of today was a show. I don't blame Daphne for putting it on. The girls will feel lucky to be included and wanted, and many other witches wanted to get into the prized, historic coven.

"If you don't mind." Daphne hands over the address.

I study it and then open a portal. A main road cuts through a small town. Most of the businesses are already closed, their signs dark. Our shoes crunch snow as we walk down a side street. When a car passes us, I'm blinded by the headlights.

Bright yellow light blooms ahead, tinted pink around the edges. Hidden in the corners of the small town is a witchcraft shop. A painted eye on an even larger painted hand covers the front window. We push the front door open, and chimes harmonize above us. The unnatural smell of essential oils twists my stomach. The whole room feels smaller, jammed with things to sell and decorations.

Pulling back a curtain of beads, a woman steps out of the backroom. Her multicolored skirt swishes around her scuffed brown boots. The charms hanging around her neck clank together at the sudden stop.

"For a psychic, you're really bad at the future." A smile breaks Daphne's stoic face.

Lily Melrose laughs and then rushes into Daphne's open arms, and they hug. "You haven't aged a day," says the woman.

"I get that a lot." Daphne pulls back. "This is Maisie. One of the witches in the coven."

Lily Melrose gives me a hug too, and I'm frozen in her grasp, my skin itching. I don't know a lot of witches who used to be in the coven. Maybe this is how they all react?

"You're welcome here anytime," she says, and I—thankfully—don't have to say anything because she turns her attention back to Daphne. "I haven't seen you in a long time. What do I owe the pleasure?"

"You brought a firestarter to my door," Daphne says.

She snorts. "It was months ago when I had that vision."

"She showed up today," pushes Daphne.

Lily Melrose walks to a cabinet, unlocks the door, and pulls out a black notebook. She pages through the book before raising her eyebrows. "Yes, Kaitlynn. Paid with cash. I didn't know she was a firestarter, Daph. I saw her standing in that old house. I would recognize it anywhere. If it's at all helpful, there wasn't any fire. Maisie, you were there too."

A lump forms in the base of my throat. "Me?"

"You're only a glimpse. Unless there is someone else in the house with long curly brown hair and piercing blue eyes?" asks Lily Melrose.

My cheeks warm. "No."

"Hmm. It was a Tuesday in September," says Lily Melrose, reciting her notes. "Kaitlynn was scared, rambling on about being sent back to the doctors who didn't believe her."

"She didn't know she was a witch?" asks Daphne.

Lily Melrose shakes her head. "I had to have the *talk* with her. She thought she was an alien."

Daphne rolls her eyes. "Her parents?"

"I think she was a runaway." She slips her finger down the length of the page. "She stumbled across me. Wanted answers. I directed her to you. Haven't seen her since." She sets the notebook down. "We both know you're going to let her into the coven, so why'd you come all the way out here?"

I didn't know that. Kat needs a coven to help her with her magic. I don't want to bind Kat's magic or have another Amira running around.

Daphne shrugs. "She said your name was Lily Melrose."

The psychic laughs. "Erica doesn't have the same ring."

"Is your mortal husband into all of this?" Daphne motions to the front room of the shop.

She scoffs. "We divorced a few years back. His pretty thing is 'normal,' though young enough to be his kid. He has a beard now. Back when I met him, he used to think beards were for hooligans. Did you get my Christmas card?"

"Your kids are growing up so fast," Daphne says.

"They're almost adults." Erica-slash-Lily Melrose steps forward. "Tell me, Daph, what do you use to keep you looking so young? Virgin's blood? Goat milk? It's nothing over the counter."

Her power. I thin my lips together.

"It was good to catch up." Daphne moves toward the front door, and I shadow her.

I want to get out of here before I pass out from the stifling scents. I should've been back in bed hours ago.

"Wait!" Erica reaches for Daphne. "That's it? We could go out to supper. Or drinks. I haven't seen you or heard from you in, like, twenty years, and you're just going to go?"

"Yes," says Daphne simply, using the same tone she did with the girls auditioning today.

Tears swell in Erica's eyes. "Daph, I know you're still angry about me leaving—"

"I may still be in the house and in the coven, but I moved on, like you have. You fell in love with a mortal and left with him. It's you who's reminiscing about the old days with…." She upturns her nose at the shop.

I stiffen. That was a petty comment in the same placid tone she used with Marina.

"Hold on," Erica says, raising her voice an octave. "This is my heritage!"

Daphne snorts. "You could predict lottery numbers, future presidents, wars, births, deaths—everything. You had the whole future in your hands. Now, you live in a small town, selling crystals and essential oils, telling random walk-ins their futures, and jealous of your mortal husband's new wife. Where is the power you once dreamt of?"

With the store so packed, there is nowhere to hide. I step toward the front door for an easy escape.

"You're one to talk." Erica jabs a finger at Daphne. "You who used to live a glamorous life but no one has ever heard of you. Who ran and hid in the middle of the woods. Who takes in stray girls, fixes them up, teaches them everything—only for them to leave you." Her eyes land on me.

My magic and embarrassment brush my skin.

"You think this girl is any different." Erica snorts. "Is she your favorite, like you were May's favorite? She'll leave you too."

I don't want to leave, but I don't want to stay here. The back of my heels hit a table, and something jingles. I cringe. Slinking away isn't a possibility.

Daphne rolls back her shoulders. "You couldn't get over that I was May's favorite."

"I never understood why," says Erica. "You're a backstabber without any power. You only stay at the coven because you have nowhere else to go—no friends and no family."

I suck in a deep breath, but Daphne says, "You're right."

Erica blanches while Daphne turns on her heel and leaves. I scramble after my coven leader. The chimes above the door announce our exit into the silent night. The outside chill bites me but clears my head. My magic recedes.

Daphne walks so deliberately but so unconsciously. I scurry after her, arms wrapped around my chest to brace against the cold. Neither of us are dressed for the Vermont winter. My exhale turns white.

"We need to go back to the house," she demands. Tempered anger and raw emotion spill into the few words. I've never heard that before.

***

Several slips of paper have been pushed under Daphne's suite doors. She is already mixing herself a martini in her kitchenette, so I collect and bring them to her dining table before turning back. While the girls may be awake in the house, I don't want to be.

"Sit. We can discuss," she says.

I squeak, "You want me to…?"

"You're my favorite." Kicking off her stilettos, Daphne sits at the table.

I sink into the seat opposite her and screen the slips of paper. Some names appear several times. There is not a lot of interest in Kat, heartfelt interest in Catrina, a polarizing interest in Johanna's friends, and fearful interest in the identical twins. Random names get one vote. I don't remember all the girls or their powers or abilities, notes or not.

Daphne reads the pieces of paper and writes in her notebook. When another slips under the door, I grab it, and she adds it to the list. An old grandfather clock tolls ten, and Daphne tallies the final numbers.

"Last chance. Get your voice heard," she says.

"You've already made up your mind," I say, even though I want Kat.

She needs a home more than anyone, and she needs someone to teach her the craft. That could be Daphne. Our leader has done it for many girls before.

Daphne gazes at me from under her eyelashes. "I value your opinion."

"I don't have one in this case," I say in a small voice.

"Is it because of what Erica said?"

My cheeks heat. "I would prefer if you made the decision."

Audrey would've said "pushover," but I don't want to make big decisions. This is the fate of our coven. Dread pools in my gut because while we are ready to accept three witches, who says the death is over? We are still on the hunt for Beatrice and Mikayla's killer.

Rubbing my forehead, I ask, "What happened between you and Erica?"

Daphne sips her martini. "I don't remember all of it, but we were friends. I wasn't in the leadership position then. Erica was power hungry, not in a bad way, but she could've taken over the world if she put her mind to it. She was also boy crazy and stir crazy. She was here less than a year." She shrugs. "I think I said something about the boy she was dating."

"Her now ex-husband?" I murmur.

She nods. "It would've been better if we didn't live in the same house. We're an odd coven like that. Most covens converge every week for a home cooked meal and some magic. We're on top of each other here."

My old coven headed to Ruth's house on Monday nights, sometimes a Thursday too. There was an occasional Saturday night party or Sunday afternoon sporting event. The whole coven and their families had potlucks. When the magic happened, we kids and non-magical spouses gathered around to watch in awe. I lived for those days when I was a kid.

Another slip of paper flies under the doors, and I retrieve it for Daphne.

"Recycle it, Maisie. They missed the deadline," she says.

I crumple the paper without looking at the handwriting or names. My choices are also thrown away.

Chapter 22

We should be thankful for the covens and all
they have taught us. They have raised some of
the very best witches. At the same time,
covens can be very closed. We need to open
the covens to all witches and mortals and
magical creatures. This is how we create a
brighter future.
—Iain Skinner, *A New Order for Witches*

The soft padder of rain hitting the window wakes me.
A fog has settled around our house. I twist in my bed,
the blankets curled around my legs. Voices rumble—
the girls are already up—and without the energy to run,
I tiptoe downstairs and close the library doors. Then
freeze.

As much as I want to turn around and run, I have to
fix this. No one else will.

Books are scattered around the library, like a
tornado has blown through and left it in tatters. The
books on the shelves are tilted and out of order. The
tables, chairs, and couches have all been moved. The
girls have left wrappers on the floor as well as crumbs

in the carpet fibers. After I stifle a scream, I collect the books and start sorting. The whole of the library will have to be cleaned.

"There you are." Lizzy has let herself in using a secret passageway between the rooms. "We've been looking for you. I should've known you'd be in the library."

"Did you do this?" I ask, my voice hard.

She holds up her hands in peace, but anger washes through me. I put the books on the table before reaching for another book hidden half under a couch.

"I would never disrespect the library. Or you." Lizzy has used the library and not left it in a mess in the past. "I came to get you because the first new girl is showing up."

"Who?"

"The firestarter. Kat."

I straighten.

Kat belongs in the coven—*needs* this coven. I don't know if Daphne chose whoever she wanted in the coven or listened to what the others wanted. Do I want to know?

"How do the girls feel?" I put books away in their assigned spots on the shelves.

Lizzy grimaces. "Not all of them are happy, especially Johie. None of Johie's friends were chosen. She was really upset this morning, and Roxie didn't help. Just shoved it in Johie's face. And none of her friends were bad choices—they're strong witches." Her voice teeters. "Do I sound like a bad friend for saying I didn't vote for them to be in the coven?"

I slide more books into place on the shelves. "I didn't want them to join either."

She lets out a deep sigh. "It wasn't personal. Their powers were cool, but they're… so Council-like, you know. It's all about power and who has the most of it. I don't like Johanna when she gets like that. It comes out around those friends. I grew up in a coven, but Johie grew up with her parents *in* the Council. She speaks so highly of it, but I remember how repressive and power-driven it was. I'm not saying right now is any better or worse, but I feel like we have more freedom."

My hands have turned clammy, and I wipe them on my pants. "What happened to Johanna's parents?"

"Her dad died in the Second Witch War," says Lizzy, and I shiver. "Her mom is in hiding. Johie doesn't talk about them often. When she does, it's like a door opening to a new world. I didn't know all these things about the Council."

"Do these things make you like the Council more?" I try to keep my voice neutral.

Our witchy world used to be very different than what it is now. I think about the people who would still be alive if the Second Witch War didn't happen.

Lizzy shakes her head.

I explain, "My old coven was killed in the Second Witch War." More than just my coven, my parents too. Even if I wanted to return to my old life, I never could. I blink tears away.

"Maisie, I'm sorry." Lizzy reaches toward me to give me a hug, but I sidestep her. She drops her hand.

"I wish I could have more sympathy for Johanna, but…." I slip more books into place, hiding the anger toward the Council and the war as best I can.

"Are you angry at Daphne?" asks Lizzy.

I grab more books and walk across the library to the correct shelf. "Why would I be?"

"Two of us are dead." She flops into a chair beside the table littered with books. "This coven isn't what I expected. Our leaders are supposed to take responsibility for our actions and for us in general. I don't think Daphne has done that. She's not protecting us. Someone is killing us, and Daphne's not doing anything."

I want to defend Daphne, but the words are lost in the back of my throat. Looking down at the books, all I wanted when I came into the library was to read. I'm now fixing someone else's mess.

The door creaks open, and Catrina pops her head in. "Is this where the cool kids hang out?"

Both of us are startled, but Lizzy says, "I didn't know you were joining the coven."

She hugs Catrina while I hang back by the books, slipping a few into place. Hugging won't clean the library.

"I'm not." The elderly woman drags her walker into the room. "I have fifteen days left, and Daphne has been so kind to allow me to spend those days here. I'll be staying in one of the guest rooms."

More death. I grab a handful of books that feel like bricks in my hands.

"We're happy you're here," Lizzy says.

"Thank you. Kat is getting a tour," says Catrina. "Would you girls like to grab lunch?"

"Of course. Maisie?" prompts Lizzy.

"I need to fix the library." It's a good excuse not to join them or the others for lunch, but the mess in the library would haunt me.

With the squeak and shuffle of the walker and footsteps, they leave together. The door closes with a soft thud. The library is still in disarray. I need to have some order to life, or everything will fall apart.

Someone has been looking through the fairy tales in the library: three fairytale books put in the spell section. I pull them out and stack them. *Snow White and the Hunter* sits on top. I slip the fairytales back into place, Red Riding Hood included. I pause. Those aren't the only hunter fairy tales we have. We have a whole section on hunting, especially for those who need to track animals and know the outdoors. I have read all the books but didn't like them. I don't like people trampling through my woods.

The library door opens with a squeal, and I jump, dropping a fairy tale book.

Paula announces from the doorway, "This is the library. And Maisie."

Standing beside her, Kat pushes a lock of dark hair behind her ear. She hides now as much as she did yesterday, though it is only the three of us.

Paula asks, "Doing some light reading, Maisie?"

"Someone did." I grab the book from the floor.

She shrugs. "Not a lot of girls spend their time here, but Maisie and Lizzy do."

I stop myself before I ask Paula who has been looking up fairy tales. She was basically dressed like Cinderella at the last party we had. Instead, I say, "Everything is set up by genre then subject then by author's last name. If you can't find what you're looking for, then let me know. I'm sure it's around here somewhere, but some people don't put the books back correctly."

Paula rolls her eyes like I'm being silly, and I press the fairy tale book into my chest.

"I'm not much of a reader," Kat mumbles.

"What hobbies do you have? I'm sure we can find something to do." Paula turns Kat away.

The library doors close again. Their talking quickly fades as Paula tours Kat around the house. How much does Paula know about the house, though? The secret passageways and the history. Has she ever been to the basement? I doubt the girls even know it's there.

With a huff, I put books away and try to connect the dots to whatever the witch was working on, but I'm confused about the mixture of fairy tales and hunting practices. I'm nearly done when I smell smoke. Flashes of what the trees have shown me and what I've seen with my own eyes flood my head. Is another one of us dead?

Zigzagging through the secret passage, I poke my head around the white spiral staircase. Roxie and Susana dig through the cabinets in the kitchen. I thought the library was in disarray, but this is horrifying. Things are strewn across the kitchen table, and pots fill the sink. People have left the old food and dishes on the counters. The overflowing garbage is rancid, and I cover my nose with my palm.

"I mean," Roxie continues, "Marina could've left after the feast tonight."

Susana sighs. "You realize she didn't get into the coven again."

"She isn't powerful," Roxie argues.

"Do you think Daphne only picks powerful witches?"

"Ask the favorite." Spinning around, Roxie eyes me. "Are you going to help or gawk?"

Too late to slink back to the library, I slip down the final couple of steps.

Roxie places her hands on her hips. "Do you know who Daphne has chosen besides Kat?"

"No," I say.

Susana pulls pale pastries from one of the ovens. "Are they supposed to look like this?"

Roxie shrugs, but I say, "Put them in for a few more minutes. You want them golden brown around the edges."

Susana raises her eyebrows, and Roxie's mouth drops open. I squirm and then glance up the spiral staircase. Could I make it back to the library? The girls would know to look for me there. I would have a better chance to be alone in the basement.

"How did I not know that you know how to cook?" Roxie demands.

"Marina didn't like people in her kitchen," I say meekly.

Roxie shakes her head. "This shit is difficult. I should leave just because Daphne ordered me in the kitchen."

I look over the recipe laying out on the counter and frown. They could've started with something easier, but Marina probably had this planned already for the feast tonight. We could've ordered pizza.

"Do we have enough eggs?" I ask. "You're going to need three dozen for the people that we have."

Susana looks in the fridge. "We need to go to the store."

"With what money?" Roxie asks. "Do you have any? Does Daphne have any? How do we buy things? I'm not using my personal money."

"I'll ask Daphne. We'll need to make a list," I respond.

Roxie sighs. "Why couldn't Marina get all of this stuff yesterday?"

"Because she was making us food yesterday." Susana places the pastries back in the oven. "I can make this list, and we can go shopping."

Needing to be outside, I begin, "I can go by myself if you start with—"

"We're not allowed," says Susana. "Didn't Daphne tell you? She's made it a rule that we are to go nowhere by ourselves. As long as we're in the coven and you leave the house—not even the property—you can only go out with at least another witch."

I bite my bottom lip. I don't want to be stuck. "Where is Daphne?"

"Last time I saw her, she was waiting for the next girl," says Susana in a careful tone.

"I'll get the money. You make the list." I follow another staircase toward the front of the house.

Daphne is waiting by the set of double doors with Johanna and Astrid. A few girls peek out the windows for a car to pull in or for another witch to appear on the other side of the gate. I don't know who it will be, though someone has probably gotten a whiff. Any gossip spreads like wildfire in the house, except for Daphne's decree to not leave the house alone. Surprisingly, Roxie didn't mention that for the days I spent in bed. Nor did Daphne mention it last night.

Meeting Daphne at the doorway, I say, "Since Marina is gone, I found Susana and Roxie cooking. I'm helping, but we need more ingredients."

"Do you have a list?" she asks.

"Susana is making it now. We need cash."

After excusing herself from Astrid and Johanna, announcing Savvy will be here soon, Daphne leads me to her suite. The cash is locked away in a safe in her bedroom. "Please bring me the receipts and the extra money. Not that I think you'll steal it."

I take the cash and put it in my pocket.

"I was expecting a question," says Daphne to my back.

I slow, hiding my cringe in my hair. I should be angry that she has made a rule about not leaving by oneself—I'm one of the few witches who ventures out alone—and angrier that she didn't tell me.

"You're not going to ask how we have money?" continues Daphne.

I don't know. I'm not sure I want to know.

It's one of those questions I thought about when I first arrived at the house and haven't tried to think about since then. However, I remember mortals coming to our house in the middle of the night, and Daphne would sneak to their car outside the gates when she thought no one was looking. Sometimes, she takes a car parked in the garage, and we don't see or hear from her for hours.

I release the breath I've been holding and face her. "How?"

"Making a few potions here and there for people who can pay is not a bad thing." She shrugs as I stiffen. So she gives mortals magic. "Due to what needed to be done by protection, vacation and health, my blood is used."

My eyes widen. "Have you always used blood?"

"Throughout my history, yes. The house used to be a finishing school, so there was tuition," explains Daphne. "When times changed, the coven could no longer function in that capacity."

"Are you healing people? With your blood?" Judgement slides into my voice.

If we would've gotten Beatrice and Mikayla back to the house when they were only injured, would Daphne's blood have saved them? Could her blood save Catrina? It's perhaps no better question than Chelsea and Chloe's magic.

She thins her lips into a firm line. "Maisie, take one of the girls with you. It's for everyone's safety."

***

After shopping, I cook with Susana and Roxie. Dinner will be served promptly at six. While the food is staying warm in the oven, I follow the smell of perfume to our bedroom floor. The girls flitter like territorial hummingbirds. I duck into my bedroom and start changing. Mikayla's bed has someone's backpack on it.

"We have a new roommate. Kat," Roxie spits, striding in. The bedroom door slams behind her.

I flinch. "It'll be fine."

"Savvy would've been cool. Johanna's jealous how much attention Savvy's getting." She laughs.

After pulling on a fresh sweatshirt, I put my hair into a new bun. I can't hide any longer, so we go down to the dining room together. Kat and Catrina speak with Ubah and Paula. Savvy is talking with Kami. I scan for the third witch, but the faces blur together. Their high-pitched voices and laughter reverberate against the walls. I back out of the dining room, but Roxie grabs my arm and hauls me to the table.

"It's Julia, the disintegrator." Roxie beams. "Not one of Johanna's friends got in. Ha."

At the other end of the table, Julia speaks with Susana. They have their heads close together like they are conspiring. I haven't seen Susana speak like that since Beatrice. At least the coven is welcoming my new sisters, even if I'm not involved.

"Can I sit here?" Kat pulls at her decaying sweatshirt.

I offer a forced smile. "Yeah."

She sinks into the seat beside me but says nothing. I don't say anything either. I wanted Kat in the coven and now she'll be my roommate, yet I can't muster the small talk expected from me. Thankfully, other girls talk to Kat. I try to block out their boisterous voices that rattle around in my skull. My head aches again. I don't know if the pain will ever go away.

Astrid and Catrina sit on either side while Daphne stands at the head of the table, wearing a crisp new outfit. Her nails are painted red. She clacks them against her wine glass to get everyone's attention. My new sisters watch her with open curiosity.

"We're hungry for food and excited to get to know our new sisters, so I'll make this quick: welcome to our coven," says Daphne. "The house is yours to explore. Your sisters are your new family. We learn and support each other here. I don't make a lot of rules, but we are in a different time. No one is allowed to leave the house without another witch by their side. I believe in freedom, but precautions must be taken."

Daphne sits at the end of her speech, but I wait for something more. A promise or to end on a happy note? Instead, I'm feeling empty. My shoulders slump as the girls dig into the food that has taken most of my day to make.

Roxie struggles to keep Savvy's attention from across the table because Susana has a very interesting story. Julia speaks with Ubah. Catrina talks to Daphne, catching up like the old friends they are. That leaves Kat and me. She really should've chosen someone else to sit by.

Clearing my throat, I say, "So you're from Vermont."

"Yeah," she says.

I scrape at the food on my plate.

"Where are you from?" asks Kat.

"Minnesota," I say.

"I've never been."

"Most people haven't."

Silence stretches between us. Other girls laugh. This is a happy moment, and we should celebrate.

"You and Roxie are my roommates," says Kat. "Am I sleeping in a dead girl's bed?"

My fingers curl into my palms.

Two girls who have slept in that bed have died, though only I and Daphne know about Audrey. And Astrid. It's a wonder the house isn't haunted by the girls who have died.

"Sorry," Kat says quickly. "That sounded mean. But I've replaced her, haven't I? That's weird." She hides behind her hair.

I chew warm, buttered carrots. I have a whole helping on my plate along with a bread roll and green beans. I helped make the pot roast, seasoning it so that it may be palatable, but I don't eat it. Neither does Kat.

After swallowing, I ask, "Do you like the house so far?"

"It's a lot. Not in a bad way." Her cheeks turn red. "It's nice."

"There's a lot to explore. Sometimes, I still find new things."

I've traveled these halls many times, and if I'm paying close enough attention, I find something from an old sister. The girls before me—and even during my time—have left their mark on this coven. The house will stand long after I'm gone.

"How long have you been here?" asks Kat.

"Almost three years," I answer.

She widens her eyes. "You don't look, um...."

"I was fifteen when I came here." And I'm short. Everyone thinks I'm younger than I actually am. Then again, I'm younger than everyone in the house.

"Have you been here the longest?" asks Kat.

I shake my head. "Daphne has been here longer." Astrid and Catrina have been here before, but those are technicalities.

Kat flicks her gaze to Daphne for a brief second. "She doesn't look much older than us."

My jaw dangles open as I scramble for an answer. What should I say? What *can* I say? I try not to look at Daphne as if her whole secret will be given away. But saying "it's complicated" may only pique more interest.

"Hey, Maisie." Roxie grabs my arm and pulls me close to her, saving me from my current conversation. "You two in?"

All the girls wear the same mysterious smirks, their eyes alight. The new girls have already blended into our new family. It's a tradition. The same thing happened when I joined, and we do it with every new witch. A scavenger hunt helps get the witch acquainted to their surroundings, even if they stampede through my woods.

Daphne meets my gaze too but then turns back to Catrina and Astrid. Neither of them are coming.

"Yes," I say.

Bottom lip trembling, Kat whispers, "What are we doing?"

"It'll be okay. You don't have to participate if you don't want to, but you should come," I say.

We finish dinner and dessert in hurried chews and large gulps. Magic crackles as we itch in our seats. Tree branches whack against the windows, like they are calling me out to play. The girls share looks as if silently passing messages to hurry up. Most of the food on my plate is left untouched.

Daphne wipes her mouth and sets down her napkin on the table. The extra moment makes the girls lean forward in their chairs until Daphne announces, "You're excused."

Our chairs scrape against the dining floor, and we escape quickly. More magic fills the house, fueled by the excitement. The girls are practically running to grab their shoes and jackets. Their laughter bounces off the grand staircase. With all the sadness that we've had, it should feel good to hear my sisters laugh, but I cringe.

Johanna walks out of the dining room behind us. "How are you doing, Kat?"

Kat nervously picks at her sweatshirt. "Good."

"Are you ready for some friendly competition?" Johanna's smile shows too much teeth.

Kat looks at me, and I answer, "Yes." Nothing about this is friendly, especially with Johanna.

I pull Kat out of the house through the kitchen. Nearly jumping over each other, my sisters vie to stand close to the hedge. Their magic is infectious. My magic is stronger outside, and tree branches shake sloppy snow off. Some of the girls jump out of the way. The snow splatters on the ground.

Roxie pulls a silver flask out of her pocket, takes a drink, and hands it off. Girls throw their heads back, giggling. The flask is extended to Kat and me, but we shake our heads. It circles the group again.

Bundled in a thick winter jacket, a scarf, and mittens, Johanna walks to the front of our group. "For the old people, you know how this game works. For the new people, welcome to the coven and welcome to a great night. Pair up."

Kat grips me, and I try not to shirk her off. She doesn't know me yet, but I will push her away. I only allowed Roxie to touch me earlier to save me from a painful conversation.

Unsurprisingly, Ubah and Paula pair up. Susana and Julia choose each other. Lizzy and Roxie latch to Savvy. Only one can have her, so Lizzy becomes besties with Kami for the night. Kami has been alone since Mikayla died and Rochelle left. If anyone in our coven leaves next, I think it may be Kami.

Johanna's eyes rest on Lizzy a bit too long, but then she pastes on a smile. It's not like Johanna can participate when she's the one who set the scavenger hunt up.

"I have hidden thirteen magical idols in the woods, all with a spell cast on them. At midnight, meet at the beach and bring the idols. This is a night of fun and winning," she says, and a few girls whoop their excitement. "Maisie, do you mind? I don't want anyone getting hurt with the gate."

I place my hand against the unnaturally green leaves, and the hedge opens, revealing the woods backed to the beach. My now awakened magic clings to two idols. I roll it back in before it gets out of hand. I don't care about winning, but these are my woods—*my* element—and I've played this scavenger hunt many times before.

Johanna says, "One… two… three!"

The girls rush through the open hedge. Johanna waves her hand quickly, motioning for Kat and me to go. Even if I don't mind a good run, running won't help us win.

Chapter 23

Modern witches, though they may not know it
and certain magical powers have evolved
since, are still one with nature. We feel the
closest to nature. We are in tune with nature.
Or we should be.
–Iain Skinner, *A History of Witches and Mortals*

The shining moon and stars light our path. Giggles bubble through the trees, alerting us where the other girls are. My magic tries to catch them.

"What exactly are we doing in this scavenger hunt?" whispers Kat.

"We can use spells, potions, our magic to find the idols. We just have to be at the beach by midnight, or it doesn't matter how many idols we have." I eye the trees around us but trust they will tell me if anyone but my sisters are in the woods.

The hair on the back of my neck stands as we pass through where Mikayla was dragged. I walk a little faster, and Kat jogs to keep up, tripping over a tree root. Keeping Kat steady, I frown at the root and warn my magic off. Just because we're on high alert doesn't mean it should be rude.

After walking a moment in silence, Kat asks, "What do the idols look like?"

"They can be anything, but they'll be infused with magic," I explain. "You'll be able to feel it."

"Will I?"

I hesitate. "Probably the more powerful idols."

An excited scream rolls through the woods, so I assume one of the idols has already been found. My magic points me in the direction of an idol, but I want Kat to learn. And I want to see what magic she can do. Like I wondered with Amira, I have a hard time believing Kat doesn't know anything about witchcraft.

"What do you feel, Kat?" I ask.

She stutters, "Um…."

"Close your eyes. Let your magic do the work."

"I don't know how."

It should feel natural to her. Magic is like breathing. It's all second nature.

Then a twig snaps, and Kat shrieks. Heat rises between us, and I jump back. Thankfully, no fire or smoke. Our sisters trample through the woods. They will veer off the paths and dig through the dirt, and I'll have to fix the woods later.

Kat needs to distance herself from the noise. She is a firestarter, so anything could set her off.

I clear my throat. "Let's try to find an idol. Close your eyes and take a deep breath."

Doing as I say, she winds her fingers through her hole-filled sweatshirt. "What now?"

"Let your body adjust to your magic and surroundings."

After I open my magic, the idols appear like dots on a radar. My magic points to Kat beside me. Her magic dims.

I remind her, "Don't fight it." *But don't light my woods on fire.*

She is still trying to fight her magic but then swallows. "I feel something."

Smoke tickles my nose, and I leave her side. Hidden under the brush—kind of close to an idol—a small fire has started. I squish it under my heavy-soled shoe. Flashes of Mikayla's burning fill my mind, and I urge the breeze to blow the smoke and my thoughts away.

"What's that smell?" Kat peeks out from her eyelashes.

"The idol is over here," I say quickly. "Can you still feel it?"

After a moment, she shakes her head. "I can't find it."

She isn't trying hard enough, so I push, "Try to feel my magic."

The plants and the ground are grabbing what they can, hungry for more. The nature is used to my magic, but I haven't been purposefully using it. However, the woods tonight are feasting; the girls are conjuring and using spells to find these idols.

I place my hand to the ground, and the magical pull strengthens. A few seconds later, I reach under a low-hanging branch and pull out an idol.

Kat peers over my shoulder. "Is that it?"

Johanna made a bra an idol. It's been done before, back when Roxie was welcomed into the coven. I lick the bra to taste the ingredients in the potion, and Kat gives me a weird look.

"It's magic infused," I explain. "If you put on the bra, you'll have bigger boobs however long the potion lasts."

I try to hand it to her, but she hesitates. The magic won't bite her nor work unless she puts it on. I stuff the bra in my jacket pocket.

We move through the woods, and the thrumming continues. The curling vines turn limp again. The branches knock against one another. The roots slither under the dirt.

"Can you find the next idol?" I ask.

"You obviously can," she says with a huff. "Why don't you just find them all and win?"

Another fire blooms, and it is larger than her previously tiny flames. She falls back. I rush over and kick dark dirt over the fire.

"I'm sorry." Tears swell in Kat's eyes. "I didn't mean to—"

"It's okay," I interrupt. "Your natural power is coming out because it's so strong. We'll need to practice magic another way." *A way that isn't so destructive.*

Starting tomorrow, she is getting a copy of the basic potion and spell book. I'll teach her the craft like I was taught when I was a child. It's what she missed anyway.

"Keep your magic open," I say, and she nods hesitantly.

Placing a hand on the dirt, I sense the magic around me: spells and conjuring from the girls, my own magic connected with nature, and then—my magic locates other magic. Following the thrumming, I find another idol barely hidden under a tree, like Johanna had gotten lazy.

"What is it?" asks Kat.

"A graduation cap. Infused with knowledge magic," I say. "Put it on."

She fits it on her head and plays with the tassel like a cat. She smiles. We walk toward the beach.

Every so often, I put a hand to the dirt and feel for idols. The girls are finding them faster now, but there are several still in the woods. I follow the magic and grab the idol from under the brush.

"Glasses. Perfect vision," I declare, but Kat isn't as impressed as before.

She looks around and jumps at every sound, including a hooting owl.

I haven't heard the other girls in a while. It's possible they've given up and are now on the beach. Any idol left over will have weakened magic—making it harder to find—and will be better hidden.

I take a hard right into the trees, following the increasing thrum, and find the prize. With a sigh, I take a hold of the energy drink. Others probably moved past this can thinking it was garbage. And none of them thought to clean up after another.

"For long-lasting energy," I announce, turning back to where I had come from.

Kat doesn't stand there.

The trees bristle and cast long shadows across the woods. Bushes are huddled close together. They act as a wall, and I can't see where I've come from.

A scream rips through the air.

My heart jumps to the base of my throat, but I stop myself from calling out. What if the killer is back?

Putting my hand on a nearby tree, I order, "Show me."

The trees talk to each other, branches and roots connecting. They bring back darkened images. I try to pick through the flashes, but the trees don't know which one of the girls is screaming. Or Kat. Everything is hidden under the cover of night.

Another scream echoes through the trees, and I run, following Kat's shoeprints. The tracks start to drag, smeared in the mud. I skid around a large oak tree.

Kat lays in the dirt, hands covering her face.

I take a step toward her. "Kat?"

Fire shoots up. I stumble back.

The little hairs on my arms are singed, but pain aches my body from the seared trees. The flames die as quickly as they started. I gasp for clean air.

She peeks through her fingers. "Maisie?"

I swallow my pain and ask, "What happened?"

She had been right behind me. How did she get so far away? I almost lost another sister. Why did we ever do this stupid scavenger hunt? Johanna barely participated before and now she was pushing for it. I'm surprised Daphne let us go.

"I want to get out of here." Kat eyes the shadows like something might pop out at any second.

I make a portal, the vines slithering out from the ground, and Kat quivers.

"It's not going to hurt you. We'll travel faster this way," I say.

When I open the portal, the beach waits on the other side. She jumps through.

Chapter 24

If you're a powerful witch, then show-the-
hell-off. No one else is going to.
—Guinevere Ravensblood

On the cold beach, the shivering Kat pulls her ratty sweatshirt around her. It won't warm her, though she could start a fire with kindling. The other girls will want a fire when they finally show up.

I check my watch. We're nearing midnight.

I set the idols beside her. "I'll be right back."

"Don't leave me!" Fear contorts her face.

I don't know what happened in the woods, and she refuses to talk about it. The only other people in the woods are the girls, so my trees tell me. I don't know what to say to her. I wish there was another girl on the beach to comfort her. Susana and Paula are the best in these situations.

"You'll be able to see me the whole time," I say and walk toward the tree line.

She shifts behind me, but the sand doesn't move like she follows me.

I stay on the beach where she can see me. I already have four idols: bra, graduation cap, glasses, and an energy drink. Another idol pokes out from the sand. Because we've made it to the beach first, it waits for us. I cringe, willing for anyone else to take it.

"What is it?" Kat calls.

"Um… something that wasn't meant to be found by us." I prefer not to even hold the sex toy.

"It definitely wasn't." Johanna laughs, coming out of the tree line. "I was thinking Kami or Roxie. Maybe Paula? I think she's got a streak in her." She winks but then grimaces when she walks back toward Kat. "Best orgasm of your life right there," says Johanna.

Kat turns red, flashing like the buoy in the distance.

I toss it into the pile of idols. Someone else can claim these idols as their own. I'll never use them.

"How much time is left until midnight?" Kat asks, crossing her arms over her chest.

Johanna pulls out her cell phone. "A minute."

Roxie and Savvy crash from the trees, carrying their idols. The burning scent of alcohol rolls off them. Roxie hasn't smiled like that since Beatrice. Lizzy and Kami are next, an unsuspecting pair. I have never seen them talking in the house, and working together in the scavenger hunt seems more like a business transaction. The two continue to discuss now, pointing at the woods and then at the idols in their hands. Is there an idol I've missed?

"Ten, nine," Johanna counts down.

A portal appears in front of us, and Susana and Julia spill out. Sand plumes up from where they have fallen.

"Where's Ubah and Paula?" Susana asks, brushing sand out of her hair.

The girls shrug, but I look in the woods. We looked to have stayed in our pairs. We followed Daphne's rule, but that doesn't mean we were safe.

Something happened to Kat in the woods, though it could've been the woods itself. People see things in there. My magic probably tripped more people than Kat. Johanna was limping, but she doesn't often go into the woods. She most likely mis-stepped.

A bloodcurdling scream resonates out of the tree line.

My magic raises for an attack. Air whooshes from my lungs, replaced by fear. But I won't let any one of my sisters be hurt again.

Julia and Susana are still lying in the sand, hiccups of muffled laughter coming from them. When I step back, I knock into the cowering Kat. This isn't funny.

A scream echoes behind us, and everyone whirls around. A figure, draped in black, bleeds dark paint on the tan sand. The features are contorted, half monster and half human.

I demand, "Really?"

"It's a demon!" Roxie smiles. "See—not the killer!"

"Is that better?" Savvy also smiles.

Kat grips the back of my jacket. "Is it really a demon?"

"No," I say, but Kat stays hidden behind me.

Julia pulls her head from the sand and frowns at me. "Maisie, don't ruin the fun."

The "demon" swoops across the sand toward us as another scream echoes from the woods. The girls scatter, laughing. Johanna crosses her arms over her chest, glaring at their backs.

Paula stands at the edge of the tree line, giggling, and Ubah, who I assume is dressed up as the demon, chases the girls.

Ubah wraps her arms around Kami, and Kami shrieks and then chuckles. Susana and Julia climb to their feet, and the girls gather around. They clap each other on the backs.

"That was good, Ubah," Roxie congratulates, out of breath. "You really got me there."

The rest murmur in agreement, red in their faces. I wait in the back for their *fun* to be over.

"It was all Julia's idea," Ubah says.

"But it's your magic," Julia says, "and damn—it was so good!"

Johanna's jaw juts out. "And how many idols did you find?"

Julia brushes her hair back. "We worked together, and we have one."

With a smile, Susana produces a rusted key from her pocket.

"Four of you worked together and you only found one idol?" Johanna spits.

"I'm not a scavenger hunt kinda girl." Julia shrugs. "Do most people like scavenger hunts? They seem childish."

"It's a tradition. Not that I expect you to understand." Johanna rolls her eyes. "Lizzy, how many idols?"

"We have four," she answers, holding two. Kami holds the others.

"Damn." Roxie drops her three idols to the ground, and Savvy huffs. White breath curls around her lips.

"Maisie?" prompts Johanna.

I reveal our five idols behind Kat and me, and Roxie mutters, "Cheater." My cheeks heat. I do have the upper hand in my woods, but the girls weren't playing to win.

Johanna declares, "We have a champion." The girls halfheartedly clap for us, and Johanna asks, "Willing to barter?"

These are low-power magic-infused idols. We trade out the prizes. I end up with the key, and Kat gets a magical pen. Anyone else can take the rest of the idols. Kat hasn't touched the bra.

"Is that it?" asks Johanna.

Roxie yawns. "These all have been done before. Not very exciting."

Johanna lurches toward Roxie, but Lizzy jumps in, "It's nostalgic. I really liked it. It really reminded me of better times. Go ahead, Johie. What did you have to say?"

Flipping her hair over her shoulder, Johanna says, "Welcome to the ocean, you've met the woods. Now, it's time to get to know your sisters." The little speech is well rehearsed.

Johanna strips until she's only in her underwear and bra. A rash has overtaken her left leg; the woods got her good. She yelps as she crashes into the ocean. Following Johanna anywhere, Lizzy runs into the waves. Roxie and Kami are quick to strip too. In their drunken state, Paula and Susana go into the ocean half naked.

Curling into my jacket, I linger on the sand but itch to be in the water. Kat waits by the burning bonfire the girls have made, and I can't leave her alone. I don't like how exposed we are. Anyone in town could see us down the beach.

With her cloak blowing in the wind, Ubah offers, "You can stay with me on shore, Kat, if you want."

Curling her arms over her chest, she nods.

Ubah sits by Kat on the log and then waves me off. "Show off your skills, Maisie."

Leaving my clothes in a bundle by the bonfire, I sprint across the sand and dive. The icy water steals my breath away, sliding across my already chilled skin. Like I'm encased in ice, I seep down. Some girls are already heading back to shore, but I only take a breath before plunging down again where it is warm and comfortable, surrounded in the abyss of darkness. I am weightless.

When I surface again, I am away from shore. There is another round of screams as girls run in and out of the ocean, drunk. They are my left, the red-blinking buoy my right. I could swim out to it like I've done a hundred times before, but the girls are on the beach. I should be with my sisters.

My body aches as soon as I leave the ocean. I drag my feet over the sand to rejoin the girls. When I'm dry enough, I slip my clothes back on but leave Kat to converse with Savvy.

Susana and Paula are only getting drunker from the flasks passed around, singing a pop song while dancing around the bonfire. Ubah starts to sing too. The three of them grab one another and dance around in a circle, kicking up sand. I flinch away, the back of my head aching yet again. The bright glow of the bonfire worsens the pain behind my eyes.

Julia tries to hand me the flask, and waving it off, I ask, "In the woods, did you play any pranks on anyone? Attack anyone?"

"What?" Julia snorts. "No. I tried the scavenger hunt, but really, I hate them. Always have. So we came up with the plan. And the woods are already creepy." She drinks from the flask. "Sorry. The woods are your thing, right?"

"Yeah," I say, ignoring how the fire eats at the wood and the brush of wind through the branches. "Kat was also freaked out by the woods. She thought she saw something in them."

"I heard screaming. I thought someone got to our prank before we did." She laughs. Her hot, alcoholic-tinged breath hits my face, and I scowl. "Geez, Maisie, lighten up. It was a joke. I'm sure whatever Kat saw was also a joke."

I'm not so sure.

Chapter 25

A young witch, whether in age or skill, needs
the most help before they hurt themselves or
others.

–Unknown

In the early morning, frost covers the destruction of
the backyard. Trees are starting to rot. The bodies of
Audrey, Beatrice, and Mikayla lay six feet under, and
the dirt is yet packed down. Thankfully. My sisters
would've had questions about why a third body was
buried. With the three bodies, they're a quarter of the
way to a coven. Their coven could rival this living one.

I touch a tree, half of the roots on display. The tree
is injured, and I cannot explain how sorry I am.
Though, I have said the exact words a hundred times. I
need to give the trees my life to let them live.

"Whenever you're ready," I say.

My awakened magic pumps my heartbeat into
nature. The tree stands. The roots snake under the
grass and into the nutrients of the soil. The branches
shake, trunk twisting. Green leaves start to grow from
buds. Everything is slow. Sweat slicks my skin.

Moving to the next tree, I repeat the process again. My magic comes easily, but I blink the dancing dots in my vision and curl my fingernails into the bark to keep myself steady.

When I can breathe again, I whisper, "I'm sorry."

I turn back to the house, and something shining from above catches my eye. Daphne, wrapped in a pink silk bathrobe, holds a steaming mug. I was never alone in the backyard, breaking her rules.

On her floor, my stomach churns at the smell of fresh coffee. I push the suite doors open and follow the scent out to the balcony. Nature cannot mask the acidity.

"You've been working hard." Daphne's tone and face are vastly different, so I can't tell if she's disappointed or proud. "In the backyard and yesterday and the day before. I know you put the library back together. You were Kat's partner. I believe that wouldn't be the easiest task."

Little did she know. "I'm going to start beginner spells and potions today," I say.

"You should ask Catrina for help. She's been around for a while."

"I'll think about it."

Being around Catrina makes me... uncomfortable. It's not her. I've just been around enough death already. I don't want to get attached to another coven sister for them only to die.

"Here, kitty kitty," calls one of my sisters below. Kami and Savvy run after a black cat in the backyard, stomping over my hard work.

"I need to go." I flee Daphne's suite.

Going down the stairs is easier than going up. My legs feel like jelly, and my head is swimming. I didn't sleep well last night. Maybe it was all the excitement. Maybe it was the girls' prank. It was probably what happened in my woods.

The girls in the kitchen have abandoned their food. Julia pokes her head out the back door. She is wrapped in a sweatshirt to keep herself warm from the oncoming winter, but I don't think it's even cold outside.

I grab a banana from the fridge and sit beside Kat. Dark circles hang under her eyes. Apparently, she didn't sleep well last night either.

"Maisie, when was the last time a cat has been at the house?" asks Lizzy.

"Not while I've been here," I say. "We would have to ask Daphne."

"Or Catrina," offers Lizzy.

"Are cats not allowed?" squeaks Kat, holding her spoon so tight her knuckles turn white.

"I don't think there's a rule, but I don't know if anyone's allergic," says Lizzy. "We might just have to get allergy medicine."

"Back in my younger days, everyone had an animal here," says Catrina, pushing her walker into the kitchen. She looks relaxed for a woman who will be dead in less than a month.

Julia scrunches her nose. "Did it smell like a zoo?"

Catrina laughs, but it comes out more as a wheeze. "They're our familiars. They help guide a young witch. They give comfort and protection. It's curious that none of you have any."

The black cat runs past the open door, Kami and Savvy on its heels. For some unknown reason, the cat hasn't run off the coven grounds. Catrina goes to the door to watch the mayhem.

Julia drops into the empty seat beside me. "Maisie, everyone says you're Daphne's favorite."

From where I sit on the bench, I raise to the balls of my feet like I'll need to make a run for it.

"Daphne seems like a hard person to please, but she's got a good style. Johanna tries her hardest but never gets anywhere close, does she? You don't try, do you? That's your secret." Julia takes a bite of her soupy cereal. "You're smart and powerful. You're quiet and small. I'm going to guess no one sees you coming."

I watch her evenly. What does she want from me? And why is she paying so much attention to me?

Kat flicks her gaze between the two of us before looking past my head at the open door. The cat runs past again. Kami and Savvy are a blur.

"There are two types of witches," continues Julia. "The common witch that hides their abilities, thus hiding themselves. Such trust issues but usually family orientated. Those are the people they've always had. Then you have the outward witch, who wants everyone to know and starts a conversation with it. It makes them feel powerful. They're usually the ambitious ones, but they probably won't get too far because they're more likely to not have self-preservation or self-control."

Why is she doing this? I'm not sure why she's talking to me.

Grabbing my banana, I stand. "We're starting training today, Kat. I'll meet you upstairs. Excuse us, Julia."

I make my way from the kitchen at a normal pace but not fast enough not to hear Julia say, "See you around, favorite."

***

I grab a copy of the beginner spell and potion book from the library. While I wait for Kat in the ballroom, I page through it. Old memories swirl from when my parents taught me this magic. I practiced it with my sister in my old coven. Marney had mastered these potions and spells at seven years old.

Kat slips into the ballroom, and I glance up, asking, "Did they catch the cat?"

"No," she says, her voice wavering.

"Good." I motion for her to come over and open the spell book to the first page after the table of contents.

It's a small telekinesis and wind spell, only meant to move something light. I have a feather waiting on the table in front of us. A beginner witch needs to start small before going big, though it could be debated that starting fires is rather big. This spell is about control.

"We'll start with some basic spells today and go from there," I explain. "Read the first spell."

Kat brushes back her hair and opens her mouth, a rush of air coming out.

"Don't!" I wave my hands in front of her face.

She snaps her mouth shut. Her eyes are wide enough to take up her whole face. I cringe. Perhaps I should bring Catrina in on the training when I've already forgotten a beginner's rule.

"Read the spell in your mind before giving it words," I say, keeping my voice calm. My heart is anything but, tense with the potential of a fire. "The words will amplify your power."

Kat reads over the spell. "Now what?"

"Do you feel that you know the spell well?"

She reads it again and then nods hesitantly.

I didn't think to bring a pitcher of water into the ballroom and regret it now, but maybe she'll surprise me. However, I take a step away from her. "Go ahead."

Kat reads aloud, "'Light as a feather, soft as a dove, take it in the wind, lift with love.'"

It's not an amazing spell. An amazing spell needs to be specific and usually have a history behind it. I've yet to see the coven's grimoire that houses the powerful spells and potions. Some witches have books of shadows, but those are more personal. The spells are specific to them. I don't have one but hope Daphne does.

With the spell and Kat's magic, the dove feather shifts less than an inch off the table, like caught in a fan's current. Then it lays flat again. Kat huffs.

"It takes time. And practice. A lot of practice," I say, trying to make her feel better. "We're using a dove's feather, which makes the spell work. Let's say we used a hawk feather or pigeon feather, then the spell would need to change. Rhyming is key in English spells."

"What if it's not in English?" asks Kat.

I can barely do non-English spells—Marney can, though—so Kat will need a different teacher for that.

"Don't worry about it for now," I say. "A lot of things, if not all, can be accomplished in English. Using a spell in another language gives the witch an advantage because the opponent probably won't speak it."

"Why would you need an advantage?" she asks.

I thin my lips together. After what she's seen with us and of her own power, she's terrified. This will only make it worse. I won't bring up the first or second Witch War. Nor do I bring up the Council or the man who destroyed the Council or the most powerful witch who ever lived. Witches have a bloody history. We can't blame mortals for all of it.

"Witches are territorial about magic. Most magical creatures are territorial too, though lack magical powers. However, witches remember our burned, drowned, and stoned ancestors. We are careful of who to trust," I say, and her eyes widen. I rush to add, "Let's try the spell again. Speak confidently. It'll help if you look at the feather."

Kat repeats the spell clearly—if not *very* loudly—and keeps her eyes focused on the dove feather. It starts to levitate and then bursts into flames. She screams, and I run to the window and open it. The breeze knocks the feather down, and I stomp the flames out. Black ash spills on the floor.

"I brought more feathers." I grab another dove feather out of my stack of supplies and brace myself for repetition. "Let's try again."

Pursing her lips, she says the spell loudly, albeit hesitantly. It's another feather I extinguish. I pull out another dove feather and make a mental note to tell Daphne that we'll need more. Kat wraps her arms around herself, shrinking back, but heat ticks up in the ballroom. Even when she's not focused on the feather, her magic wants to burn.

"Powers are tied to our emotions." I take a few deep breaths, and she mimics me. "Back in the olden days, you'd be praised as a fire god. The witch in you is in there. You need to harness it."

Gulping, she turns to the new feather. It lights on fire too.

She slumps her shoulders. "I'm not getting any better."

"You are," I assure weakly. "The last fire was smaller."

She gives me an exasperated look. "I can't control my magic."

"There are some witches that argue we are not supposed to control it." My magic brushes my skin, and I shove it back. "I think differently. Control doesn't come naturally. Or easily. Your power is like an extra being. Either you have to work with it or have it control you. Control is something people have to practice, especially because you haven't had training. Usually, parents would teach you, but..." I cringe.

"There were eight of us in the foster house. I don't know who my mom is," says Kat, voice hard.

In my old coven, we had an adopted witch. The man who adopted her was a friend of a friend of a friend of her mother. Letting a witch grow up with mortals without support is dangerous. Both Kat and Amira are firestarters. Amira claimed her family

232

members aren't witches. Powers can be inherited from both parents, but power dissipates with mortal generations mixed in. Where is the magic coming from?

"I lit a fire in the house," Kat admits.

I stiffen. Amira and the guys from her school. Did we let a killer into our coven?

"It was an accident," adds Kat quickly. "No one was hurt. But the doctors put me in a group home with really fucked up people, so I ran away."

"And ended up at Lily Melrose's doorsteps," I finish.

"She told me to come here. She said you'd help."

I'm trying. But where are my other sisters? Or Daphne. I wanted Kat in the coven, but I'm not trained for this. We've never had a witch like her in our coven before, the kind of witch that needs this extra training. Any witch who has joined our coven has either mastered their powers or knew spells and potions.

We do the spell again. Kat lights another feather on fire, and I get rid of it. Only a few embers glow on the next feather, so she's gaining control. The next feather is burned around the edges but no flames or embers. The next feather is darkened but not burned. The next feather lifts into the air and isn't currently on fire.

A smile crosses her face. "I'm doing it!"

"Keep control," I demand, not giving into the potential hope. However, my heart thunders.

Control of the spell has taken most of the day, but witches learn to control their magic over years.

"Hold it," I tell her.

The feather trembles but stays put. Kat holds it just under the ceiling for ten seconds as I count silently in my head. Sweat glistens her skin, starting to bead under her chin.

"Release," I call out.

Smiling, Kat lets her magic go and nosedives against the table. The feather flutters from the ceiling like fresh snow. It's almost as pure, much like her giggles.

"You worked hard today. I recommend chocolate and a nap. Stay hydrated," I say, collecting the excess feathers.

Kat falters. "That's it?"

"For today. You need a break."

"But I just managed to do it."

"I know." Like I know she'll feel like she's on a high before she crashes from the adrenaline. With a sigh, I say, "Read the whole beginner's book by our next lesson. I'll find some other books for you to read to get started."

Kat grabs her reading assignment like she'll start straight away. I hope she doesn't try any of the spells aloud, or I'll be cleaning up more than burned feathers.

Chapter 26

Covens are not built on blood but common
understanding and the love of magic.
–Unknown

I walk into the library, and Savvy and Catrina sit at a
table. I've just cleaned the library and scan for another
mess. Thankfully, none. After giving my polite
acknowledgements, I slip by them to the witchcraft
bookcases for more materials for Kat. Perhaps a couple
history books or books about other creatures? She'll
need to know what witchcraft means in the larger
context of our world.

"How's it going with Kat?" Catrina smiles, showing
off her bright white dentures. They match her stark
white hair.

"She's doing some reading before our next lesson,"
I say, skimming the titles.

"Speaking of reading, do you want one?" Catrina
shuffles a deck of tarot cards.

I paste a smile on my face. "No, thank you. I've
done my own."

Marney did it often when we were kids. While the cards are meant to offer guidance and enlightenment, I usually just get anxiety.

"Have you ever had one by a psychic?" Her eyes twinkle. "It's a popular power, I know, but mine's strong. That's how I know when I'm going to die and why I returned here. My heart will finally give out. It's been a long time coming, and barring the killer gets me, I've got fourteen days left. Bury me in the back with the others please."

A lump forms at the base of my throat. "How much can you see?"

"I can't see the killer, if that's what you're wondering." Catrina lets out a small wheeze. "Daphne already asked, and she knows my powers well. Do you want a reading?"

"I don't want to know my future," I say earnestly.

"How about your past?" Savvy asks, hands empty.

Savvy is good with potions and spells, besides being a very nice person, so I didn't question why people wanted her in the coven. Or that Daphne chose her.

"You told Johanna you don't have a power," I say, confused.

"Johanna seems like a mean girl who I don't want to spend time with. I expect Ms. Duvay," she says in a thick southern drawl, "already knows my worth."

"I know my past, thank you." I'm scared to be standing between the two of them. All they need is a mind reader.

"Let me know if you change your mind. I'm great at parties," says Savvy.

"Thanks." I turn to the books before whirling around and bursting, "How does it work?"

"I read objects." Savvy grins. "Find one, and I'll give you a free show."

There are a lot of old things in the library, let alone the house, but I want an object that looks like it has an interesting history. Random trinkets throughout the years of the coven have been discarded in the library at one time or another. The library had been popular once in the coven's history based on the many things hidden away and forgotten about.

I grab old spectacles off a history bookshelf. It's a scuffed pair with metal sides and circle frames. I found them my first year in the house when I was doing a deep clean of the poorly kept library.

Savvy blows dust off the frames. "Don't interrupt me." She sits deathly still.

A shudder runs down my spine. Catrina smirks, excitement glinting her eyes. Then, Savvy's knuckles turn white on the metal. As much as I want to not interrupt Savvy while she works her magic—it could be dangerous to do so—I don't want her hurt either for what's supposed to be fun.

"The 1930s, I think. Looks like the Depression. Lack of technology, the radio is really big. I don't recognize any of these women—hold on, they're having a party." Savvy runs her thumbs over the lenses. "The glasses are men's. And he's with a lady friend. Going off in private, are we? How scandalous. We're in the library now.

"They stopped kissing. Yelling at each other." Her eyes shift quickly under the lids. "Boy doesn't want to

237

commit. Girl is not cool with that. Ouch!" Savvy touches her face. "She slapped the glasses right off. They went flying. Lost in the books."

That explains how the glasses got sandwiched behind a bookcase.

"She's a witch and she is not letting him go that easily. What are you doing, girl? Oh." Savvy chuckles and opens her eyes. "She cursed him. Turned him into a frog. No wonder he no longer needed his glasses."

My stomach twists. "Do you know who she was?"

I don't mess with curses, but some witches use them too easily, especially on those unsuspecting, innocent, or weakened.

Savvy looks at Catrina, who frowns and says, "I was here fifty-seven years ago, girls. Fifty-seven years ago wasn't in the 1930s."

"I don't know for a fact that it was the 1930s. I can only guess," says Savvy.

I walk over to one of the cabinets that line the north wall, but they don't go as high as the bookshelves. Then again, I packed them better than the shelves. The coven receives the local newspaper every Sunday, after it stopped being daily. I shuffle through the filing cabinet until I find the 1930s. A witch turned someone into a toad, like the evil witch in a fairy tale. I doubt the punishment ended after the night based on how Savvy described the scene. If a person went missing, then it would be in the local newspaper.

The library door opens, and Susana peeks in. "Supper is ready." She helps Catrina up from the chair, and they leave.

Savvy pauses in the doorway. "Are you really gonna look for him? It was forever ago."

"I'm going to figure this out," I say, taking out the first stack of newspapers.

"I don't think messin' with what other witches did is a good thing."

"I don't think turning mortals into animals is a good thing either. And like you said, it was *forever* ago." I walk back to the table she and Catrina had been sitting at.

Savvy purses her lips. "I'll bring somethin' up for you after supper."

"Thanks." I probably won't eat it.

The library door closes behind Savvy as I shuffle through the newspapers, skimming headlines for the mention of missing people. That stack mentions no man missing, but several women had gone missing. Not related to the coven or my current search. I hope to know that they were found safe, but like the current chase I am after, I doubt I'll find an answer.

Would it be so wrong to have a concrete answer? My world right now is ebbing waves, me on a raft. So far, two of us have drowned, and I've nearly died. The storm isn't over.

I pick through another stack of newspapers but don't find a mention of a missing man. Savvy didn't know if it was the 1930s, so I go back further. These newspapers are thicker, showing off the hometown life filled with farms and the small town and then radiance of the night life, including one or two bootlegger busts. It was all the buzz in the town with the reverend and bankers and a homemaker giving quotes about the "recent crime spree." This was also before Daphne's time. I move to the 1910s. A good summarization is that there were a lot of arguments against women voting.

I run my ink-stained fingers through my hair, ready to pull it out. The text is blurry, spilt on and the yellowed pages ripped. We have a large historical collection of newspapers, probably rivaling the town's library or town hall. Before I came to the coven and organized all these dates, the newspapers had been bleached in sunlight and insects had started to make nests.

I try to imagine the library in the 30s. Savvy said a big radio, so I should look at that timeline before radios were portable. Pulling my hair into a bun, I reach into the cabinet of 1940s newspapers. Unfortunately, all the news is about the war, and many local boys are dead. Some issues are just filled with obituaries of dead sons at war and little of anything happening at home, minus a couple of articles on the war effort. I pull the newspapers out.

Knocking on the library door, Lizzy walks in with a full plate. "I brought you food. Savvy got distracted because one of the girls challenged her to a reading. Did you know she could read objects?"

From where I sit on the floor by the filing cabinets, I say, "She showed me today."

"Daphne must've known, right? I'm surprised neither of them said anything. Like shouldn't we know because we're their sisters?" She sets the plate of food on the table. "Maisie, what are you doing?"

I shift through the newspapers. "Do you know how long curses last?"

"I would have to do more research, but I think it depends on the type of curse and how powerful the witch is. If they pre-planned it or in the moment."

"In the moment. It couldn't last long, right?" *I hope.*

"Not unless the witch is well versed in curses?" suggests Lizzy. "Maybe if the witch has a natural tendency toward them, then they would last longer?"

"Like, if they were her power, you mean? I don't know a power like that."

"Neither do I. But there are always new powers to learn. I didn't know a power like Savvy's existed. Why are you asking about curses? Do you plan on using one?"

"No." I won't do that to anyone. "Savvy saw a witch curse a man into a frog."

"While cursing someone into a frog is frowned upon, may I ask why it matters?" Lizzy sits on a chair next to the table.

"A theory," I say.

"What is it?"

I tug my bun. "Maybe it's connected. Maybe she turned him into a frog. And now he's no longer a frog and now killing us to get revenge."

Lizzy blinks at me.

I know this all sounds... *odd.* Not crazy because this is magic. Power does what it wants. But I can't wait around for another one of us to die or for Daphne to find answers.

"I know it's a longshot," I say, curling my knees to my chest.

"But it's something." She huffs. "It's better than nothing, which is what we had ten seconds ago about who could be killing us."

The stack of newspapers lay at my feet. "Maybe there is a report of him when he went missing?"

"Give me a moment before I help." She leaves me in the library, and I continue to skim.

Reading newspapers doesn't move as fast as I want it to go as I pick through the headlines. I need to get out of the Second World War, but these newspapers are packed with names. Everything in the town moved to smaller headlines. I blink to return my vision to normal, the back of my head throbbing.

A few minutes later, Lizzy returns to the library, Julia and Susana behind her. "We need more eyes," she says.

We settle into silence on comfy chairs and on the floor, scanning stacks of newspapers. I thought the Great Depression era was bad, but the early 1940s isn't much better. Besides the death notices of the fallen soldiers, there are many from women dying in childbirth and children dying of hunger. The notices burn into my mind, and I try to shake out the fresh pain.

I find random and very gossipy articles about the coven and the house. Some say we're haunted; others say we're a cult; some say we're prostitutes. There is only one mention of witches, and it's in the Halloween-edition of the newspaper. That rumor is squashed by the time the next newspaper was printed.

I find the end of World War II. Wedding and birth announcements fill almost every page. So many birth announcements. The mansion is mentioned again in another gossip-like column. We are known as a finishing school, but one of the unwed girls gave birth. The article of gossip is filled with many quotes from the townspeople. I begin to understand why some of my sisters are prone to using curses.

"Here's something," Susana says, pointing at a headline.

I perk up. "Is someone missing?"

"No," says Susana.

I can't get distracted, so I flip to the next page of my stack. The man would be reported missing, or a man would've been rambling about being a frog.

"It's about the coven," continues Susana. "There's a picture."

"Let me see!" Julia snatches the newspaper from Susana's hands.

I flinch at how the paper crumples. They are holding a piece of history.

Julia widens her eyes. "Is that Daphne?"

I stare at the newspaper laying on my lap. The words have morphed like the whole newspaper has been soaked. If I don't move, maybe the girls won't ask, and I won't have to lie.

"It's not her," says Susana, and I release the breath I've been holding. "Look at the names under the picture. Three from right on the top row: Doxsie Dick."

Julia snorts. "What a name."

"That woman must be Daphne's relative or her mom," says Susana.

"Or grandmother," Lizzy interjects.

I peek out of the corner of my eye. They are getting further away from the truth. Good.

"They look so close, don't they?" asks Susana, shoving her face closer to the picture. Julia's nose practically touches the page.

Lizzy leans in too. "The photograph is bad. All the people look the same."

Susana laughs. "That could be just the era."

This is my chance, so I say, "You should listen to Lizzy. Her hobby is photography."

Susana lowers the newspaper. "I didn't know that. Can I see sometime?"

Lizzy flushes pink. "Yeah. It's my passion, but I don't share much because it's an artform, you know. It's all about lighting and mood."

I read the headlines in the current newspaper on my lap as the girls talk about Lizzy's photography. Any more talk about the specific photo that is definitely Daphne from many years ago will give me a migraine. Though, it could all be the loud voices, fluorescent lights, and the musky smell of the old paper.

I finish one newspaper and move to the next. The stacks are being reformed, and I'm going to have to reorganize them all before putting them away in the filing cabinets.

April 1953, a missing person is reported: Gary Michael Williams. He lived on Rogers Street. He was last seen at a party at the house, courting one of the local girls. The headmistress—May—of the finishing school spoke with the police, and apparently, witnesses saw him go into the woods. Heart pounding, I know that's not true.

"Focus April 1953 and later." I dive into the next newspapers.

"Did you find something?" asks Lizzy.

I hand the newspaper off to her. The girls take turns reading the article and staring at the picture of the man-turned-frog. I'll need to check with Savvy if this is the person she saw in her vision of the past.

"He's cute," Julia remarks. "If it's him Beatrice and Mikayla went with, I can understand why."

"I don't know," Susana says. "Too big of a nose, eyes too close together, his forehead and chin are most of his face."

I bend my face further to the newspaper like I could climb inside. Maybe they won't talk about my features then.

"Lizzy, what do you think? Would you sit on his face?" Julia asks.

They're all giggling, like this is funny. This man had part of his life stolen away from him because a witch decided to hex him for a reason that I don't think is justified.

"Beatrice went on many dates, and Mikayla was drunk." I raise my head, and their laughter dies. "I'm saying that it may or may not be him, but both of our sisters had different types of attractiveness. We need to find out whether Gary Michael Williams ever returned."

"Why?" Julia asks.

"He still could be a frog?" I offer. "Then we would be looking for a new suspect."

"He's a suspect now?" Susana asks. "Of the killings? Why?"

Because I have nothing else to go on. It's been a month, and we have no answers to our sisters' deaths. What if something in the coven's past is coming back to haunt us?

"Are you sure this isn't a dead end?" Julia asks. "I'm all for helping, but I need to know if it's worth it. The girls are partying downstairs."

"I can't guarantee it," I say.

"Then it can wait. I'll be here tomorrow, but there's only one tonight."

Julia stands up, and Susana gives me a sad smile. They leave the library. I glare at the doors as they close. I need answers. Can't this be one?

Chapter 27

A witch has magic. Power comes from a
collective.
–Iain Skinner, *A New Order for Witches*

In the morning, I stumble into the kitchen that's already filled with girls eating breakfast. Why are they up so early? I check the clock. No, it's me who is up late. Without being able to go for my normal run in the morning, I've lost my schedule.

"Maisie!" Roxie yells excitedly.

I flinch. My body still aches after the night I spent in the library.

"You're coming to town with us," says Roxie.

I don't have the energy to argue, let alone think. My bones are jelly. I want food, which they stand in the way of.

Later, we walk through a portal and into the outskirts of the seaside town. The girls start to make their way to a cute shop that's open for mostly tourists, but I only have one place to go.

"Roxie," I say, pulling on her jacket. "I'm going off by myself."

"Rebel," she says, surprised. "Where to?"

"The library."

She rolls her eyes. "Have fun."

I wait until the girls go into one of the shops before I jog up Main Street and the library steps. Stripping off my jacket, I walk inside. The musky scent of books and the old building burn my nostrils. Humidifiers puff to keep the books in good condition, but years of use have left them worn.

The singular librarian looks up from her computer, her glasses hanging around her neck. "Do you need help with anything?"

"Yes, ma'am." I stand at her desk. "Gary Michael Williams went missing in April 1953. The library houses the city records, police records, and extra newspapers, building permits, the like?"

She draws her eyebrows together, wearing a quizzical look. "Yes."

"I would like to take a look at them, if I may." I keep my knowledgeable but innocent pretext. Being small and unassuming has its advantages. "I have looked through the newspapers all the way through 1959, but I haven't found anything else on his disappearance."

While this might be an odd request, she takes me over to a line of computers against a wall. Most of the computers offer internet access, but one of the desktops is marked for internal records use. I sit down on the lumpy chair and roll myself under the table, kicking the hanging wires.

"Thankfully, we went digital a few years back, or you'd have a lot of work ahead of you. All the town's written records are kept here. By typing in a name, you should find records," she instructs. "You'll need to move the cursor to zoom in and out, some of them are picture slides. It won't be easy, though. Sometimes, the computer is wrong too."

"Thank you, ma'am," I say, keeping my voice two octaves higher than usual.

With a kind smile, she hobbles back to her desk in the middle of the library. I'm in full view of her, but I doubt she can see anything I type. I'm only here to research Gary Michael Williams anyway, which I've told her, but I stop myself from typing in the address of the coven house. I'm scared of what I would find.

The computer loads, and I pull up the internal search engine for the town records. I've already tried an internet search for Gary Michael Williams, and there was nothing. In the town's search engine, I type out his name. The buffering symbol keeps circling. My heart hammers in my chest.

When the results pop up, there are a lot: Gary, Michael, and Williams, and the results don't relate to 1953. I run my fingers through my hair and then change the search settings. It's another minute before 100 results populate.

With a huff, I click on one link. A blurry picture pops up. Gary Michael Williams is in the middle row, ninth from the left in his football jersey and helmet— or what was considered a helmet at the time. According to the description, the picture is part of the 1952 high school yearbook. I back out and click on the next link. It turns out Gary Michael Williams also played basketball. This research is going to take a while.

"How does it go?" The librarian wheels a creaking book cart past my computer.

"There are a lot of results," I summarize.

"Well, Williams is a popular name around these parts," she says. "It's one of the founding families. Is this for a class project?"

"No." I don't know how to explain.

Her hands flex on the cart, but I thin my lips together and say nothing more.

"Call me over if I can help you." She gives me a nice smile and then pushes the cart away.

I search through the history of Gary Michael Williams: a homecoming picture, academic lists, an essay about losing his older brother in war. Finally, I find the article from the newspaper that announces Gary Michael Williams' disappearance. In the archive, a scanned-in handwritten note from the police sheriff states the police had looked through the woods and on the beach. I click on more results, and there are remembrances of Gary on the one-year anniversary of him going missing and again on the five-year. After seven years, he was officially declared dead, and an empty coffin was buried in the local cemetery. That appears to be the end of any records of Gary Michael Williams.

"Here." The librarian slides a book across the table for me. "It's by a local author about the town's founding families."

"Thank you, ma'am." I page through the book, though I'm not sure if Gary Michael Williams can be involved in the murder of my sisters. Questions outnumber the answers.

"Is there anything else you'll need today?" she asks.

"A library card."

***

As I walk back on Main Street, a black cat crosses my path, and I still. Black cats supposedly mean bad luck, but I don't believe that superstition. However, this particular black cat has been lurking around the house. It blinks its big yellow eyes at me and then saunters into an alleyway. It's obviously not interested in me, so I let it go.

Paula, Ubah, and Kat are walking down the street, the same direction the cat came from. The other girls must be nearby.

"Maisie, there you are! We've been looking for you everywhere," Paula calls.

I join the girls with a tightlipped smile. The book on the founding families is tucked under my jacket.

"Look at you breaking the rules." Ubah smiles. "I'll try not to mention it to Daphne."

Word will get back to her one way or another. I should be the one to tell her.

"What have you been up to?" I ask.

"Went shopping," Paula explains, "got lunch. We split off a while ago from the others."

With Paula and Ubah complaining about the cold and mist—this is the Pacific Northwest, after all—we transport back to the house. I force myself up the front steps at a regular pace and past the landing to the library. Eventually, I reach Daphne's suite and run my fingers across the library book. Maybe I should investigate more before I bring this up to her. Really, I only have theories. I could be going in the completely wrong direction.

I probably am wrong.

"Come in, Maisie." Daphne's melodic voice rumbles under the door before I knock. How long have I been standing here, hyping myself up to ask something I know nothing about?

Here goes nothing. I shut the suite doors behind me and ask, "Do you remember Gary Michael Williams?"

Daphne looks over her shoulder at me from where she sits on the couch. Paper is laid out like she's working on something, and I avert my gaze. She'll tell me if she wants me to know. I consider how much I want to know anyway. It's gotten me in trouble in the past.

"He went missing in April of 1953," I continue. "He was turned into a frog in the house, cursed by one of the witches."

"Hold on." Setting aside her work, she hops up from the couch.

With her bedroom doors wide open, she picks a painting off the wall and reveals a safe hidden behind. I haven't seen it there before, but I've been more interested in the paintings and pictures of her. She turns the clicking dial. With a squeak, the safe door opens. She takes out a notebook from the back and closes the safe, but other things—like a large leather-bound book—are hidden inside. That must be the coven's grimoire.

Paging through the notebook, Daphne says, "When I first showed up, my leader—May—said journaling would be good for me. But I never got into it. I don't even have a book of shadows." She turns another page in her notebook. "Here's 1953. I only write a sentence or two in each entry, and that's wherever I felt like it. After World War II, everything seemed rather boring." She reads the notebook. "Lisa cast the curse. I don't say what kind."

I've never heard of Lisa before. "Did it have something to do with her power?"

"Just well-practiced. She could fly. Absolutely loved to take a broom out and wreak havoc on the locals." Daphne flips through the pages before closing the notebook. "There's not another sentence until 1963. You said Gary Michael Williams?"

I inch toward her. "Does that name ring a bell?"

"Williams is one of the founding families. Why the sudden interest?"

"Savvy's power showed Lisa cursing him." I wait for Daphne to say I misunderstood. "I'm grasping at straws, but my new theory is Gary Michael Williams is the one killing us. I went to the library today, and there's no record of him ever being found. He has a death certificate without a body."

Daphne walks over to her desk. "Lisa made a lot of enemies in her life, but she was a good friend. She cursed mortals so others wouldn't have to get their hands dirty." She pulls a stack of letters out from the bottom drawer. "I know Lisa is dead, but I can't tell you when."

I still. This happened in 1953, of course it's possible she's dead. "Why does it matter when she died?"

"You don't know a lot about curses, good. They give witches' a bad reputation." She sits at a table and then flips through the letters. "Curses are flexible and complicated for the person who is cursed. For a witch, they can be hard to master. The desired outcome is rarely death."

"It's about revenge and control," I say, remembering my old coven's teachings. My parents told me to never use them, but I don't recall Daphne mentioning curses before.

"And humiliation," Daphne adds. "Witches control the timetable, make it move from person to person, give pain, so on. However, when a witch dies, the curse dies along with them. Magic works itself out." She flips from one letter to the next, obviously looking for something specific. "You said Savvy saw him turned into a frog, he would be stuck in his human age until the curse ends. Will you help me go through the letters?"

Sitting at the table, I take a stack of paper. "Is there anything you don't want me to read?"

Daphne laughs. "Maisie, you already know more about me than others. Take the opportunity to learn more."

I skim the letters, looking for keywords and Lisa's name. I prefer learning about Daphne's life through her voice. A lot of the letters are nostalgic, remembering times when they were in the coven with Daphne. Since they know Daphne is now the leader, they ask about how it goes and when the next party is. I don't know if Daphne ever sent responses.

"Here it is," she announces, and I put down a letter. "Lisa died over a year and a half ago. She was murdered."

Chapter 28

The history of witches is bloody, but it
doesn't need to be. We can let our petty
angers go. We do not need to fight amongst
ourselves or with mortals.
— Iain Skinner, *A History of Witches and Mortals*

I don't know how this is all connected. It has to be... *or* we have nothing to go on. And a killer who is still hunting us, no matter how much we ignore it. We've done a very good job at ignoring it. Some of us better than others.

Walking over to the bookshelves in the library, I start pulling books. The curse section is rather full, and I don't particularly remember the contents. After setting them down on our shared table, I grab more.

Lizzy pages through the founding families' book. "I know we're not doing a seance, but it would be really helpful if we could ask Lisa."

"Wasn't there a powerful witch recently that could communicate with the dead?" I ask.

Lizzy grimaces. "I wouldn't recommend it. Johanna doesn't have positive things to say about her. Something about the Council or whatever."

I skim pages as Susana pokes her head into the library, yawning. "Have you seen Julia?" She wears her pajamas, though it's nearly noon.

Lizzy looks up from the book. "Ask Johanna. I saw them together yesterday."

"I'll go find her." Susana leaves the library, and the door closes.

I collect all the books I need before settling into a long day of research. After I spoke with Daphne yesterday and the public library search, I have more questions. Any chance of answers relies on the books in front of us. Research is the best thing to do when a brewing storm thrashes wind and rain against the windows. Finally, I sit down and open a book. I have a fresh notepad and basic timeline to start.

Catrina pokes her head into the library. "Maisie, Daphne wants to see you outside."

I clench my hand around my pencil. So much for research on our only lead.

"I got this. Go to her, *favorite*." Lizzy rolls her eyes.

***

Daphne waits by the front doors, wearing a royal blue dress and a long tan overcoat. She checks her watch. "She's a busy woman. This was the only opening she had."

"Who?" I ask, tying my shoes.

"Lisa's daughter, Melissa," says Daphne without further explanation.

Chicago's blistering wind lashes between buildings. We enter a skyscraper and take an elevator up. The foyer is open and wide with floor-to-ceiling windows. People in matching gray suits walk past, and one guy cuts me a look. I shrink in my leggings, sweatshirt, and muddy tennis shoes.

When it's our turn, the receptionist shows us to Melissa's office. Her floor is dark hardwood to match her desk and bookshelves. I linger back by the door. The office is sterile, and my shoes are dirty.

Daphne pastes a smile on her face. "It's great to see you again."

Waving off pleasantries, Melissa pulls a large journal from a desk drawer. "I don't have a lot of time before my next meeting. You mentioned my mother and a curse of hers. Mom was good at keeping her book of shadows up to date. Do you know his name?"

Daphne glances at me, so I peep, "Gary Michael Williams."

Melissa flips through the book of shadows. Ink fills every page.

Over by the windows, Daphne says, "You have a nice place here."

The clouds are hanging low today, and it's darkening by the minute. We can't see anything outside.

"I got it for a real deal after I cursed the last leasers," says Melissa in a dismissive tone. "Use what your mom gives you. And she was really good at curses."

"Can you fly like her?" Daphne asks.

"Wouldn't you like to know." She snorts. "Here he is. Was turned into a frog. How fashionable for the time. Less than thirty years ago, though, the curse ended. Mom put a timetable on it."

"What?" I blink at her. "When Gary returned to mortal form, he became his own age again, right? He would age normally. That would make Gary Michael Williams older."

Melissa gives me a pointed look, like I've just personally called her *old*. "Were you looking for someone young?"

Yes. Maybe a few years older than me. Beatrice and Mikayla wouldn't go off with a man older than thirty. Gary Michael Williams would be in his fifties or sixties now.

The puzzle I was building is now in pieces. I was wrong. I don't know where to start. If I can restart. Two of my sisters are dead, and we're nowhere near finding their killer.

My magic brushes my skin, but everything green in this office is plastic. Melissa watches me, and I curl my fingers into my palms, holding back my magic. And my tears.

"Thank you for helping us." Daphne softens her face. "I'm sorry for your loss."

"Me too. She was a damn good witch, but some mortal hit her with his car and drove off," says Melissa with pure malice.

"Was the murderer ever found?" I question.

"No," says Melissa. "I tried spells and cursed so many people. No one ever found him. We only know that he has some janky truck with a bed on it."

I stop. When the trees showed me Mikayla's death, she was loaded into an older truck with a bed on it. It was night, and I wasn't able to make out the man, the kind of truck, or the license plate. I had thought it was a dead end.

Melissa puts her hands on her hips. "My next meeting should be here any minute. You can watch. Whatever he says, he's cursed. He owes me money and hasn't paid me back."

"Thank you for the offer, but we must be off. Maisie," orders Daphne.

I numbly follow her out of the office. How much time have I wasted in search of Gary Michael Williams?

***

Ubah and Paula wait by the front door of the house, arms around each other. Paula's face is wet. A scream builds in my throat, but I lock my teeth together, unable to breathe.

"What happened?" demands Daphne, walking through the gate that surrounds the house. I grab the gate before it slams in my face.

"Julia's missing," says Ubah, her face ashen. "They think—*we* think too—the killer got her."

"Has her body been found? Has there been a fire?" My magic doesn't feel it from the trees. I don't smell smoke.

Ubah shakes her head.

The girls have gathered in the library because it has the most comfortable places to sit in the house. They take up every couch we have. Susana sobs loudly, a tissue curled in her hand, and Catrina has her arm around her shoulders. Kami sits on Susana's other side, staring off into the distance. Ubah and Paula take their seats as if they have been assigned. Roxie—wearing Beatrice's quilt—and Savvy sit furthest away. Johanna and Lizzy are close by, drawn faces mirroring one another. Kat is by herself.

I should sit beside her and tell her everything will be okay. Can I lie? I don't move from Daphne's side as if she'll offer protection.

Daphne says, "I realize that some of you have tried to contact Julia or track her but have been unsuccessful. It is possible Julia left us by her own account, but I will not stop until I know what happened to her—"

"And Beatrice and Mikayla," interrupts Roxie. She wipes her tears away with Beatrice's quilt.

"I will contact Julia's family and the police," continues Daphne like she didn't hear Roxie. "We will work to locate her. For tonight, let us get a good night's rest. We do not know what tomorrow will bring." She leaves the library.

That's it.

After everything that has recently happened, with the dead bodies piling up, it's all I should expect.

The girls begin to filter out, but I'm stuck where I stand, as if my feet are glued to the carpet. If I start moving, I'm scared I'll leave the house and become the killer's next victim. None of us should've left the house, Daphne or me today. We left and look what happened. I shouldn't have gone off by myself yesterday. How stupid can I be?

Susana returns to the library, arms filled with candles and a Ouija board. "Maisie, will you help me? You're one of the most powerful witches in the coven." Her bottom lip trembles.

Throat tight, I nod. How do I say no to her? This won't end well because seances and connecting with the dead rarely do. I don't know how the Council witch did it.

In the ballroom, Susana puts the supplies on the floor as Lizzy and I place the candles in a pentagram and light the wicks. The smoke starts to rise toward the ceiling, and I crack a window. Lizzy tells me I need it open more for Julia's ghost, but I don't want her ghost to arrive. We shouldn't be messing with any sort of death magic. Yet I open the window more.

Susana brings others into the ballroom for the solemn affair. We step up to a point on the pentagram. The magic builds. I try to fight it, but my magic has gotten a taste. It's hungry for more. Savvy, Roxie, Kat, Lizzy, and me on our five points are held together by magic. We are a concoction of magic, ranging from high to mid-range. Each of us has a distinguishable power.

"Julia, hear us now, cross from the divide. Follow our voices, follow our magic." Susana picks up a knife from the floor and pricks her finger. Red blood bubbles at the surface. "We call to thee to let your soul be free. We want the truth to sleuth. You are our sister from past to future."

The ballroom is still in the night.

Wind blows the curtains in. The candles flicker. A high-pitched whistle breaks through the pentagram.

"Please," Susana begs, "show yourself. We can help you move on."

"Can you?" Julia's voice echoes.

A shiver runs down my spine. I want to back away but can't break the circle. Julia could escape our magic and be stuck in the house. Enough ghosts already live here.

"Yes, we can," Susana presses. "You are our sister. We love—"

"I was barely here!" Julia's ghost appears, foggy around the edges. Her face and her hair are stark to who she was, even if her body has morphed into a transparent projection.

Susana draws back. "Julia, tell us what happened to you. Who did this to you?"

"I came to the coven knowing what happened here, trusting my sisters to help me grow as a witch. You take, and what you can't have, you steal! Why haven't you realized that, Susana? You thought I could just replace Beatrice, be your new friend. I was stupid to believe I could." Julia turns to Roxie, and my roommate stiffens. "Then there's you. The dead talk to each other."

Roxie grips the quilt so tight that her knuckles protrude from her skin.

"Julia," I say, "we want to—"

She whirls around. "Audrey has got a lot to say about you. We have a lot in common."

I peek from the corner of my eye, like Audrey will appear. If she and Julia are talking, then Audrey hasn't moved on. I want to say I'm sorry, but my lips are thinned together.

The ballroom doors burst open, and one word of Latin breaks Julia's ghostly hold. The power slashes across my body. My magic breaks. I stumble but don't break the circle. Neither do my sisters. But with just one word, Julia is gone.

Daphne stands in the doorway. Fury burns in her gaze. I think she might yell at us. Maybe cry after another of one of us is dead. But she storms away.

Roxie wears a smug smile. "I guess you're no longer the favorite."

My magic flares, and she steps back.

Chapter 29

According to the police, Penelope
Ravensblood was accidentally killed by offseason hunters. The police have decided not
to name any participants at this time to
protect confidentiality and so no one else
would be harmed. Chief Mauer said, "The last
thing we want to do is start a witch hunt."
Penelope Ravensblood is survived by her
daughter, Guinevere Ravensblood, who was
remanded into her godfather's custody.
—*Lake Superior Gazette*

Morning light cracks the sky. Walking to the nearest
tree in the backyard, I curl my hand into the bark.
Already, my magic flows.

"Please, show me the night Julia died," I beg.

The branches bob in the breeze. The message runs
from root to root. The trees know Julia from the
scavenger hunt and strain to find anything else about
her recently.

"Is Julia within your land?" I ask.

The trees smack against each other in the growing wind. The past victims have been burned at the stake, even if it's taken some time, but the trees show me nothing of Julia.

"Thank you," I murmur and then move around the side of the house.

Cold nips at my exposed skin, but I'm not ready to go back inside and be with others. I'm breaking the rules by being outside alone, but I've broken them before. I just need peace before meeting the storm of others or the tension in the house with Daphne. Last night, it seeped through the cracks and wound around my neck as I slept until I woke up, gasping. I halt at the hedge.

Two police cars with flashing lights sit on the street. A third police car, a plain-looking one, sits in the middle of the driveway. Its driver, the detective I've seen before, speaks with Daphne.

"Go inside, Maisie," orders Daphne like I'm a child.

The detective watches me, and I quicken my speed inside.

In the library, I hunker down with the book about the founding families. I'm only pulled out of the book when I hear gravel crunch under tires. Daphne pulls away from the house in her sleek black sports car, Astrid in the front seat. I should be with Daphne. I'm Daphne's favorite.

Girls are awake as I walk into the kitchen. I can't eat but need to keep moving. Maybe just a quick sprint around the house. Maybe I'll go further than that. No one is here to tell me otherwise. Daphne didn't say anything to me after this morning. She was heading toward town, and the local police were at the house. Whatever happened didn't occur in the woods.

Kami reads a letter at the kitchen table, Ubah and Paula looking over her shoulder. She announces, "Rochelle's pregnant, starting off her journey to have many witch babies." I think back to the party we had a while ago.

"She's the first one to have a baby." Paula tears up. "I hope she sends pictures."

Ubah nudges Paula. "You'll probably be next."

"I hope so, but I have to find a nice man first," says Paula. "And get married. Just a few steps between."

Giving a tightlipped smile, I excuse myself from the kitchen but trip on Kat on the back step. I catch myself before falling face-first into mud.

Doodling with the magic-infused pen, Kat cringes. "Sorry."

I wave her off. "I should've been looking where I was going."

We're not supposed to be alone, but Kat is within five feet of the other girls. Not to mention, she could incinerate anyone who tried to hurt her. So could Julia—*disintegrate*, that is.

"Did you catch the cat?" I ask. The likeness between Kat's drawing and the actual cat lurking around the house is uncanny.

"No." She covers her drawing with her sweatshirt sleeve. "Where are you going?"

"Into town." I hate it as I say it.

We need answers. Gary Michael Williams is a bust, so I need a new method.

Her bottom lip trembles. "You should have one of the other girls go with you."

"You should find the cat," I offer, and she ducks her head.

Suddenly, Savvy steps from the back of the house, wearing a polite smile that suggests she knows everything. I thought she only saw the past, but she looks like she can read my mind and see the future too. I wonder how long she's been watching for me to make this move. Was she watching Daphne too?

"I brought my coat," she says, tapping her thick winter jacket. It's not that cold outside. "Lead the way, Maisie."

"Fine," I mutter and turn on my heel, walking toward the back gate.

We step through the squeaking gate, Mikayla's blood washed away by the near-constant mist of the Pacific Northwest. We stand close together as I build a portal. Having been to town enough times, I know where the police station is and where to best empty out into the woods. I have no interest in being caught by mortals.

"Why are we at the police station?" whispers Savvy.

"I think Julia's body has been found," I say.

Savvy's eyes widen, horror striking her. So she doesn't know why Daphne left. There goes my theory about her reading an object Daphne touched as she left the house.

"I don't know the answers," I add quickly, "but Daphne and Astrid were heading into town. Julia's body wasn't found in the woods."

She draws her eyebrows together. "That doesn't match."

I admit, "You're probably the best person to have here. If Julia was dumped and someone tried to light her on fire—"

"Then I can read the object and get the asshole." She sighs. "Where do we start?"

"Main Street and then on to Smith Street," I say.

Those are the most traveled streets in town. The town is small enough that we should just follow the flow of local traffic.

Still, hope pumps with each heartbeat that this isn't about Julia. Maybe they found Beatrice and Mikayla's killer? The police wouldn't have shown up with three cars if that was the case. They suspect we're the killers, and they now have another victim on their hands.

"Do y'all do any witchy things to the tourists? Besides the big parties." Savvy means, do we mess with the tourists or sell potions and favors. Daphne might.

"We prefer not to be looked at like that," I say, shying away from the mortals walking the sidewalk opposite of us.

"It may be too late." Savvy inclines her head to a man following behind us by twenty feet.

I put my head down and scramble ahead.

More mortals walk in tandem with us. More mortals are out than I've seen recently when I've been in town. They crowd the intersection of Smith Street and Main Street. I slow my walk, but Savvy takes my hand and pushes through the milling and whispering locals. We stop at police tape. A few news channel crews are pointing toward a scene filled with police officers. We've discovered where Julia was found. Unless something else happened in town.

The caution tape cuts off the sidewalk and street. Blood lies in the middle of the pavement but has splattered up the wall. The police tape is held up by the power line poles. The building itself is long, heading back further and an alley. The front is a store for tourists with swimsuits, surfing gear, postcards, and t-shirts. It's closed for the offseason.

Savvy heads across the street, and I jog after her. The police officers are watching us closely—along with the locals—but the officers turn back to the stagnant crowd. Outside the closed business is a bench, and she sits.

"What are you doing?" I ask.

We're exposed, and my sisters' killer could be near. I shouldn't have come here. How could I be so stupid? The police are nearby, but we're surrounded by mortals. What could happen before we realize it? It's not safe. We need to go home.

"Keep watch." Savvy places a hand against the wall down the street where Julia's body was found.

The wall has been repainted several times after being graffitied. I remember drunk people vomiting on the wall during summer from the bars nearby. One time, I saw people making out against the wall. Children slide their fingers across when they walk. The old building has a plaque at the front saying it was erected in the 1950s.

The crowd glances toward us. While we are not casting spells or making potions, Savvy has her head down and eyes closed. She could be meditating or having a moment of peace, yet the locals spread the rumors that swirl around the house. The boy who had been walking behind us stands at the back of the crowd, eyeing us suspiciously. My magic raises its head, slipping through the cracks in the pavement. I reel it in before it creates more issues for us.

"Found it," Savvy says, and I bend my head toward her. "Julia is stumbling, hand touching the wall. There's blood—she's coughing blood."

Coughing blood doesn't match the other two deaths from our coven. Beatrice and Mikayla had blunt force traumas to their heads and bodies. The back of my head throbs.

Savvy shifts on the bench, fingers digging into the aging wood. "Julia has to lean up against the wall to keep herself upright. There's the other person. Huh."

Fear climbs up my throat. "What?"

"It's a girl."

"Are you sure?"

"I think so."

When Beatrice and Mikayla were murdered, the killer was a guy. Just the way he walked, so heavy and firm. But his clothing had been baggy. The trees showed me, and everything was cast in shadows. Maybe I was wrong.

"I can't see who it is. Person has light hair. Julia is screaming for help, her life." Savvy's eyes flutter under her eyelids. "Julia has fallen. The woman dumps gasoline on Julia. She's got a lighter…."

We aren't in the woods. And Mikayla and Beatrice weren't doused in gasoline. They were already dead and lit on fire.

Savvy blinks mist from her eyelashes. "Maybe Julia had enemies?"

I say, "Or maybe we have more enemies than we think."

***

Back at the house library, I turn another page and skim the contents of the founding families. The town has a long history, but I'm more interested in the coven. Still, I bark up the tree of Gary Michael Williams.

Will I have to start over on my research to find Beatrice and Mikayla's killer? Julia's death is so different that it makes me think it's someone else, but the killer could be getting smarter or bolder. Maybe the killer ran out of time? Maybe Julia's death was personal?

When I finally get to the Williams family in the library book, I read the pages thoroughly. There is a family tree, and the Gary Michael Williams listed has a birthdate but no death date. The book was published during his time alive or when he was a frog.

The library doors squeak, and Lizzy walks in, a camera hanging around her neck and tracking sand in from her shoes. I stifle the urge to tell her to take her shoes off and to get the vacuum. I took off my muddy shoes before stepping into the house.

"Roxie told me I could find you in here," she says. "The waves were kicking up, so Susana and I went to the beach. I thought it was best to get her out of the house."

I push away my annoyance. "Did it help Susana?"

"I think so. When Beatrice died, Susana was sad but had purpose in revenge," Lizzy explains. "But with Julia dead, she couldn't get out of bed, like she had lost all hope. I think Susana will leave next. She has nothing to keep her here."

"We're her sisters. We did a seance for her."

"Others are talking about leaving too."

They did the same thing after Mikayla's death. They'll continue to talk about it. I wish we talked less and did more. I'm the only one doing anything to find our sisters' killer.

"How's it going with this research? Are you still looking into Gary Michael Williams?" she asks.

"I'm thinking. Trying to come up with something." Ideas bounce through my head, none of the dots fully connecting, but it's the start of a new idea. "Lizzy, do you have any pictures of the party?"

She starts clicking through the pictures on her camera. "I haven't had time to upload them yet."

"The time?" I ask. It's been over a month since Mikayla's murder.

"The patience," Lizzy amends. "The want, the motivation. Mikayla is going to be in these photos."

Like Beatrice and me, Lizzy and Mikayla rarely spoke, but they were sisters. We care for our sisters. The losses of Beatrice, Mikayla, and Julia punch holes in me. I am slowed, aching with each death.

The clicking slows when Lizzy gets to the pictures of that night. "We looked so beautiful. Beatrice died, and we were so sad—but the party lifted our spirits for at least a little while." She clicks again. "Here's Mikayla. God, she was gorgeous."

We all looked great, but Mikayla was stunning in her blue jumpsuit, golden accented like a goddess. Mikayla was always beautiful in the stereotypical kind of way.

Lizzy clicks through the pictures of people and the setup of the house, us in our dresses and masks. Lizzy was focused on us witches and how much fun we were having. Well, how much fun my sisters were having. I brood in each of the photos.

"Wait. Go back," I say.

Lizzy clicks a photo back and then more.

"There. Do you see it?" I ask.

Ubah is center with her yellow dress, also gorgeous. In the corner are Mikayla and a boy in a horse mask. For a masquerade where most girls wanted to look gorgeous, this guy didn't try to fit in. How did he get Mikayla to talk to him? His suit is baggy.

"Are there more pictures of him?" I ask.

Huddled together on a chair, Lizzy and I study picture after picture after picture. So many faces. His mask starts to morph with others wearing animal masks. There is not one direct picture of him, but there are enough photos of him where he's lingering in the background. He's always around a coven witch. Besides Mikayla, he was nearest to Daphne at one point. Her back was turned to him.

Lizzy points to the screen on her digital camera. "Is that you?"

My head aches.

Chapter 30

Death is not the end for any soul. Ghosts
linger on our plane for those who hold on and
have something to hold onto, but do not trust
them. They are vengeful and wanting. When
your time comes, go to your next life with
open arms.

–Unknown

In the morning, two men scurry out of the dining room, leaving Julia's body on the table. The men skid to a stop when they see me in the shadows of the house. Their eyes widen, and they practically run. I know I didn't sleep well last night, which allowed me to hear the car drive on the gravel this early in the morning, but I don't think I look that scary.

I start backing away. I don't want to be in the dining room if Julia's ghost returns.

"Come in, Maisie," says Daphne. "I see your shadow in the doorway."

Fighting a grimace, I step in. The scent of death lingers, and acidic bile claws at my throat.

"Her mother will be here at noon to collect her, so we should start," says Daphne, standing over Julia's body.

Before I can ask what she means, she unzips the black body bag and exposes Julia. She's unnaturally still and pale.

I didn't see the other bodies, burnt to a crisp, and besides the direct aftermath of Audrey's death, I didn't see her body. I haven't seen many corpses in my life— not my parents' or my old coven. I stumble back.

Astrid stands in the dining room doorway, lugging a shiny steel machine on wheels. What are they doing?

"Maisie, if you walk out those doors, you won't be allowed back in," Daphne warns.

I stop.

If I leave, I won't be allowed back into whatever they're doing in the dining room, and perhaps I may not ever be allowed back into Daphne's secrets. I won't know her life, and I won't know all her teachings. I won't be her favorite.

I shut the dining room doors and then stare at the wood before turning on my heel toward Daphne and Astrid.

"What does that mean?" I inch closer to the body. It's a shell of a sister we barely knew.

Daphne flicks a button on the machine that looks like it should be in a hospital, not a coven house. The machine wheezes and shakes, sucking air in through a tube. What are Daphne and Astrid doing? We focus on magic, but this isn't magic. The way Daphne and Astrid move together is like they have done this before.

Astrid inserts a tube into Julia's arm, and the machine pumps red blood out, emptying into the bottom of the attached container. I'm horrified, wanting to run from the room, but curiosity brings me up to the machine. More blood spills out, moving faster than it should from a dead body. It washes up the side of the container as the machine gasps for more.

"This is the most blood we've gotten," says Astrid to Daphne.

"Do you do this often?" My voice has pitched up an octave.

"With the bodies," explains Astrid dismissively, Daphne a statue behind her. "Beatrice was crisp, so not there. Mikayla was preserved a little. Julia will rival Audrey."

I gulp. "You did this to Audrey?"

Who haven't they done this to? Would they do this to the living witches too?

"It would be a waste not to," Astrid answers. "She was young and healthy."

I whip around to my leader, looking for a response. A why in the chaos of death. There has to be a reason!

Daphne watches the machine pump blood, her face hard set. She almost looks… hungry. Her glossy eyes are distant.

Astrid chuckles. "Julia's mother was part of the Council. The pretentious bitch. Imagine when she learns her daughter's body was *accidentally* delivered to the house."

Raising her head, Daphne mutters, "Make sure she doesn't cause any *accidents* here."

Astrid smiles. "There's only ever been one witch to best me, and I am preparing to meet her again." A deadly note hangs in her voice.

Scars mar Astrid's exposed skin. She has taken off her black gloves to work the machine. At this early in the morning, she doesn't wear a veil. I would hate to be the witch against Astrid. I remember how she's stolen my power before, crushing it into oblivion until I couldn't move.

Daphne bends beside the blood-filled container. "We need to leave some blood in Julia. Her mother may want to embalm her for the mausoleum."

"What will you do with the blood?" I ask.

A strange fascination has glued me to the floor. I should run. No one would blame me. Three of my sisters are dead, and I could be next. When I look at Daphne, I know I must remain here. I want her to choose me above everyone.

Astrid scoffs. "Daphne, I thought you told her what we're doing."

No. She had never mentioned anything.

What could Daphne have said to prepare me for this? I wouldn't understand unless I was seeing this with my own eyes.

"Did you take all of Audrey's blood when she died?" I ask, voice wavering.

"No one was looking for Audrey. She had no family or previous coven," explains Daphne. "The police didn't know she was dead, so I took her blood. All of it."

I blanch at her harsh voice and harsher words. Audrey was our sister! But when Daphne has lived as long as she has, maybe that doesn't mean much if she'll treat one of her sisters like this. Am I any different if I died? No one would claim my body. I take a step back, but neither Daphne nor Astrid look at me, like they trust I won't say anything. What am I becoming?

Turning off the machine, Daphne pulls the filled container out of the holder, careful to not let the blood slosh. She takes it upstairs before any of the others wake.

Julia's body looks deflated to me, a new kind of pale in her deep sleep. I hope Julia's ghost didn't watch what we did to her.

Astrid wraps Julia in white satin, covering up a crime. My skin crawls at how she touches Julia after stealing from her.

She growls, "Are you just going to stand there and watch, or are you actually going to do something useful?"

I lift my hands to help, urging myself forward. Her skin is clammy like warm wax, but her bones are hardened. No matter how much I pretend this is sleep, Julia is dead. Her ghost is with Audrey's.

Astrid chuckles. "You should get used to dead bodies."

I mumble, "No one should be used to dead bodies."

"We'll need to keep it cold in here unless we want her to smell. I'll open the windows."

I pull the satin across Julia's face and use golden ropes to keep the sheet together, hiding her. She looks like a mummy. Mummies rise. Dead bodies rise too with a necromancer. Voices murmur around me, and I whip around.

The ghosts are here to haunt us—Julia has returned—but no, the other girls are awake in the house. Their voices slide through the airducts and under the door. They'll see what we're doing. They'll be as horrified as I am. But Daphne won't be here to make them understand. I don't really understand.

"Maisie, you need to keep it together," snaps Astrid.

Clearing the lump in my throat, I urge, "I am." I could be doing a lot worse.

***

Susana's sobs fill the house. Catrina offers comfort to others, but we need more than comfort. The open windows whip cold air at my cheeks, and I rub them with my hand and then smell Julia on my fingers. I tuck my hands behind my back.

Savvy stands off to the side of the group. "I can't stop thinking about what Julia said—about this coven."

I still. "It really is a nice place."

We can't lose another sister.

"I don't dispute that—" Savvy stops as Johanna sweeps into the dining room, joining our sisters late. Savvy lowers her voice. "Julia said this place took from her and we aren't sisters. Julia's killer was female. Lightish hair. We can rule Susana out. She's not a shifter, right?"

"Medium level of power. Why do you say 'rule her out?'" My heart skips a beat. "You think one of us killed Julia?"

Suddenly, I am looking at the girls like Savvy is, wondering who it could be with lightish hair: Paula,

Lizzy, and Johanna, Daphne too. It's not hard to lighten one's hair with a simple potion only to be washed out, so that adds Kat to the list, though I don't think it's her. Susana and Kami are possibilities too. All of us could be potential suspects.

I want to shake these thoughts from my mind. For better or for worse, these are my sisters. I cannot believe one of them would kill Julia.

The doorbell rings, and I slink away from the group. I'll do anything to escape the pain and the lingering scent of blood. On the ground floor, I close my eyes and breathe. I need a moment to collect myself.

"Girl, are you going to let me in, or do I need to force my way inside?" yells someone through the window beside the front door. A middle-aged woman with the perfect likeness to Julia stands on the other side. "I don't have all day, mortal!"

I open the front door. "I'm not mortal."

"You're certainly not a full witch. Something taints your blood." The woman pushes past me. "I told Julia not to come here. She was stuck with morons."

"I thought I heard you, Angela." Astrid stands at the base of the grand staircase, plastering a too-sweet smile on her face. "You know mortals and how idiotic they are."

Angela eyes me. "Not just them. Honestly, Astrid. I don't know how you keep such company."

"Neither do I," says Astrid as they walk up the stairs together. I trail behind them.

Magic wafts off Angela. She pushes open the dining room doors. I know Astrid won't allow anything to happen to us. Per Daphne's order. But Daphne is missing.

Johanna steps forward, and Angela teeters back on her heels and then smiles, saying, "My, you grow prettier by the day."

"And more powerful," Johanna coos. "Just like my parents taught me."

"It's good Julia had one powerful witch in this mix." Angela flicks her gaze to us. "Where are your servants to help?"

"Do you mean 'staff?'" asks Kami.

Angela rolls her eyes. "Covens. You'll never know real power."

"I'll get them for you." As she passes Ubah, Astrid whispers, "If she steps out of line, send Angela on her ass."

Ubah nods, and Astrid disappears into the lower levels of the house.

Chapter 31

Magic is not always the answer, but it usually
brings about a solution.
–Unknown

With Julia's corpse gone, Lizzy and I sit in the library. Lizzy is light haired, but I don't know if she could kill Julia. Which one of my sisters could it be? If it is one of us.

"You're staring." Lizzy closes a book. "What's going on?"

"At the scene, Savvy said that a woman killed Julia, not a man." I peek through my eyelashes up at her, trying to gauge her reaction, but I'm not an investigator.

"So we don't think Gary Michael Williams is involved?" She pinches her eyebrows together. "Because I do. There are too many coincidences."

"I'm not saying that. Julia's death is different. The town versus the woods, the lack of blunt force trauma." I do sound like an investigator.

Pursing her lips, Lizzy nods slowly. "Where do we start?"

I run my fingers through my hair, catching the knots at the end. "I don't know. There's a lot I don't know."

In the hallway, Johanna crosses the open library doors. She's still dressed in black while many of us have changed out of mourning clothes. Perhaps she's still putting on a show for Julia's mom, though she's gone. Johanna didn't wear black so long with Beatrice or Mikayla.

"Johie!" calls Lizzy, and Johanna sticks her head into the library, frowning at us.

I shrink in the seat, but her gaze drills into me. "Johanna, I'm sorry about Julia. I didn't realize how good of friends you were," I say.

"We weren't. I was being a good sister." She looks at me off the tip of her nose. "I'm trying to speak with Daphne about our new opening. Zelda's still available. Catrina won't be alive much longer anyway, best to get a jump on it. We don't want to be caught unaware. Again."

"She's already looking for a new witch." The lie flies out of my mouth. I'm startled by how quickly I speak. "She's gone to Seattle."

"That's why she wasn't answering her door." Johanna huffs. "I'll talk to her later. Lizzy, can we do something? I'm bored, and you have to be bored in here." She motions to the library.

"Yeah, sure, Johie. We can do something." Lizzy gives me an apologetic smile over her shoulder as she leaves with Johanna.

While I should focus on the never-ending research, I push up from my seat. A surge of adrenaline pumps through my veins, forcing me forward before I think. I haven't seen Daphne either. I thought she would come to see Julia off.

Lizzy and Johanna head downstairs, so I tiptoe away from them and then sprint to Daphne's suite, locking the doors behind me.

She isn't in the sitting room and kitchenette. Nothing's brewing on her balcony. The suite is so still. Maybe she isn't here? But a chill wraps around the base of my spine.

Knocking on the closed bathroom door, I say, "Daphne, are you in there?"

There is no voice or splashing. Or any sound.

Maybe Daphne isn't in the house. Maybe she left without me realizing. But all the cars are here. So are the girls.

I push the bathroom door open, and Daphne lies in the bathtub, naked. Immediately, I glance away and mumble, "Sorry."

Silence responds.

"Daphne?" I peek from the corner of my eye.

She's slumped in the bathtub. Her hands have sunk like stones at her sides.

Running to her side, I tilt her head back. Her breath tickles my skin, but her eyes don't open. Her chest rises and falls, but she's ice. Water beads down her pink-tinged skin as whatever the extra substance is starts to clot. The iron scent clogs my nostrils.

I don't know what is going on with this blood, but it has to be Julia's. Who else has bled this much without dying? I don't see any open wounds on Daphne.

I try to pull Daphne out but can't get a firm grasp on her slick body. She slides from my hands and lands with a thud on the bathtub floor. I jump into the large bathtub that could fit three people. The water splashes me. Grabbing her again, I slip and fall.

My head aches. The pain is dulled quickly by the adrenaline rushing my system, but it also calls upon my magic. It won't help me in this situation.

Daphne's face has fallen beneath the surface of the water, so I pull her back up, pressing her to the side of the bathtub.

"I'll be back," I promise her.

Blood and water covering my skin and clothes, I run out of the suite and down the stairs and pound on Astrid's door. She doesn't answer. I need to get Daphne out of the bathtub—someone to help me lift her. Running, I reach the landing, and Lizzy gapes at me.

"Where's Johanna?" I ask because Lizzy stands alone.

"She left, and I didn't want to go into town. It's not safe. Is that blood?"

"I need your help." I sprint back upstairs.

"Wait, Maisie!" She barely keeps up with me, yelling questions at my back.

I'll explain, but I don't have answers. My mind tries to connect the dots, but survival has overtaken me. I need to save Daphne and need help to do it.

Leaving the suite doors open, I run to Daphne, making sure her head isn't in the water. I jump into the bathtub and pull Daphne up, but I'm sinking under her dead weight.

Lizzy stands in the doorway, dumbfounded.

"It's not her blood," I say.

"Whose is it?" She stands at the edge of the bathtub.

"We need to get her on the bed." My skin is stinging, and tears burn my eyes.

"Maisie, stop," says Lizzy.

I heave. "We need to get her to the bed."

She grips my shoulder. "I can move things with my mind. Get out of my way."

My magic tingles at the reminder, but I shove it aside. And myself out of the bathtub.

With little effort, Lizzy lifts Daphne out of the water and into the air. I grab a towel. After Lizzy lays her gently down on the bed, I cover her with the towel and try to dry her. The pink has stained her skin. Some now seeps into the towel.

Lizzy demands, "Tell me what happened."

"Daphne's immortal. She bathed in Julia's blood," I explain.

Could she have gotten blood in her mouth? I don't think she drinks blood, but until this morning, I didn't know she stole blood from my dead sisters. Or bathed in it.

Lizzy thins her lips. "Immortal?"

"As far as she's told me," I say.

"She can't die."

"Technically, she can."

"But she's not. Maisie, stop scratching your arms."

Raised scratches are up and down both of my arms. My dead skin is deep under my fingernails. My blood begins to bubble to the surface. If I can't scratch my arms, I'll scratch my legs. The rest of me too.

"Maisie, you were in the water. Like Daphne. Get in the shower. Now!" Lizzy runs into the bathroom and turns on the shower. "We need to get you washed off. You have been poisoned!"

I balk. "What? Poison?"

I look at Daphne on the bed, but Lizzy claps her hands.

"Come on, Maisie!" she demands.

Water streaming from the head, I get into the shower and scratch, trying to free myself from the itchiness eating me. It's everywhere. I pull at my sloppy clothes that hang on my body, and the clothes slap against my skin. I'm weighed down.

"Poison." My teeth chatter. "I've been poisoned."

"Start screaming if it gets worse." Her footsteps thunder the floor. "I'm making you a salve. Don't panic, Maisie!"

I don't know how much worse this can get without me dying. Salves take time to make, like any brew does. That is why witches rely on their brute force of powers and spells. But I don't know a spell that takes poison out of my body.

I've been poisoned by… Julia's blood.

Bile is building in my throat. The world spins. My blood mixes with what I can get off my skin. Everything burns. I let out a shriek.

Lizzy runs into the bathroom. "Open the door. Turn off the water. Stay still."

I do, and she starts pouring the liquid over my skin from a bowl. I clench my teeth to hold back my howl of pain.

Through rushed breaths, she says, "It didn't have time to solidify."

The salve turns my skin cold, and finally, the burning stops. I want to scratch, shredding my skin off my body, but it is now a secondary thought instead of what I need to do to survive. The brew sits on my skin for a few minutes before I wash it away, yet I stay in the shower long after the water has turned clear around my feet. I'm scared the pain will return once I step out. And I don't want to see the blood in the bathtub or on Daphne.

Lizzy brings me a towel, and I wrap myself in it. She checks Daphne on the bed, who is still alive and breathing. I loiter in the bathroom doorway, pinching my eyes shut. Unfortunately, all I see is blood. It haunts me as much as the scent of burnt flesh does. It will follow me forever.

"Her immortality is keeping her alive." I force my eyes open. Enough of this emotion. I need to fix this. "We have to figure out the poison to make a salve."

Lizzy crosses her arms over her chest. "Maisie, it won't work."

"What the fuck is going on here?" Astrid yells from the doorway. Her magic flares like a storm, and mine dims. She hobbles around us and checks Daphne's pulse.

I stutter, "I went looking for you. Julia's blood was poison and Daphne—"

"Shut up!" Pacing the length of the sitting room, Astrid is scary enough for neither of us to say anything. "No one can know about Daphne, and we need to wake her up. Now."

***

Astrid, Lizzy, and I create salves. We keep the balcony doors open as we go back and forth on brews. I want to go to the library to research poisons and potential solutions, but Astrid won't let us leave the suite until nightfall. When the girls are asleep or out. I want to tell them, but Roxie may dance on Daphne's early grave. She may not be the only one of my sisters.

On the balcony, I brew. We need the potion to boil and then solidify into a salve by cooling. The night air brushes my raw skin, and I shiver.

"Come here please." In the backyard, Kat nears the black cat.

It smells her outstretched fingers and then brushes up against her, flicking its tail. I'm happy watching Kat with her cat. It's been hers since the moment she arrived. The moment quickly ends when someone knocks on the suite door.

Astrid puts up a hand, motioning for us not to move. I hold my breath, but white steam rolls into the night on the balcony. Kat could see us up here. Others must know.

Another knock rattles the door, and the voice says, "Maisie, I know you're in there."

Astrid motions for me to go, and Lizzy and her duck into the bathroom.

Quietly, I walk over and check the peephole. Two girls stand on the other side, neither Johanna. I open the door only a little, trying to block the view of Daphne. Roxie puts her hand on the door and pushes it open, propelling me out of the way.

"Why is there blood in the hallway?" Roxie asks and stops short, Savvy a couple feet behind her. Concern is written on her face.

Blood waits in the hallway and has been tracked across the pink plush rugs. The bathroom and bedroom are far worse. The kitchenette and sitting room are wrecked. Many potions are brewing. So far nothing has worked for Daphne, who lays in her bedroom.

Walking out of the bathroom, Astrid slams the door against the wall. "Close the doors!"

I do.

Savvy and Roxie have a lot of questions, and Astrid gives a quick rundown. Neither of them look like they want to be involved, but they don't have a choice now. They followed the blood trail. This is what they get for being curious and good sisters.

"Do we think Johanna is Julia's killer?" Roxie asks.

"What? Johie. She wouldn't." Lizzy crosses her arms over her chest.

"Are you sure?" Roxie arches an eyebrow. "Lizzy, you're a smart girl. A nice girl. So how come you don't see Johanna as she truly is? You have to know something is off."

"It wasn't Johanna." Lizzy kneads the salve she's been working on in the kitchenette. My salve cools on the balcony.

Savvy looks around the sitting room. "What do we have going, and what do we need to do?"

As we continue to work, the potions and salves begin to stack up. Once we find the poison, we'll be prepared. I test them on Daphne's skin. More welts boil on the surface, or warts bloom like flowers. My skin aches at the thought. I return to the potions to start again.

Savvy has her own ideas, so we make those too. Out of the salves and brews she makes, a couple give some relief to Daphne's skin, but most do nothing. Daphne is a statue lying in bed. She had to have been in that bathtub for hours, so the poison had its time to work into her blood.

My skin is starting to itch again, and Lizzy puts salves on me. She says that if I keep scratching, my hands will be bound. Honestly, it doesn't sound too bad.

"How are you not dead?" Roxie asks, stirring a metal spoon in a black cauldron.

"I wasn't in the bathtub as long. And it's only on my skin." For the most part, I was protected by clothing. "We are already working on salves and potions to fight against belladonna, hemlock, aconite, foxglove, and arsenic."

"Sounds like overkill," mutters Roxie as Savvy says, "We should make something strong enough to fight off all of them at the same time."

"I don't know anything like that," I say, wracking my brain for the magical answer. "Potions are all about dosage. Whatever the potion, or *poison* in this case, dosage is most important. This person planned this murder and even technically executed it well, but they don't have the expertise. But…" Dread fills me. "We have everything in the house. We use them in potions."

"Even the arsenic?" Savvy draws her eyebrows together.

Things like these are very dangerous. It doesn't mean we use them in wrong ways. If the police knew—besides the other things we have in the house that could create bombs and whatever else to kill each other—then we would all be under arrest.

"It's not used often, but it does have properties to be used in potions. I've seen Daphne use them before." Lizzy looks at each of our faces. "Daphne is lucky she isn't dead. I don't think there is a way to save her."

I gasp, chest constricting.

"I'll help," Savvy promises quickly. "There has to be a way."

I nod slowly. I need the hope. Or the lies from my coven.

"Is anyone wondering, you know," Roxie asks, "why Daphne was in a bathtub of Julia's blood? Has no one been thinking about this?"

"I think she bathes in young blood—Julia's blood—to keep her youthful." I look to Astrid for confirmation, but she says nothing.

The girls look at me in horror, and I hate that I'm the one who has to say it. I just found out.

I shift uncomfortably. "I'm going to check our public stores. We should see what we have."

Astrid snaps her fingers. "Roxie, go with her. You're not doing anything."

Begrudgingly, Roxie comes with me. I tiptoe down into the mansion's stores as she drags her feet. I remain quiet not to bring anyone else into this mess.

Daphne is vulnerable right now, hovering on the edge of death. That was me not too long ago.

We have our potion-making ingredients in multiple places and check the kitchen and then a hidden panel of the wall on the landing. Each of the girls know where these things are and are welcome to take them to make potions, but any girl rarely does. Minus me.

We knock our knuckles against the hollow wood. The paneling slides open, revealing a dark room. I step in, Roxie hanging back in the close quarters. I flick on the hanging lightbulb. Dark cauldrons, mixers, and lighters line the path first, and I shuffle those out of the way. The ingredients are in alphabetical order based on common name. I look for the five possible poisons.

"Who's in charge of keeping this in order?" she asks.

"Kami and Mikayla," I reply.

They are to ensure everything's in order and in stock, the same I do with the library. Everything is covered in dust and mostly running low. I cringe. I won't know if anything is truly missing or used from our storerooms.

Roxie mocks, "Kami's doing a great job."

"When was the last time you did the backyard?" I snap.

"That's why I'm friends with you." Roxie turns ingredients around. "And you'd just come in after me and redo it. The leaves are meant to be on the ground. Some shit like that."

Ignoring her comment, I count the ingredients in the storeroom. "The supplies are lower than the last time I was here a few days ago."

Roxie arches an eyebrow, though she smirks. "Were you using poisons?"

"No." A shiver runs down my spine. "I got aluminum, which is next to arsenic. Also hemp next to hemlock."

"What a naughty girl you are, Maisie," she jokes. "Doing drugs like that."

"It was for a sleeping and relaxing brew. We didn't even get to potions that day," I say, remembering how many feathers Kat burned.

"Hey—" Roxie lowers her voice— "do you think Kat is pretending to be bad with her magic?"

I don't want to tell Roxie Kat's secrets, including those of her being sent to doctors who made her feel crazy. The doctors pumped her with drugs that are given to mortals when they start doing "crazy" things, but they masked her witch abilities. That is her story to tell and a horror I don't want to think about.

"She seems genuinely incapable of control, freaking out anytime she lights a fire," I say, leaving the storeroom. Supplies spill from my hands, and Roxie grabs what falls.

Before we can make it far, Johanna steps out into our path, holding a bowl of cereal. She doesn't seem to notice us in the middle of the night as she starts up the stairs, wearing a pair of short shorts. She doesn't wear socks or shoes, leaving her legs exposed. Her swollen ankle is scarred, but she doesn't limp. Whatever salve she used has healed her well enough, but I know those marks.

Astrid is covered in them.

I step up, asking, "Is your ankle feeling better?"

Jumping, Johanna mumbles, "Yeah. Thanks."

Roxie says, "It looks like a bur—" My hand grips her tightly, and Roxie grunts. "It looks like a bitch."

Johanna rolls her eyes. "Goodnight." She walks away.

The scar is most definitely from a burn. Probably from Kat in the woods during the scavenger hunt. She and I were separated, and she said she was attacked. I couldn't find anyone. Everyone in the coven was paired up, except for Johanna.

Chapter 32

Do not wonder what makes a powerful witch. Once you have joined a coven, you are powerful. This coven was built on history and fertile land. This coven shall stand longer than any one member or the house that was built.

–Daphne, written in the coven grimoire

Salve after salve is tried on Daphne and me. I no longer feel like I'm dying from the poison, but I'm not healed. The bindings have been pulled back for now, and I hiss as Lizzy applies a salve to my blistered arms.

"Sorry," she says.

"It's okay," I say, holding back my tears.

"You've been quiet since getting back from the stores. Now that some of the poisons are missing, it makes our sisters look guilty." Her words are monotone but still strike me to my bones.

Too much emotion won't allow me to think straight. My magic will be wild. Everything is building up in me, and I'll explode.

The words rush out anyway. "What happened to Johanna's ankle on the night of the scavenger hunt?

You saw her limping. Where was she on the night of Julia's death?"

Lizzy's face reddens. "Why don't you ask her?"

"She could lie to me."

"Then make sure she doesn't," Lizzy urges.

I lean back on my heels. Her tone is spiteful, like we've questioned Johanna one too many times. But I've seen Johanna's ankle and her wrath before. Lizzy is taking it one step further by suggesting I use a truth potion or spell on Johanna. Could I? I don't think so, but that's the old me talking. Before I lost three of my sisters and almost lost my leader.

"If Johanna did poison Julia, she didn't mean to hurt Daphne or anyone else. Stop blaming Johanna for everything." Lizzy leaves, slamming the suite doors shut.

The whole of Daphne's suite silences. Roxie and Savvy look at me. They haven't overheard much— probably—but the words thrum through my blood, executed by the shock. How vicious it was. How wrong it can be and goes against all I believe in.

My magic latches onto the idea and won't let it go. It is a seed planted in my mind, and it grows like vines, curling around my bones and driving through my veins. It wants to force me to move, no matter how hard I root myself to the floor.

Bypassing Daphne in bed, I pull down a picture from the wall and focus on opening the safe door. I remember how Daphne opened it last time, though she made sure I would see. I'm her favorite. It had to be her plan. Sitting directly inside the safe is our coven's grimoire. I grab it and head back into the sitting room.

"What do you have there?" asks Savvy from where she chops herbs in the kitchenette.

"Our grimoire." I page through the leather book, the parchment thick and yellowed.

Roxie yawns. "I didn't know we had one of those."

"Every coven has one. Keep stirring, Roxie." Savvy moves around the counter. "Maisie, what are you doing?"

"I'm looking for a truth potion." The old ink dyes my fingertips black.

"There are truth potions down in the library. Why are you looking in the grimoire?" asks Roxie, barely stirring the potion.

Truth potions are so wrong. I shouldn't do it. But I don't stop flipping through the pages, hearing them crack like sticks in the woods. I smooth down a page only for the spine to crack too. A shudder runs down my arms.

"Because the grimoire's potion will be more powerful," Savvy answers Roxie. "It's based on our magic and our history, those of the ancestors of the coven. Did you find the potion yet? I bet it had to be used at some point."

"Not yet." I flip through the pages, easily distracted by potions and spells I've never seen before. All are stronger than the books in the library.

There are vast stories and reasoning from the past coven leaders, and I want to read them. Still, I have only one mission: find a truth potion. Undoubtedly, it will be complicated to brew and expensive. I'll have to enlist Savvy's help because she's the best potion maker in the coven. Minus Daphne. I flip through the pages until I find it. Daphne entered the potion into the grimoire. Her initials stain the bottom of the page.

Crowding around the book, Savvy reads the potion a couple of times. This is more than just me. I don't want to drag everyone into the truth potion, but I'm not the only one who considers Johanna a viable suspect in Julia's murder and Daphne's potential killing. To get everything done in a timely manner for the potion, we are going to have to work together. Some of the ingredients need to be fresh too. I start to do the mental calculations.

Roxie takes one look at the page and groans. "Can't we try one of the books downstairs? This is going to take forever."

"Then we should get started," says a new voice. I hadn't realized we weren't alone.

How long has Lizzy been standing in the doorway? Why would she come back after how she left?

I want to apologize, but it's the one thing I keep silent.

"It's not Johanna," says Lizzy. "She didn't do this to Julia, but we should figure out the truth with Johanna. Maybe then you can put Julia to rest."

"And the other girls?" asks Roxie. "Beatrice and Mikayla? They're dead too."

"One killer at a time," mumbles Savvy.

I bite my tongue before I say something. Savvy wasn't there with our other sisters. She doesn't understand all the pain that has consumed us and drives us forward. Finally, we have a possible answer, and we're chasing it.

"We need to know if we have a killer in our coven," continues Savvy. "Then we'll find Beatrice's killer. Roxie, I promise we will. Maisie, where do we start?"

I tell them my plan, and we enact.

First, we gather the ingredients that we already have. Second, we take stock and start making. Third, we go to bed. Gray morning light slips through the curtains. While I should feel tired, I'm buzzing with energy. I can't stop myself from moving.

Before leaving Daphne's suite, I check on her again. The redness of her puffy skin hasn't reduced. Her power is keeping her alive, but I don't know for how long. I don't know what kind of poison could make her almost dead, but I'll make Johanna tell me.

Reaching the steps to our floor, Savvy takes me aside. "I know you trust Lizzy, but she's so stuck on Johanna that she doesn't see the obvious."

"She won't compromise the potion," I disagree. It was Lizzy's idea. "And she wouldn't hurt Daphne. She's been trying to help her."

Savvy eyes me. "Okay."

***

When I slip into my bedroom, Kat is lodged under her blankets. Her drawing is exposed on the nightstand, the magic-infused pen laying on top. It's run out of ink and magic. The picture is incredible, and I stop myself from staring at it.

A breeze from the open window knocks the pen off the nightstand. Going over to the windows, I'm about to close them, but the black cat with big yellow eyes sits in the flowerbed. By the dirty pawprints on the windowsill and in the room, the cat comes and goes as it pleases.

"You're Kat's familiar, aren't you?" I ask, and the cat blinks at me. "You've followed her, probably all the way across the country, just trying to help her. I'll leave the window open for you but tell her to give you a name."

I turn back to the sleeping Kat, knowing I should be like her. Burrowed deep in the cocoon of blankets, sleeping soundlessly. But I stay near the window, watching the day wake.

Chapter 33

Witches rely heavily on their individual powers, but the strongest spells and potions require sacrifice. That was what our ancestors gave. It is what we are called upon to do too.
—Daphne, written in the coven grimoire

After a much-needed shower, I brush out my hair. Kat is perched on the edge of her bed, watching me from under her eyelashes. I brush harder, peeking toward the bedroom door. I can't make a run for it—I would be a bad roommate. She has been waiting for me.

"I know you're really busy." Her words rush out with her exhale. "But when are we going to have our next lesson? It's been a couple of days. I read the book a couple of times. And I even read some books from the library. I didn't speak aloud, like you said. I'm ready."

To say *there's a lot going on right now* seems like a lame excuse. We haven't told the others what's going on with Daphne, and so far, no one has been asking about her. Besides Johanna. Kat needs to start with the basics of witchcraft, but we need more help.

"It's going to be hard," I warn.

She nods, almost too quickly. She doesn't know what she's getting into, and I don't tell her either. She won't have time to back out.

We go upstairs to Daphne's suite, and Kat murmurs that she's never been up this way. Daphne's suite is something to behold, or it used to be. Now, it looks more like a warzone. Besides the blood on the floor, used pots and pans are dirty in the sink and on the stove. Salves and brews press together in jars, lacking any original thought. Library books are splayed out with our last lackluster idea.

Savvy gives me a weary look from where she stirs the potions, and I whisper, "You said she was a good student."

"I really don't think bringing someone else in is a good idea," murmurs Savvy, but Kat steps into Daphne's suite. "If the girls find out, we could lose more sisters."

I don't want to think about more of my sisters dying, but they could leave if they think Daphne is going to die. Daphne cannot protect us. Three of us are dead, so maybe she could never protect us.

"Kat's a firestarter. Better to have her on our side." I walk further into the sitting room, and Kat trails after me.

"Make her do a blood oath," says Roxie, stifling a yawn.

"I'm not doing a blood oath," I say. "I'm not making *her* do it. And you didn't do one either." I've seen enough blood recently. More blood—and blood magic—won't make this better.

Kat's eyebrows knit together. "What's going on?"

"Johanna killed Julia," Roxie sums up.

I grimace. "We don't know that for a fact. The evidence is… heavily pointed in Johanna's direction. It's possible—"

"It's definitely Johanna," Roxie interrupts.

"You and Johanna don't get along," I argue.

"She doesn't get along with anyone!"

"Roxie, keep stirring," Savvy snaps, and Roxie rolls her eyes but stirs. Savvy softens her voice. "Kat, are you in or out? We need to keep this quiet."

"We should mention that whatever poisoned Julia also poisoned Daphne, and she's now in a coma," I say, pointing to Daphne's bedroom. The door is half closed, hiding her lying on the bed.

Kat gulps. "I'm in."

Another knock rattles the suite door, and we freeze. Blood litters the hallway, and it'll bring more girls to our door unless we clean it up. With everything going on, it doesn't surprise me that no one cleaned up— usually it would be me—but it does surprise me that no one else has followed the blood. Maybe after all the death, we're immune to it.

Savvy lets Lizzy in—thankfully, it's *only* Lizzy—and Lizzy takes one look at Kat and sighs. "It's possible it's her," Lizzy says.

"Could also be you." Roxie crosses her arms over her chest. "But we haven't kicked you out. Yet."

"We need to get moving on the other supplies," says Lizzy, dismissing Roxie and walking further into the suite. "The ingredients are going to take long to get, and we're going to need a lot of magic. We'll be in a time crunch if we don't get moving."

"We? You? No." Roxie throws down the spoon in one of the pots. "I have been stirring this pot for the past I-don't-know-how-many hours! I have been here the whole night."

"You want to go, so go." Lizzy shrugs.

"I want to go to bed. Sleep, you crazy people! You got to sleep. It's my turn." Roxie abandons the cauldron, leaving Daphne's suite and presumably going to bed.

I take over with the stirring since we can't have the contents scald. Then we'll have to restart the potion. I'm not willing to restart the truth potion this late in the game. If we get Johanna to take it and tell us what she put in the poison, we can save Daphne.

There is a spell that would conjure the spoon to stir without one of us doing it, but if it fails or goes wonky, then we have to start over with the potion. And who's to say that something else won't need to be added to the potion in case it starts to turn color? We have other potions going too, though they need less maintenance. We can't leave the brews and potions unattended for even the smallest amount of time, but we're running out of people to get supplies for the truth potion.

"I'll stay," Savvy says with a hefty sigh. I trust her with Daphne too.

"I already tracked where we can find the ingredients. Maisie, are you ready to go?" asks Lizzy, and I nod.

"Kat, you should go with Maisie," says Savvy.

I try not to make any sudden movements, wondering if this is a good idea. Kat may slow us down. She could light our ingredients on fire.

"You'll learn a lot with Maisie," adds Savvy, giving me a pointed look. "Maisie can probably teach you how to make a portal."

"Um," I begin while Kat's eyes widen, "we'll travel through a couple, but we'll keep the portal making to Lizzy and me. You can get used to traveling first."

***

For the ingredients to remain fresh, we need to move quickly. Which is why Kat shouldn't have come along. While it's wonderful that she marvels at everything, I don't have the proper time to teach her. She can't truly see what magic has to offer and what we witches can do.

Lizzy slips through the crowd with ease, so I chase her, dragging Kat with me. Starting in Tokyo, we stepped through a portal to a busy street. Most shops are closed at night, so we head into the guts of the city and further in until the cigarette smoke fills our way. I stifle a cough.

"The potion calls for a certain type of seaweed only found in this area of the world," explains Lizzy, holding a piece of notebook paper. We've copied down the ingredients and planned out an estimated schedule.

The lights are on in a bar with a flickering sign out front. Men in suits eye us wearily, and I slip behind the two taller girls. It doesn't matter that I'm a witch and have strong powers; I would still prefer not to be looked at. Ever.

We push forward to the counter in a bar, and in broken Japanese, Lizzy says, "We spoke on the phone."

The bartender replies in perfect English, "I missed your American accent."

The seaweed is in a plastic bag behind her on the counter. My magic curls toward the unfamiliar plant, but the plastic bag repels it. My magic looks for another source.

"What are you looking to do with the seaweed?" asks the bartender.

"Does it matter?" Lizzy asks defensively. "As long as we can pay."

The bartender lingers her gaze on me for a second too long. "How desperate are you for this? You can wait until the morning when the market opens. There will be plenty of seaweed there."

"It's the properties of that certain type of seaweed." I wouldn't be able to replicate it with magic, though I could make it look similar. However, I would need to research—and touch—the specific plant.

The bartender frowns. "What do you have?"

"What do you want?" Kat asks.

I cringe. I wish she wouldn't talk. It may get us into more trouble, especially with how the bartender watches us. It's like she knows how suspicious this is. Does she suspect what we are? How would she know?

Pulling out her cell phone, the bartender scrolls through the pictures and then shows us. "It's my mother's birthday tomorrow, and I forgot. I'm not sure I'll have time to stop and get her the flower before I see her. You get me this and can have the seaweed. Or you can wait for the markets to open."

I know she's testing us. We could get the seaweed in the morning, or we could break in somewhere and steal it. If we were different witches, we would just take it from her. Thankfully, we're not those witches.

"That flower?" I question, and she nods. "I'll be back."

Soft rain falls outside, and I shake out my hair. In between the cracks in the pavement, weeds grow. Reaching down, I pull the weeds from the ground. I imagine the Japanese apricot with its rounded white petals that melt into pink. Yellow balled stamens stick out from the center. I'm putting my full magic toward making these flowers, and my magic answers the call. It tickles my skin. The flowers bloom, bringing in brightness and beauty. The edges form and color nicely. When the flower has met my high standards, I bring it inside the bar.

The bartender narrows her eyes on the flower. It is gorgeous but comes without a pot and dirt. Pulling out a beer glass, she holds out her hands for the flower, and I gently give it to her. Our skin touches for a split second. That's all it takes.

Energy runs across me like a shockwave, and I stumble back. My magic flares because it doesn't know what else to do, but I know what it is. What she is.

Dumbfoundedly, I say, "You're a witch."

"So are you." She studies the flower. "Good job. Did you conjure?"

"No," I say, almost snorting.

Conjuring wouldn't have this good of a replica of a flower. No one can smell a conjure.

"Portal and pick?" asks the bartender.

"Grew," corrects Kat.

Trying to fight my grimace, I hesitate to give any additional information about my magic to a stranger witch. It's another thing I'll need to teach Kat. She especially needs to be cautious with a power like hers.

The bartender hands over the seaweed. "You are making a powerful potion to need this, but most witches wait for the markets to open."

"We don't have the time." Lizzy tucks the bag in her backpack.

"Not even for a drink?" She places four glasses on the bar. "It's on the house. I'll start: Hi, my name is Haruka."

"Maisie." My name slips from my mouth.

I'm high on magic, the taste lingering on my tongue. It isn't my own magic, however. My magic tries to fight it off, rearing its head toward the waving flower.

"We don't have the time." Lizzy steps away from the counter. "Thanks anyway. Kat."

Haruka smiles. I smile too and then am gone. The rain washes the high sensation away.

We hit the street, make a portal, and leave Japan. That feeling of ease leaves me too. I gasp for breath. It's like I've shaken off a dream, as if Marney's power is walking with me, but I'm still awake. I pinch my thigh just in case and feel the bite of pain.

Next, we make our way to Belgium, where we need to get some Bosc pears. Unlike the seaweed, these are easier to get. We buy a bundle. I'm not entirely sure what the pear is needed for, and while I like pears, this specific pear seems browner than other types. We move to the next ingredient for the truth potion.

"A star?" Kat asks as we stand on the peak of a mountain. "How are we going to get one of those?"

Thunder rumbles the sky; lightning will soon follow. The air is painfully dry. Electricity crackles around us, and my hair begins to frizz.

"We're not." I bat down my rising hair. "We're going to catch lightning in a bottle. Add ingredients. And make the closest star we possibly can." Hopefully, it will be enough.

"We have to make a potion to put in a potion?" asks Kat uncertainly.

"That happens a lot with upper-level potions," Lizzy explains. "We can't always create or have on-hand what the potion used in the past. Sometimes, we have to be creative."

"It calls for a star," says Kat, dumbfounded. "I can chalk things up to magic—obviously—but even that seems impossible."

"Kat, we're witches. Magic doesn't make sense," I say.

It's not about *what makes sense* or *what is possible* because magic will do what it wants. We only act as conductors. We can focus and control it. Or magic will control us.

I hold out a glass bottle as another rumble crosses the sky. Lightning zaps down, but we need to bring it closer to us.

"Lizzy, if you can bring it to me, I can harness it," I say, grimacing at my words.

Lizzy needs to do this because she has the power to bring the strike closer to me. Even though Kat is a firestarter, she would be just as injured as I will be in a moment. I try not to think about that.

Grabbing Kat's arm, Lizzy pulls her twenty feet down from the peak. Rumbling thunder nearly knocks me off the top of the mountain. Digging my feet down into the hard rock, I brace myself.

My flaring magic fills the peak. Down to the base of the mountain. The roots of the tree. The stems of the grass.

I am a beacon.

We stand in the eye of the storm. My magic fights nature, but it won't win. Nothing does.

"Now!" Throwing the bottle up in the air, I heighten my magic.

The wind picks up, and the mountain feels like it's tilting. But it might just be me. I can't breathe, the oxygen thinning. A lightning strike shoots from the sky. Lizzy's magic overtakes my own, pushing the lightning straight into the vibrating bottle.

I am knocked to the ground.

A shock seizes my body. Bright dots fill my vision. Blood pulses past my ears, and though someone is yelling, I can't make out the words. Everything about me is buzzing. The glass bottle burns with white light.

Someone grabs my hands. "Maisie! Kat, grab the salve from my bag. We need to put it on her hands."

"We need to get her to the hospital," Kat urges.

My hands start to cool as solidified salve is applied to me. My skin might be scarred forever. Lizzy rubs the ointment across my arms too, but the lightning has numbed me. Thankfully. I'm hovering in a sack of skin, bones, and blood.

"Maisie, can you eat a pear? Kat, feed it to her," orders Lizzy.

She presses the fruit to my lips, and I take a small nibble. My burnt tongue aches. The whole of me is crisp.

Lizzy mumbles, "We need to get out of here."

"Back to the house?" Kat's hand trembles, but she shoves the fruit to my chapped lips.

I take another small bite. The pain... the numbness... I'm just tired. Can I go to sleep?

"We need to get the other supplies. Maisie will be okay in a few minutes. Eat more," says Lizzy.

The force of the lightning went into the bottle. Astrid survived a direct lightning strike, and I cannot imagine how. The back of my head throbs with an extra heartbeat, the pain growing. I try to push myself up. I can't make it to my feet, but Kat helps me up. I sway, but I'll survive.

We jump through another portal. Sun shines down on my shaky body. I dig my fingers into the damp dirt. The ground is filled with nutrients, and my magic latches on, sucking the soil dry like I'm a vampire. The tickling slides across my skin.

"Kat, stay with Maisie," Lizzy says. "I'll get the cow's fresh tongue, blood still attached."

A scream builds in the back of my throat. I should've looked at the truth potion better. Why would Daphne make something like this? We should've chosen a different potion. No one—not even an animal—deserves to die for a potion.

Kat tries to press the pear to my mouth. "You should eat this."

I take another bite to satisfy her. The juice runs down my chin and into the dirt. I grip the dirt tighter. My heart returns to its regular rhythm. Everything adjusts around me. I should feel guilty about stealing the nutrients, but there is a lot I should feel guilty about.

"Got it." Lizzy runs back, a freshly cut cow's tongue in her hand. Blood drips to the ground.

I almost vomit. Guilt sinks its teeth into my skin. What have I done?

Chapter 34

Kindness is free, but are you weakened by it?
–Unknown

In Daphne's suite, Savvy has kept the potions brewing. Roxie, wrapped in the quilt made by Beatrice, sits on the couch with our coven's grimoire. As I pass, I swipe the book from her, and Roxie yells after me. Holding the grimoire in my hands, I consider throwing it into the fireplace flames.

Nothing like this should exist, but this is old magic. The type of magic that Daphne performs. The type of magic that the Council and whoever else of powerful witches wouldn't blink to use. None of my sisters gawked at it. I'm the odd one out.

Throwing the grimoire into the flames is rash, so I put it back in the safe and lock it away. I won't use it again as long as I'm in the coven. Not even to save Daphne.

The ingredients have been cut up, except for the tongue. The smell slides up my nostrils. I shouldn't have made Lizzy do it.

"Five drops of your blood should be good," says Savvy, stirring a spoon in a cauldron. "The potion requires any witch who helped make the potion add their blood."

I have seen enough blood today but slice my finger open and put in five drops. I would give more if it reversed time. There are many things I would redo. The others form a circle to give their blood to the truth potion.

I remind myself that this is for the truth of Julia's death and this could help us learn the truth about Beatrice and Mikayla's deaths. We need to save Daphne. We are doing this for a reason.

With all the blood in, the potion boils. Roxie is back on stir duty. Savvy checks over her shoulder often, but we have another potion to make.

We have a bottle filled with lightning. Put some other stuff together and we still don't create a star. But we are as close as we're going to get.

On the balcony with a pot on the ground, fire flickering underneath, we move quickly: Lizzy puts in the hydrogen peroxide—the best we have, Savvy puts in the helium from a canister, I drop the lightning in the bottle in the pot, and Kat is quick to put on the cover and hold it down. We give her an encouraging nod. If it does go boom, she would be the only one to stop it with her magic. If she doesn't stop the explosion, we could all die.

Kneeling beside Kat, I ask, "Can you feel the heat? The pressure?"

Sweat beads at her temples. "Yeah."

"This is your next lesson, Kat," I whisper. "Listen very carefully: if it becomes too much or too large, you'll need to shrink it down. Take in the impact."

Her eyes widen.

"I don't mean sacrifice yourself. Sorry," I add quickly. "What I mean is you have the power to create fire but also have the ability to condense, not to destroy but to shrink. Keep it until it can be released."

I have done research on firestarters since meeting Amira, but the existing research is mostly hypothetical.

"Keep your focus on the heat and the pressure. In a few minutes, it will subside when our 'star' is formed," I say.

Taking a deep breath, Kat keeps her weight on the shaking pot. All we can do is wait.

The few minutes are agonizing. I'm mostly stuck in my own thoughts. My thoughts are a dangerous place to be. The fresh pain and guilt gnaw at my bones, sucking me dry as I've done to the earth. I deserve it.

My magic whistles through the trees, and the branches lean toward me. I curl my fingers into my palms and wait for my blood to flow. My magic opens its mouth.

"The pressure is gone, but the heat… it's less but still there," says Kat.

"Time to move to the next stage of the potion," says Savvy.

Inside Daphne's suite, we stand around the big cauldron again. The pear has already been added, having been cut up into small pieces and now turning to mush. Next, we put in gold flecks, arguably the most expensive part of the potion. It bubbles. Much of what

Daphne has hidden in her personal storeroom costs a fortune, gold flecks aside.

When we put the fresh cow tongue into the potion, it lands with a thud at the bottom of the cauldron. I grimace. The recipe didn't call for us to cut the tongue up. In the past, we grilled or pickled them, having them in slabs especially if dried. With all the blood mixing in from the tongue and us, the brownish gold tints red.

Lizzy, with her power to move things with her mind, is in control of this next step. None of us want to be within five feet when our created star is added to the potion.

"Ready?" I ask through ragged breaths. "Three... two... one!" I whip off the top of the glass bottle.

Lizzy lifts the infused, glowing conglomerate that counts as a star. She moves it quickly, dropping it into the potion. She and I duck behind the pink sofa that acts like a shield.

An explosion shakes the room. Each of us stay hunched as things fall, shattering on the floor. Flashes from my earlier brush with lightning occur in my mind, and I shake my head. I'm safe.

We stand from our hiding places, but none of us are quite brave enough to see if the truth potion turned out correctly. I've never seen anything like this potion before.

The boom has quieted my hearing, but I look to Daphne, waiting for that noise to have awakened her. It didn't. We wait for girls to be pounding on Daphne's door, wondering what's happening up here. The rest of the coven must think Daphne is the one making the potion because they don't come to investigate. I would've, but then again, I'm Daphne's *favorite*.

Walking over to the cauldron, I stir the potion with a wooden spoon. "It's good. It'll need to simmer. Then it can be administered. I can stay."

"Maybe you should go take a nap," Lizzy offers. "You were struck by lightning today. I can stay."

"I can stay too," adds Savvy, stepping beside the cauldron.

"I'll do it," I say through clenched teeth.

***

Lizzy and I stay in Daphne's suite. Part of me listens for any sound from Daphne, like she might magically wake up. Since we're witches, it seems like a possibility. And an improbability. We've tried hundreds of things. I don't know what will wake her or how long she'll be in a coma.

Lizzy stares off into the distance, not really paying attention to me or anything, so I say, "Thanks for the cow tongue. It must've been hard for you." My voice wavers.

"Hmm?" She blinks rapidly. "Not as hard as it would've been for you."

I grit my teeth. "I could've done it."

It would've taken me a few minutes to gain enough confidence. I wouldn't have been able to look in the cow's eyes, and I probably would've cried.

"I know," she says softly.

"Thanks," I repeat, a sour taste in my mouth.

We're in silence for several long seconds before Lizzy says, "Thanks for taking a lightning strike."

"It was the bottle," I brush off, though my eyes avert to my haggard hands.

The salve has been reapplied, and it helps a little. The scars may last forever, but I don't mind scars. Maybe they'll keep people away from me.

"You were still hurt," says Lizzy.

"I'm hurt often. You fixed me up like you did after I was attacked," I say.

"We should've taken you to a hospital. They would've helped you more." She shakes her head like she's furious with herself.

"You did a good job," I say. The reminder of the injury spurs a headache.

"I was stupid," she spits.

"You're not stupid."

She stirs the potion quickly, whacking the spoon against the sides of the pot and scraping the bottom. "You have to think I am, Maisie. Look how I'm defending Johanna."

I had done the same for Audrey. "She's your friend."

"The evidence is against her. I want to deny it but can't. I want to defend her, but she makes it so hard." She runs her fingers through her bleached hair. "I haven't told her."

"Told her what?"

"What you're doing—what we're doing. I haven't warned her."

We don't want her to be warned. Johanna wouldn't take the potion if we told her what it was, but she could surprise me. My sisters surprise me every day… or maybe I'm not paying enough attention to them. My sisters join the coven and then leave me. I used to try to learn everything about their lives, but at some point, it became a hassle.

"I'm a bad friend," continues Lizzy.

"You're not," I say. "You're doing this for the coven. For your sisters. And if she didn't do it, then we'll know. It won't be an issue."

Then we'll have to figure out who is the one hurting us, if not Johanna. Who killed Julia? Why did they do it? If it is one of our sisters and I'm not wrong again.

The fumes from the potion rise. At the same time, my magic is brimming at the surface, and I ball my hands into fists in my sweatpants.

"I didn't vote for Johanna's friends at the audition. I missed her birthday a couple weeks ago. I should've taken her side at the scavenger hunt," Lizzy lists in one breath. "It's a wonder she keeps me around. I don't know why she stays in the coven because she doesn't seem to like it and could be doing other things."

"You follow Johanna around like a puppy," I snap. Anger washes over me. "The day we realized Beatrice went missing, you read the tea leaves. They gave you a death omen. Johanna kept telling you that you were wrong. You were the only one that had an idea, but she didn't believe you. If we had only believed, then maybe we would've…."

What exactly? We wouldn't have found her body faster. We probably wouldn't have stopped Mikayla's killing. What about Julia's?

Lizzy's shoulders slump. She's almost as short as me now.

"I'm sorry," I say. "I shouldn't have said that."

"No, you're right." She slows her stirring. "I just feel high around Johanna, like she can be funny and light. She knows how to make a person feel good about themselves, like I'm the only person in the world. And then after, it's like drowning, like I'll never be good enough. I've spent hours analyzing what she said and what she meant. I get jealous of her talking to people, like her other friends or Julia. Are you going to kill Johanna?"

I jerk back like I've been slapped. Where did that come from? I just want the truth, and once I have it, I will.... What will we do? We can't go to the police, and the Council is gone.

"I'm not going to kill anyone," I say, but Audrey lays in the backyard.

I didn't kill her, I remind myself. Daphne said it was a power inducer that went wrong.

"Johanna won't go without a fight," pushes Lizzy.

"She'll see the error of her ways."

"She never does," she says coldly, her voice so controlled and thick. She glares into the potion like she's a firestarter and not a witch with telekinesis.

"I need to check on Daphne," I say and leave her to stir the potion.

Chapter 35

The mortals say not to trust a witch, but it is not witches who should not be trusted. It is the individual person who houses such power. Those who use their power greedily will always choose magic over anyone else.

– Daphne, written in the coven grimoire

Just as I fall asleep in my bed, I wake to a loud obnoxious banging on my bedroom door. It brings back memories of me being hit across the back of the head. Night oozes through the curtains, morning far off still. Kat cowers on her bed, her black cat hissing at the door.

What's happened? Which sister is missing now? I throw off the covers and run to the door, swinging it open. My heart beats wildly for what I'm about to walk into.

Savvy demands, "Where's the potion?"

"Roxie was stirring it last." I look at her empty bed.

"Both her and the potion are gone." Whipping around, she stomps down the hallway.

I quickly follow, Kat hesitantly on my heels. Her cat comes too.

Savvy bangs on the bedroom door of Lizzy, Johanna, and Susanna. It rattles. Soon, she's going to have the whole floor awake. We don't need more of our sisters involved in our scheme.

Susana opens the door, bleary-eyed. "What's going on?"

Savvy looks ready to barge into Susana's bedroom, so I quickly step in, "Is Lizzy here? Johanna?"

Susana checks the room with one sweep. "Neither are here. I haven't seen them since last night. I went to bed early. Why?" She yawns.

Savvy storms down the hallway on a mission, and Susana stands in her doorway, confused. I say, "Sorry," and jog after Savvy. I want to tell Kat to go back to bed but might need her power.

Savvy looks through the guest bedrooms. We check the library, the ballroom, and the dining room—also empty. Heading downstairs to the kitchen, we stop when Johanna comes out with a bowl of sugary cereal. Her hair is in a messy bun, and she looks like she only recently woke up, her pajamas loose.

Through a large bite of cereal, Johanna asks, "What's going on? It's the middle of the night."

"We're looking for you," answers Savvy.

Johanna straightens. "Why?"

Suddenly, Roxie appears behind Johanna, potion in hand, ready to put it in Johanna's cereal. I still.

I want to warn Johanna or yell for Roxie not to do it. This isn't how it was meant to be done, but the truth needs to come out. The evidence is pointing to

Johanna that she killed Julia, but it feels wrong to go against our sister. Why would she hurt one of us? Julia and Johanna were both raised in the Council. They seemed friendly enough toward each other, like we all are with our sisters.

Savvy points down and asks, "Is this cat yours?"

The cat shrinks between Kat's legs, and Kat bends to pet the animal. The two of them clearly belong to each other. It's a wonder how I didn't notice before.

"No," Johanna replies as Roxie sneaks up beside her. Her hand is outstretched, the glass vial in her fingertips.

"It has your initials on its collar," Savvy adds.

"I'd know if I owned a fucking cat," spits Johanna.

"I'll show you."

As soon as Savvy reaches for the cat, it jumps away. Its wide eyes stay on the advancing Savvy. Kat can't save the cat now.

Sighing, Johanna hands the bowl off to me without a second glance and then reaches for the cat. Kat stands protectively in front of it before Johanna shoves her aside. Roxie is quick to put the potion in the cereal. I grimace. All of this feels wrong, like somewhere along the way I made a massive miscalculation.

The smell wafts to my nose, smelling different than last night, but I don't say anything. The color of the cereal remains the same. Once the potion is in the bowl, Roxie bleeds into the background of the front entryway. She wears too much of a satisfied smirk to be completely unnoticeable. I wish I could be invisible. Or not here at all.

"The cat isn't wearing a collar," snaps Johanna.

"My bad," says Savvy. "I must've gotten it confused with another cat."

Rolling her eyes, Johanna takes her bowl and a bite of cereal.

Before I know it, I'm leaning in. While Johanna makes a weird face after her first bite, she continues to eat. The cereal must've tasted different, including a star and a cow tongue. Even the gold flakes. The smell alone should give something away. My stomach groans, not with hunger. I'm going to be sick the longer I stand here.

Standing by the doorway, Roxie asks, "Did you kill Julia?"

Johanna chokes on a piece of mushy cereal. "What? No."

Maybe the potion isn't in her system yet? Maybe she hasn't eaten enough of the cereal? Maybe we're wrong.

Johanna swallows a sizable chunk of cereal. "Why are you on my ass? Honestly, don't you have other things to be doing? I know you don't like me, Roxie, but seriously, leave me alone." She brushes past us and stomps toward the landing.

Biting the inside of my cheek, I shift through my memories of Johanna. When I was injured, I went in and out of consciousness, my mind pulling me to the night Carmella ran away. My mind pulls me to Audrey. Of all the things, I need a more recent occurrence than that to believe Johanna could be the one who killed Julia.

As she's walking away, I yell, "What happened to your ankle?"

"Kat burned me when I attacked her in the woods during the scavenger hunt." Johanna drops the cereal bowl. Its contents spill on the carpet, looking like pale vomit.

Kat's eyes widen as I stifle my gasp. The potion worked. And I was right about Johanna's injury. I don't feel any pleasure in the answer, only horror.

Johanna covers her mouth with her hands. "I don't know why I said that."

"Because it's the truth." Roxie laughs like a madwoman.

"Why Kat?" I demand.

"She's the weakest," Johanna responds, unable to stop herself. "She has a strong power, but she can't control herself. She has been stripped of her self-esteem." Her eyes narrow on Kat. "You're scared, and they pity you. You'll never become a good witch. You'll just be the screw up until someday you light yourself on fire."

Kat breathes, "You tried to kill me?"

"No. I don't *like* killing. I wanted to scare you off." Johanna scoffs. "Daphne takes in sad causes. Look at Paula. Beatrice! I mean, Daphne got smarter this time and at least got power, but you are... nothing. Your mom is undoubtedly some mortal, knocked up by a powerful Council witch wanting a good night."

Hating that this has fallen on Kat, I step in front of her. "Why? There were others."

Johanna rolls back her shoulders. "You know who was easy? Carmella. Do you remember her?"

"I remember her," I murmur. "I remember everyone."

They are my sisters. Even though they have left the house, they will always be part of the coven.

"Zelda should've taken Kat's place," says Johanna. Venom laces her voice. "I should've taken Carmella's place. Or Jo's or Rhonda's or Jane's or Eva's or Marie's. I had to go through so many witches until I got Tori's spot." She smiles smugly. "I finally got Daphne to let me in. And she won't let in my friends. She seems confused about power, but then again, she considers you her favorite, Maisie."

My fingers have curled into my palms, threatening to draw blood. My control is slipping, and my magic stretches. I barely have enough time to reel it in.

Johanna cracks her knuckles. "Zelda is more powerful than you. Robyn and Ashley too. You're just Daphne's pet. I tried to be your friend, but you're very boring. Maisie, you're fine at potions and spells, and you can make wonderful trees. But you're not a powerful witch. You don't deserve to be at Daphne's side."

I spit through my gritted teeth, "She needs someone like you?"

"You're getting it!" She looks around for confirmation, but no one agrees. "Daphne may not be the most powerful witch ever, but she's immortal." Her face reddens. "She's been alive for a long time. She's done amazing things. She could teach us more than we could ever think." She hacks. "Daphne has been spending too much time on Beatrice and Mikayla. It has made her weak."

"She's powerful," I say, jutting out my chin.

"The Council," Johanna says suddenly. "There's real power. I know what you say about the Council, but you don't understand. You've only known the coven power. The Council could do—"

"Damage," I insert.

She frowns. "Don't be so judgmental, Maisie. That's such a Roxie thing."

"Hey now!" she retorts, flaring her magic.

"And—" Johanna swings over to Savvy— "who are you? You show up here, and you start… what? Brewing potions. This is you, isn't it? I'm under a truth potion. Seriously! I didn't kill Beatrice or Mikayla."

"How about Julia?" Savvy questions.

Johanna snaps, "Ask Lizzy." But she isn't here.

Kat steps around me. "What do you mean 'the Council?' Why do you think my mom is a mortal? What do you know?"

"Half-breeds. Crystal-gazers," says Johanna.

My cheeks heat. Johanna has said these things about our sisters before.

"Your blood is tainted," says Johanna to Kat. "You can light things on fire, but you have no place in this world. Maybe those doctors were right. You're crazy, Kat."

Tears in her eyes, Kat flees the front entryway. I turn to catch her and then decide to let her go. Her cat follows. Anyway, Johanna knows the truth about Julia.

Johanna starts to prowl like a predatory animal. "How many times have I said I should be Daphne's favorite? You're in my way, Maisie."

My mind can't come up with a retort. Her vicious words strike me in the belly, and I gasp for breath.

Johanna raises her chin, though she already stands taller than me. "I've killed before, but the truth is that I respect you, so fight back, Maisie. Go out with some dignity."

A scream builds in my throat. I hold myself back, but my magic rears its head for the challenge. It's blatant and deadly. I stumble back.

"Killing?" Savvy steps into Johanna's path. "Why don't you try some dignity? The door is right there. Leave."

Roxie interjects, "Also, do you remember how she kicked your ass last time?"

"She kicked your ass too, but don't worry. I can feel it," says Johanna, rolling her shoulders back. "The power inducer."

What? My heart nearly stops. I didn't... The metallic tinge of magic pulsates around us. The potion was only a truth potion. I brewed it myself. What is she talking about?

"My magic is growing. I can feel it all. You won't win this time, Maisie, and I'm not leaving quietly." Johanna sighs with a soft giggle. "I didn't think you had it in you, Maisie. When did you figure out the power inducer in Audrey? When did you figure out it was me?"

I stutter. What?

Everything Johanna says spins around me a million miles per minute. I'm powerless to stop it.

The night of Audrey's death stares at me, a night very much like this and how she acted... like Johanna does now.

"Oh. You didn't know?" Johanna laughs loudly. "My bad, but since we're here: Audrey."

"Who's Audrey?" asks Roxie.

"The pre-you." Johanna waves her hand dismissively. "Maisie, you've got a type."

Her words buzz like background noise.

"You killed her." The words tumble out of my mouth, filled with disbelief.

"No, you—shit. I can't lie. This is tricky." She moves her body as her magic grows. Soon, it will have to be released. It could be disastrous inside the house.

Magic inducers were used by witches in the Second Witch War and other times in history to boost power, but it does things with the mind. I would never put that in the potion. Who did that? Was it Roxie? Savvy? The words die on my lips, about to accuse another one of my sisters of a heinous crime.

"I gave Audrey a power inducer when I was stopping by and trying to make friends with some of the girls, not that she knew what it was," Johanna explains. "And I pointed her in your direction. Audrey was so jealous of you, and you're not a very receptive friend. You and Audrey fought. You obviously won. I wanted to know what made you tick, and I saw it."

She bends to become eye level with me. It makes me feel smaller. I'll melt into the carpet until I'm just a single atom. I should've run away when I had the chance, but she knows more than I thought she ever did. How wrong I've been.

"Audrey was in so much pain and was angry," says Johanna, voice husky. "You went inside the house and you even tried to save her—all out of guilt because she was already dead."

"You killed her." My voice cracks.

"I don't feel bad about it." She bops me on the nose with her pointer finger. "You blamed yourself for Audrey's death whe—"

"You killed her."

Her breath burns my skin. "I wanted a spot. *Your* spot. To be Daphne's favorite. When you can't beat them, you join them."

I shake my head to escape her fingers, yet she keeps touching my face. Her fingernails turn into makeshift claws.

"Daphne let me in the coven knowing I killed Audrey," she continues. "She let you go on believing that you had killed Audrey, your best friend. The reason why you carried so much guilt."

"No." It's the only word that comes to my mind.

"Daphne's not your friend or mentor, Maisie," says Johanna. "She's not the person you think she is. She used you."

"Shut up." My magic curls around my neck until I can't breathe.

"Maisie," Savvy warns, "don't do this. Don't play into her hands. She wants to—"

"Shut up," I snarl. "This isn't your business."

Like a mortal and with the possibility of mortal-tainted blood, I send my fist flying. My magic would be easy, but it would be easier if we were outside. My fist connects with Johanna's face, and she tumbles to the floor. Blood leaks from her lip.

I open the front doors. "You want to be the favorite. Come and get me."

Savvy and Roxie yell after me, but I run outside. My magic answers the call.

Chapter 36

A witch war broke out between Powell and
Skinner-Ravensblood sides. Many covens
were disbanded, and many witches were killed
or went into hiding. The war itself lasted mere
days but left thousands of witches and mortals
dead. The war ended when Ravensblood
killed Skinner, joined Powell's side, and then
went into hiding. Powell took power.
—*A Collected History of the Witch Wars*

I head around the house and into the backyard,
Johanna behind me. Her loud magic bangs against my
aching head.

With a flick of my wrist, I open the hedge. Once
she's through, I close the green bushes. It's only us
now. As it should be. No one else needs to be
involved. She made this personal.

I continue to walk, exposing my back to her. She
follows, dragging her feet over the ground.

Johanna has been the sliver in the corner of my eye.
A ghost in the shadows of my life for the last three
years. She has played me and played with me. I've been

blind to it all. She's morphed my life by pretending to be my sister and friend. She could claim to be my sister in the coven, but she never was.

"Where are we going, Maisie?" Johanna's voice is low. "You know you're losing blood."

It drips from my battered hands. I dig my fingernails in deeper. I fear if I release the hold, then I release control of my magic. We're not far enough away from the house. From my sisters. I can't let any of them get hurt for my mistakes.

Daphne's mistakes.

Only a month or so ago, Daphne asked me about being leader of the coven someday. She hadn't said soon. With Daphne comatose, I have taken over the coven. Savvy, Roxie, Lizzy, and Kat followed me through making this potion and administering it to Johanna. With something extra in the potion too.

"Maisie," sings Johanna behind me, snapping branches.

I hate to bring her into the unprotected woods, but there is nowhere safe to go. I couldn't leave her at the house or take her into town. She may not care for our sisters or mortals, but I do. With the woods, I can protect them… as much as my magic protects me.

"Maisie!" Johanna's voice ricochets off the trees. "How long are we walking?"

As far as I can keep going.

As long as I can hold her back.

We're deep in the woods, so this would be as good as anything else. However, I can't bring myself to stop. To face her. My anger has relented some, but I know if I face her, it all will crash into me again.

She yells, "I'm bored!"

Her magic hits my back, and I slam to the ground. My hands break my fall, releasing my fingernails from my palms. I open my mouth, ready to tell her to not do this—it isn't worth it—but she hits me with her magic again.

She throws me against a tree. *Crack!* My vision blurs. Pain floods my head. I fight to stay afloat. The sounds of the waves from the ocean blow through the trees and collect in my skull.

My magic slithers through the dirt, and I try to pull it back.

"Don't make it easy for me to kill you." She twitches.

Her magic will take over soon. She won't even know what she is doing is wrong, not that she truly understands now. Or ever understood before.

Johanna steps closer to me. "Everyone's waiting."

A tree root wraps around her leg, and I push my fingers into the frozen soil. With a jerk, she falls to the ground. Dirt sprinkles her strawberry blond hair that spills out of its pony.

Using the tree for balance, I stand. The world spins.

Lifting her head from the dirt, Johanna laughs. "Is that the best you have?"

Her conjuring magic focuses on the root, and I let out a hiss. The root burns, so I burn. More pain flitters up my fingers, the little hairs on my skin fluttering.

My magic vibrates down my bones, burrowing deep into the soil. The ground moves. Power ripples the earth, and the trees lean away.

The root releases from her ankle, but the dirt has started to sink. She sinks along with it. Her fingers dig in as she tries to climb out of the hole I am creating.

"This is a coward's way out, Maisie. Just so you don't have to fight me." Johanna hauls herself out of the hole, muscles taut. "You're not going to kill me. You're a 'good person.' You think so highly of yourself. So high and mighty on a horse. You think you're so great."

"I'm not great," I respond, breaking my silence.

Snow begins to fall. Thick clouds have covered the moon and stars. The heavy darkness stretches between us. It offers a place to hide and my magic to bloom.

"Look at that control," Johanna coos tauntingly. "You didn't have that a year ago. Or even a month ago. Remember what you did to the backyard. Why keep control, Maisie?"

My fingernails curl back into my palms. More of my blood spills. My magic licks it up. The ground opens for a taste, and then the dirt opens further under her.

"It's control, isn't it? That's why Daphne likes you. You take her orders." She spits dirt. "You're trying to come up with a plan. You're trying to be smart. Lizzy's smarter than you."

Suddenly, the wall she is holding gives way. She falls into a ten-foot hole, landing with a thud. The woods silence, including Johanna. The trees don't move.

Cursing myself for losing control and possibly hurting Johanna, I move toward the lip of the hole. "Johanna, let me help you out."

Magic shoots up from the ground and hits me in the chest. Knocked back, I cry out. Pain thrashes in me, my heart thundering. I try to block the invisible conjured force with any spell I can come up with, but no words spark in my mind. The force weighs down on me, pinning my legs to the ground.

In one quick move, I slam my hands on the dirt, and it rumbles. The hole crumbles. The invisible force on my body breaks. Coughs escape my throat as I wheeze for breath.

The hole has caved in, leaving a slope. Her legs stuck in the mud. Johanna glares at me. Her chest heaves, but I don't know if it's from the power inducer or the panic she must feel from almost being buried alive. Tears sparkle her eyes, but I bite back an apology.

"Just do it, Maisie," she says, covered in dirt.

I stand over the hole, breathing heavily. "Get out of here, Johanna."

She draws her eyebrows together. "You'll let me leave?"

"Yes," I force myself to say. I force myself to believe it too. "You can say you won. Say you're more powerful and I cried, weeping for mercy. Just leave, Johanna. Enough people have been hurt." I won't lose another sister because of her.

Nodding slowly, she hangs her head but then whips her hand from the dirt and finishes off a spell in her mind. I throw up my hands but lack a spell to block. The conjuring magic blows past me, but I stumble back.

The wind picks up, threatening to create a vortex around me. It brings more than just a tornado: a nightmare from years ago when Audrey digested a power inducer. I've seen this before and how it ends.

I yell, "Don't!"

A form—conjured by Johanna—swoops through the bushes. I duck. The being slams into a hundred-year-old tree, snapping it like a twig. The tree collapses into two. They tumble like dominos.

The monster charges at me again, and I run.

When it's about to drop, I jump behind a thick ancient tree. The solid monster bangs against the tree that threatens to crush me. I place a hand on the bark, sending my magic to make it sturdy. The mass beats at it again. A hole forms in the trunk.

"Enough!" I hurdle around the tree.

The mass without eyes focuses on me. My heart beats wildly. I've made a grave mistake, but I refuse to die today.

"Johanna, please," I beg. "Stop this. Don't do this—"

The conjured monster flies at me again, and my magic answers. A tree root grabs Johanna and slams her to the ground. The creature stops without a command.

Johanna looks up, dazed, but the form rushes me again. Sprawling out of the way, I bring in another root. It grabs her other leg. It doesn't stop her magic.

Looking more human-like with limbs and a torso, the monster snaps another tree. Branches connect with other branches. Snow and leaves fall. They blind me for a second.

Johanna has her hand stretched out toward her monster, so I take two more roots, wrenching her down to the soil.

"Don't, Johanna," I warn as the roots curl around her neck.

The monster throws a limb at me. I roll away but bang into a tree. I'm surrounded. The monster hovers over me, raising the tree limbs to impale. I slam my bloody hands to the ground. A hole opens from under the monster's feet.

An earthquake rocks us.

The ground gives way, crashing almost thirty feet down.

Trees, bushes, trails, and everything else fall into the pit too. The world is flattened in the cavern—and I fall along with it.

Chapter 37

The Council would say witches are territorial,
but covens would say otherwise.
–Rise Against the Council pamphlet

When I open my eyes, the earth is torn apart. Distorted. The world is covered in white powder. The snow covers my destruction—something I would prefer not to remember. I don't think I lost control of my magic, but the world is turned upside down.

I have destroyed what I love. Again.

The incline is steep. I cling to the sides to climb out of the hole I have created. The snow sticks to my clothes but melts on my skin. Each breath is white, clouding my face. Reaching the top of my hole, I freeze.

Johanna hangs, suspended mid-air by the roots holding her by her limbs, like she was almost pulled apart. A root is wrapped around her neck tightly. Her face is purple and eyes bulging. She stares off into the distance.

I teeter, vomit burning the back of my throat.

I killed her.

***

The girls poke from the house curtains. I'm battered, bruised, and bloodied. Pain aches my skin and joints. My hair keeps my vision thankfully short.

Astrid stands at the top of the landing. My magic is weakened because of her magic. But my magic is already weakened with how much I used of it. Not looking for another fight, I sidestep her. I don't speak to the others.

Taking the stairs to Daphne's suite, I don't have the energy to talk.

To explain.

The worst part is, I don't care.

***

In my dreams, I walk in the woods by my parents' home in Minnesota. Marney and I spent our weekends exploring and playing in the woods, following the creek to the great Mississippi River. The woods were one of the first places Marney and I practiced magic by ourselves. We used maple, poison ivy, mud, and oak for potions.

The canopy of green leaves hangs above my head. Golden light cascades down to warm me. A soft breeze brings the scent of crabapples. Dreams have neither of those things, so this isn't mine. Someone else has hijacked my sleep.

"Marney?" I ask.

"Behind you." Marney stands between two large oak trees.

Losing all breath, I slam into her. She is solid and whole. She is here, though she's not. She's a dreamwalker, creating this world around us based on a memory.

"I was so worried." Marney hangs onto me, head on my shoulder. "What happened? We felt the earthquake. Not physically. Magically. It woke us from our sleep."

I don't ask who the "we" is. I'm just happy that she is okay and here after not seeing her for so long.

Pulling back, she searches my face. "Are you okay?"

Physically, I think I'm fine. I've been worse. Mentally, I don't know. Emotionally, probably not. I don't feel the void that has been carved in my chest. I'm all right with it missing.

"Mais," she says tenderly, "we don't have long. I needed to make sure you're okay. While I can't be with you, I needed to make sure you're... *alive*. I can't lose you too. Not after Mom and Dad." Her voice cracks.

I don't want to think about them. Or the coven we lost in the Second Witch War.

Marney's eyes flash to the woods to her left. Wherever she is in reality, she's not alone. Her hand twitches.

"I wanted to give you a fair chance with your new coven, so I didn't visit you. I dreamwalked with some of your sisters, though. They all had wonderful things to say about you. Mais, I knew you were doing okay." She wipes her thumb across my cheek, rubbing away my tears. "You will get past this. You will be better than whatever this is. I love you, Maisie."

The words clog my throat. "I love you too, Marney."

She disappears from my sight, like she wasn't here to begin with. She can't be with me. I don't have enough energy to ask why. Marney's still around because the woods stay as does the crabapple scent and sunny warmth. That slowly fades.

Chapter 38

Silence like a still night, sleep comfortably in
your bed. Silence in your mind, peacefulness
in your life. Silence of your body, like a slab of
stone. Silence of your heart, death will take
you as its own.
–Unknown

The doors to Daphne's suite rattle. The pounding continues, refusing to stop until the doors are broken down. Let them. Everything else is ruined.

I still, dead like the almost-dead Daphne.

The doors to Daphne's bedroom slide open, and a shuffle of feet draw close to the bed. "Is she okay?" someone asks.

"No." Heavy hands land on my shoulder, knocking me on the floor.

I land with a thud. My eyes flutter open.

Somehow, I'm alive. I shouldn't be. I don't want to be.

"See," Roxie says to Kat and Kami in the doorway. The shadows of more people hover in the back, like the rest of the living coven has come to see my demise.

"You really did it now, Maisie," Roxie begins with a sigh.

Kami snaps, "Don't. She's been through enough."

"Don't you want answers?" Roxie kneels beside me. "What happened in the woods, Maisie? Did Johanna admit she killed Julia?"

"We know she's dead," Susana adds softly.

"Huge earthquake by the way," congratulates Roxie, beaming. "Did good."

Susana pushes Roxie out of the way and bends in front of me. "Maisie, we just want to make sure you're okay. Let's get you up and get you something to eat."

I don't want to, but they won't leave me alone until they succeed. They'll pick me up and carry me out. That might be easier. I can play doll to their dreamhouse.

When I take Susana's hand, Kami helps me to my feet. We walk into the sitting room of Daphne's suite, where Paula and Ubah are cleaning up the mess they weren't involved in making. The girls brought toast with jam and white cheese and a pear.

My eyes stay on the pear longer than they should. The pear starts to brown and mold, deteriorating before my eyes—and everyone else's.

"Oh my God," Roxie groans, gagging.

"Drink some water." Susana hands me a glass. "Maisie, I understand that this is hard. No one should've been put in that situation. You must be feeling a lot right now."

I should have guilt about Johanna's death. I should have anger toward Daphne. I should be sad about what

I did to the woods. I should be happy about seeing my sister. Any emotion shies away.

"Hey, Maisie, are you still in there?" Kami pokes my shoulder.

"Maybe we should take her to the hospital," offers Paula.

"And tell them what? She caused an earthquake and killed another girl?" Roxie asks. "She'll be fine. She always is."

"She doesn't look fine," Ubah argues.

"I agree she needs help, but we can't go to the hospital," says Susana loudly, cutting through the noise in the sitting room. "You saw the news. They're reporting the earthquake. The police found Johanna's body. They're going to be suspicious. None of us should leave the house right now. Not until this all calms down."

"What about Beatrice and Mikayla's killer?" asks Roxie.

"He's still out there," answers Savvy. "We'll get him next."

***

Days come and go, ushered in by the unseasonable sun. The girls bring food and then collect when it has not been touched. Sometimes, they try to get me out of the bed that I share with Daphne. I have no interest. Daphne keeps breathing, so I keep going.

Sometimes, the girls talk to me. It's only background noise, like the birds outside or the rustle of the wind. When the girls come in, I have a hard time recognizing them. Their faces are in shadows, and their voices all sound the same. The girls ask what they can do to help. The girls ask what happened. The girls think they can fix it.

A girl will sit on the end of the bed. She never touches me. She never says anything. She is *my* favorite.

Daylight is breaking when I hear Daphne's doors bang open. Roxie stands at my feet. "I know you're going through a lot, but Catrina is dying."

I don't need more death.

"We are your sisters! Isn't that what you always say? Are you going to abandon us when we need you the most?" Roxie literally throws me off the bed.

I land with a thud, my chin hitting the rug. There should be pain. I feel nothing.

Roxie pulls me to my feet and then drags me out of the suite. The air is foreign, but I walk with her. My legs are like sticks. I slip sideways before Roxie uprights me.

On the guest floor, girls spill out of a bedroom, all lined up for Catrina's last day. We don't know when she'll go but stay with her. That's what sisters do.

Two of us aren't here: Astrid and Lizzy. I don't question where they are because no one else does. Do I care? My sisters leave all the time. Or they die. I don't know what happened to either of them. It's better not to know.

Susana sits on Catrina's bed, holding her hand. "Her eyes haven't opened, and her pulse is slowing. Does anyone have any final words to say to Catrina?"

Kat lowers herself beside Catrina, whispering in her ear. Paula hovers at Catrina's side, Ubah by her shoulder. We've gathered here today for another death and another body to be buried in the backyard. Where is Johanna's body? Has she been buried with Audrey, Beatrice, and Mikayla?

Roxie's warm breath makes the hair on the back of my neck stand. "Do you remember Catrina coming into Daphne's suite? She would stay with you for hours."

I remember but don't remember her.

"Lizzy's gone. Left right after Johanna died. She didn't even say good-bye. It was like she didn't want to be here anymore. Astrid left for her revenge," Roxie murmurs with a small chuckle. "I'm going too. Once Catrina dies. I stayed for Beatrice and then her killer, but this is too much. You should leave too, Maisie. This coven is garbage. There's nothing left here for anyone."

I want to tell her to stay, but it's her life. I can't promise her safety. Four of our recent sisters are dead—five, if I count Audrey. Six if Daphne dies. How many more of us will die? We haven't found Beatrice and Mikayla's killer. We need those answers and to bring that killer to justice. Johanna's death, however, proved there's no justice.

Waiting for someone to die isn't an easy task. We want to celebrate Catrina's life but want to give her peace. This world hasn't been kind. We want to give comfort because she gave it to us, but none of us quite know how or can do it.

It takes hours for Catrina to die. Susana checks her pulse and then confirms that Catrina is gone. When I turn around, I find many of my sisters gone. I don't know if they'll ever come back. Or if I will ever come back. After everything I have lost, I should lose myself too. The killer out there can have me.

Maisie's story continues in *The Least Kind of Controlled Enchantments*

Coming January 2025

Turn to the next page for a sneak peek…

Chapter 1

Life is not made up of fairy tales, because if it was, witches would always be considered evil. They are hurt and are in pain like us, and they celebrate and love like us. The world is more than what you know, think, and can see before your eyes.
–Rise Against the Council pamphlet

The death may have stopped, but the nightmares haven't.

It doesn't matter that months have passed since Beatrice and Mikayla were killed. It doesn't matter that I live in a quiet house with vacant rooms and even quieter roommates. It doesn't matter that I sleep next to someone who is basically dead.

In my nightmares, history replays itself: Johanna swinging from brown tree roots, face purple, eyes bulging.

I killed her.

Daylight shines through the canopy of leaves in the woods as I push myself harder. Every day is going to get better—be better than the last—or that's what the self-help books say. The books also say I need to keep a routine. Thankfully, I like books enough to believe them.

Gravel crunches under my feet in the front of the house after my run. Sweat beads down my neck and collects under my armpits. Keeping to the routine as the books say, I head into the kitchen, refusing to back out when two of my sisters sit at the long kitchen table.

"Good morning," Savvy says as Mercedes barely raises her head from her coffee mug. "How was your run?"

I shrug, chugging a glass of water.

"We're going to the beach today. Want to come?" asks Savvy.

The books say I should go. Spending time with those who care about me is key. I should learn to step out of my comfort zone in a safe environment.

Mercedes adds, "Kat is coming too."

"And Kami," says Savvy.

We're the only ones left in the coven. Everyone else is gone. Besides Daphne.

"Plus," Savvy says, "I need to talk to you about something."

Anxiety bubbles in my stomach. Savvy must be kicking me out of the coven. I have nowhere to go. My family is dead. My sister is in hiding. I've been here for the past three years.

Savvy quickly adds, "It's nothing bad, Maisie."

Susana said it was nothing bad and then left our coven. Ubah and Paula interviewed other covens and then left us. Astrid had left in the middle of the night, chasing revenge of the witch who scarred her. I look down at my own scarred hands.

The light in the kitchen is too bright. I blink, and it's like a flash of lightning. It rushes up my arms. I ball my hands into fists to keep my magic back, but it has awakened. It's hungry for more.

"Really, Maisie," Savvy promises loudly. "It's good."

I nod, having to believe her, and keep to the routine.

In the suite that takes up the top floor of the house, I check on Daphne. She breathes in her constant vegetative state. Dead but not really dead. So close to it.

I get into the shower and grab the soap and just let the water wash over me. Exhaustion weakens my bones. I could let water melt me, and I would run down into the old pipes of the house and be burped out into the ocean. I only realize I haven't been moving because the thoughts creep into my head. *Beatrice, Mikayla, Julia. Johanna.* The last at my own hands.

When I step out of the shower, I check on Daphne again. Nothing has changed.

According to the books, it helps if I get ready. I'm going to the beach, I remind myself, so I slip on a bathing suit and then a t-shirt and pants. I run a brush through my hair like I should. A few months ago, my hair got so knotted that Kami suggested I cut it. It would've been easier than the hours I spent tearing at the knots, clumps of my bushy hair falling to the floor.

The girls didn't say when we are going to the beach, so I wait. Waiting makes the thoughts come back, so I run through a list of things I need to do: mop the west spiral staircase, knock down cobwebs, and wash the windows. I mopped the west spiral staircase a few weeks ago, but the girls track mud in the house. Anyway, I'm the only one who cleans. The staff are gone.

Kat knocks on Daphne's door, entering the suite slowly. "We are almost ready to go."

She smiles, but I can't give it back to her. It hurts too much. Yet I follow her through the house instead of locking myself in Daphne's suite. One step at a time.

The large backyard is encased by a green hedge. A garden—another thing in my routine—a flowerbed, and a wooden swing are held inside. It is nature at its finest, letting the environment do what it wants instead of manicuring it to fit my needs.

I take a deep breath, and my magic stirs deep in my belly. I give it a chance to move in a non-destructive way, and the hedge peels open. The trees clap against one another like thunder. My magic flows from my bare feet into the grass, deep into the dirt, and through the veins of the earth. We are all connected.

"The others went ahead," Kat explains.

My magic withdraws. Its claws retract back into my body, yet the magic is all around. Anywhere nature is, my magic is.

"Mercedes said something about scaring tourists off the beach," Kat continues, rolling her eyes.

Memorial Day is in a few days, but the tourists are already flocking to this town, the beach, and the water. Tourists will be driving by the coven house. We're marked on the maps for several reasons: it's a historic house, one of the first houses built in this part of the country and still has its old Victorian look; the house used be a finishing school and other things but has always been owned and run by witches; and four girls that lived in this house died last year with no suspects arrested and no one charged. The police have only recently stopped sniffing around us, and the case has turned cold.

Fire creates a circle suspended mid-air, and I startle. *My nature!* But the branches and trees aren't singed. The ground is left untouched.

Kat has just created a portal, coming a long way since she first joined the coven. I'm guessing Mercedes taught her, seeing that she is the only other witch—besides me—who can build portals in our coven. Guilt twists my stomach. I was supposed to be teaching Kat. Daphne assigned her to me when she first joined the coven.

Through the portal, Mercedes and Savvy sit on the beach. Kami puts on tanning lotion, the coconut scent flittering in the breeze.

"I can't do long distances," says Kat meekly. "Or places I haven't been."

I want to tell her how good she has been doing. How far she's come. How good of a witch she is. Yet the words are lost in my throat.

I shuffle through the fiery portal, and sand squishes under my feet. The portal closes.

"Maisie," calls Kami, "you have clean hands. Can you take a picture of me and make it internet worthy?"

I take her cell phone, and Kami poses, throwing out her hips and letting her curly bleached hair flow in the wind. Her skin is golden any time of the year, but she shines now. Her deep brown eyes stare into the camera and then off into the distance before she puts on sunglasses.

"Work it, Kami!" Mercedes cheers.

Moving like a wave, Kami flips her hair. She could be a model.

"Okay. That's enough. Even for me." Taking her phone, Kami swipes through the photos. "These are great, Maisie. Thanks!"

"Maisie, you should take everyone's photos," Savvy says, looking over Kami's shoulder at her cell phone. "You're so good at it."

Lizzy used to do photography. She's gone too, leaving many questions behind. Answers I may never have. Lizzy taught me a few things, but this was all Kami with the good photographs.

"We should get a photo together," suggests Mercedes.

The girls agree, even Kat. I can't blend into the back fast enough.

"Kami, you should take it." Savvy hands over the cell phone. "You take so many selfies."

Kami positions the phone to get a good angle of us. We are careful to not blink. Kami moves the camera again, getting creative with the shots. Kat is on one side of me, and Mercedes hangs off my other. They touch me, and I try not to pull away.

Mercedes is our most recent addition. She auditioned months ago but didn't get into the coven then. One day, she showed up at our doors and was welcomed with open arms. While she's powerful, we're dwindling. We're not a coven anymore. It's my fault.

"Let's talk," says Savvy, calling the photo session to a close. "Maisie, by me."

I sit beside Savvy as instructed, and the rest of the girls create a circle on the towels. Our knees brush.

Savvy begins, "I have been enjoying our time as the Fab Five."

Not including Daphne. Who I spend my nights with. Who I wait to wake.

"And a half," Savvy adds quickly like she can hear my thoughts, but that's not her power. "I think it's time we start looking toward the future. We need more members to be a complete coven. We shouldn't be hasty, but it's time to add good witches and witches who need our help. This coven has a long and beautiful history."

I stare at the sand. I knew this day would come but don't know if I'm ready.

There is safety in numbers, but we died anyway. I couldn't figure out why we were being killed before. I wasn't smart or strong enough. I'm not sure I'm either of those things now.

Taking a red candle from her bag, Savvy lights it in the center of our circle. She and Mercedes unload supplies from a backpack, including a large spell book. Mercedes holds a bird's skull as Savvy explains, "We're going to put a call out for witches."

"That could draw in some crazies," says Kami.

Daphne looked for Kami and me specifically and then brought us into the coven. However, she let the magic bring Kat, Savvy, and Mercedes to audition. Twenty-seven witches tried out last time. I don't know how many witches will come now if they feel the pull.

The candle flame dances in the breeze off the ocean. Five different bird feathers poke from the skull. Mercedes takes out a knife from the backpack and slices her finger open, letting her blood roll onto the bird's skull. Kami's squeamish, so Mercedes slices open Kami's finger and I hold the skull. Kami's blood drops, and then she snatches her hand back, nursing the small wound. This isn't the first time we've used blood in our magic, and it probably won't be the last.

Without hesitation, I slice my middle finger open. My blood dribbles over the skull. A few droplets of blood is nothing compared to what I have spilled. I pass the bird skull and knife to Kat. They continue around our small circle.

Placing the bloody bird skull on top of the red candle, Savvy sucks her bleeding finger and skims the oversized book. It is filled with yellowed pages and hand-painted pictures. It smells like clover, lavender, and apples from all the potions brewed.

The scents of witchcraft, minus the metallic scent of power, used to give me ease. Now, the scents alight something deep inside of me. The tiny sand grains begin to tremble, and I sit on my hands.

Savvy tucks the five feathers into the bird skull: a mourning dove, mallard, sparrow, starling, and robin. The feathers flutter in the wind. We hold each other's hands and breathe together. I try to clear all thoughts from my mind, but they start to creep in. The names and the faces and all the pain and death. I try to shake them away.

"Maisie."

I don't focus on being calm—it's impossible—so I focus on my magic. It answers my call after moving the sand. I should just be happy a hole doesn't open underneath our circle and swallow us.

"Witches of the past coven, hear our plea," chants Savvy. "Bring the witches to me. We have vacancies."

Together, we repeat: "Witches of the past coven, hear our plea. Bring the witches to me. We have vacancies."

The Favorite Kind of Wild Magic Playlist

"Into the Woods" by Phidel
"Rise" by Denmark & Winter
"Running with the Wolves" by Aurora
"All the Magic" by Karilene
"Don't Need Nothing" by Aly & AJ
"It's Happening Again" by Agnes Obel
"There's a Ghost" by Fleurie
"Dance with Druids" by Karilene
"Savage Daughter" by Sarah Hester Ross
"Under the Giant Trees" by Agnes Obel
"Drumming Song" by Florence + the Machine
"Back to Forever" by Lissie
"Into the Mist" by Eivor

Acknowledgments

I would like to thank you, the reader, for taking the time to read this. Thank you! I'm a writer because I have too many ideas, and you as a reader didn't have to pick up this book.

This book is very personal to me because I focused on some hard truths for myself, including anxiety and depression. This story wasn't easy for me to write, and it continued into book two in the duology.

I would also like to think the people who helped me create this book, including Giorgi and Melissa, who beta read for me. It is because of them that this story is in the world.

As always, there are more people to thank than I can possibly remember or put into words. Such as my parents for allowing me to live rent-free as an adult in their house. To my dogs for allowing me to snuggle with them. To my coworkers who will ultimately buy this book to be nice.

Once again, thank you all who read this book and support me as an author.

-Sophie

About the Author

Sophia-Rose Johnson, who has also written under S. Johnson, is from Minnesota, USA, and she is a northerner by heart and accent. She graduated from the University of Wisconsin-Superior in 2018 with a writing degree, and she argues about commas constantly. While she first published in 2022, she's been writing since 2011. When not working at her day or night job, she enjoys reading, hanging out with family and friends, playing with her dogs, making sarcastic comments, being a fake blond, chugging energy drinks, and wearing high heels as a tall woman.

Stay connected with her via social media or website:
https://www.sjohnsonbooks.com/